Knights of the White Company

Book One of the Magna Societas

J. A. Fabre

Knights of the White Company

Olympia Publishers
London

www.olympiapublishers.com
OLYMPIA PAPERBACK EDITION

Copyright © J. A. Fabre 2024

The right of J. A. Fabre to be identified as author of
this work has been asserted in accordance with sections 77 and 78 of
the Copyright, Designs and Patents Act 1988.

All Rights Reserved

No reproduction, copy or transmission of this publication
may be made without written permission.
No paragraph of this publication may be reproduced,
copied or transmitted save with the written permission of the publisher,
or in accordance with the provisions
of the Copyright Act 1956 (as amended).

Any person who commits any unauthorized act in relation to
this publication may be liable to criminal
prosecution and civil claims for damage.

A CIP catalogue record for this title is
available from the British Library.

ISBN: 978-1-80439-366-6

This is a work of fiction.
Names, characters, places and incidents originate from the writer's
imagination. Any resemblance to actual persons, living or dead, is
purely coincidental.

First Published in 2024

Olympia Publishers
Tallis House
2 Tallis Street
London
EC4Y 0AB

Printed in Great Britain

Dedication

To the editors of Olympia Publishers who were kind enough to reply with, *"Your work is well-written with a consistent and absorbing narrative."* And to the memory of Sensei Bob Elder (1952–2022), 8th Dan, Zen Nihon Toyama Ryu Iaido Renmei, who taught me a lot more than martial arts – *Perseverance*.

"From that time on, all went ill with the kingdom and the State was undone. Thieves and robbers rose up everywhere in the land. The Nobles despised and hated all others and took no thought for usefulness and profit of lord and men. They subjected and despoiled the peasants and the men of the villages. In no wise did they defend their country from its enemies; rather did they trample it underfoot, robbing and pillaging the peasants' goods. The regent, it appeared, clearly gave no thought to their plight. At that time the country and the whole land of France began to be put in confusion and mourning like a garment, because it had no defender or guardian."

– From the *Chronicles of Jean de Venette,* circa 1356.

Prologue

On the thirteen day of April in the year of our Lord 1360, King Edward of England rides with ten thousand men to claim his ancestral rights on the throne of France. The king is middle-aged, bearded, with long hair and masculine-cut features. He is franked by his young commanding knight, Sir Guy de Beauchamp. His father, Sir Thomas de Beauchamp, the Earl of Warwick, has already built quite a reputation on and off the battlefield. Sir Guy is expected to command the invading army with the same intelligence, integrity, and bravery as that of his father. King Edward, suddenly pulling on his reigns, which made his horse neigh loudly, and leaning on his saddle's cantle, says, "Another city that refuses to meet us in open combat – Sir Guy!"

"What do you expect, my king; they fear us on the open battlefield," said Sir Guy, taking off his war helm, which let down his long, blond hair, and adjusting himself on his saddle.

"Paris refused to fight, and now, Chartres does likewise, hiding behind their walls and fortifications!"

"My king, we have built a formable army ever since our victories over Sluys, Crécy, and Poitiers. The use of our longbows and dismounted tactics have caused the king's army to have an edge on the battlefield like never before. The French now know almighty God is on our side. Their only impasse is to hide behind their fortified walls. A war of siege is at hand. I will send for siege weapons and craftsmen to build us ladders, catapults and trebuchets."

"Fear! What good is fear to me now? I need to conquer these cities and settle these lands that my forefathers once held. William the Conqueror, Richard the Lion Hearted, King Henry… all those heroic kings and warriors whose blood run through my veins… my ancestry… my land! But, most importantly, my dear late uncle King Charles… making I the true male inheritor to the French crown. The rest of the French nobles will have to recognize this claim. They must!"

Sir Guy de Beauchamp hunched on his saddle. "Aye, my king; but it looks like we will not get any battle, or even a parley from Chartres this day." Sir Guy motioned to his squire to remove his gauntlet and armor pauldron. No words were needed to transpire with his squire; many years together took care of that. His squire was older than Sir Guy and an experienced warrior of many battles. He wore a large dagger and was dressed in chainmail with a helmet. Sir Thomas de Beauchamp handpicked the squire himself for his son. The king looked at them incredulously and at the same time remembering the agreement he made with his father. The Earl was to look after the prince during chevauchée. The king was to reciprocate during the invasion. The Earl kept his part of the bargain; now it was up to the king to keep his end. After the plated armor was removed leaving only his chain mail, Sir Guy took out his free arm and rotated it all the way around until his shoulder made a popping noise. "It's an old tourney injury, my king; it usually acts up when bad weather is about to happen." He looked up toward the sky, contemplating the cloud patterns. "And I'm expecting some possibly before the end of the day."

"You're still very young – Sir Guy; it might still completely heal. I had many injuries in the past that healed over time, and a few that still linger." The king chuckled a little, then stopped chuckling, and immediately adjusted his seat like an old injury had just poked at him and said, *I'm still here.* But just then the king shrugged it off, just like he must have done countless of other times before. "I know you have your father's intellect, but tell me, my young commanding knight, what do you fear most?"

"I fear nothing, my king. I competed and won many victories at tournaments. I earned my spurs in a bloody battle. I've crossed the sea in command of this grand army." But then, for a moment, he rubs his head and, moving his head from one side to the other until a small snapping sound was heard, "But, I would say, my king, I do fear two things." Grabbing his horse's reigns more comfortably now without his pauldron and gauntlet, he said, "I would say… I fear my wife. I hate upsetting her so. She has an awful temper, you know."

"Aye, indeed!" These words brought laughter to them both. "And the other is… I fear God… I fear to lose God's favor over us."

"What do you mean?"

"Losing God's favor will bring failure to our great endeavor."

"God is with us. This is evident over the many victories that we have accomplished so far. My son, the Black Prince, through his successful chevauchée has softened the French countryside for us. He told me himself that he has set a table before us. All we have to do now is eat this bountiful feast."

"Aye, my king, but it will only take one among us whom has done a great sin to undo all these great deeds; one might bring God's wrath upon us and undo this great conquest." Sir Guy looked up toward the sky, observing the fast-moving clouds and following a flock of birds flying in the sky.

"Ha, if that's what you're worried about… then fear no

more. If God looks down at you, surely all the sins that this whole army of cutthroats have done will surely be washed away compared with your goodness, grace and chivalry – Sir Guy." Suddenly, King Edward indicating toward Chartres, "The trebuchets you mentioned – can they reach over the walls?"

"Sire, I will have to confirm with the craftsmen, but I do believe they can be constructed to do just that."

"Good. Requisition a large quantity of plague cadavers, as well. When the trebuchets are ready, I want them aimed over the walls at Chartres." The king had an expression of staring into a faraway distance. "We will bring fear to whoever wants to hide behind walls. We will force them to come out and fight like men." Then, King Edward, coming back to his senses, began looking around and pointing with his finger at the immediate horizon, "That open field over there looks like a perfect spot to camp. Command the men to encamp for the night, Sir Guy. I want Chartres' defenders to look at our vastness of our army. Let them tremble when they see us. Let them get no sleep tonight. Let them know we are here to stay until we defeat them. Align the rank and file as is our custom. Now, hurry up, lad, give the orders!"

Sir Guy advanced forward to give the order on his high-spirited steed. A gift from his father before he departed. It was a destrier horse, bred specifically for war. The colors of the horse were dark gray with a black mane, and he had one eye that had an unnatural white-blue color including its pupil. Some thought that he was blind in that eye, but he wasn't. This gave the horse an unnatural malicious look about him. Maybe it was the animal's aura, or his high spirit that had a part in the name that the Earl had chosen for him, 'Lucifer'. The Earl, before he departed, was noted as saying that 'Only Lucifer can take you to the gates of hell and back.'

As it was the king's custom to watch the rank and file, he watched mounted on his steed as they slowly moved in and aligned themselves to set up camp. Not an easy task for such a large army. Ten thousand men consisting of four thousand men-at-arms, five thousand archers, and seven hundred mercenaries with support units making up the rest. The king waved and nodded and smiled at his men-at-arms from time to time as they went by. This was the least he could do for them. These were all his men even the mercenaries. Less and less true, noble knights would beckon his call these days, so, he would have to rely more and more on men-at-arms and mercenaries to account for his royal invasion force. This change of a professional fighting force instead of the knightly class must have taken a toll, but the exact cost he often wondered to himself. Nevertheless, they were all expected to die for him, and at this time they made a formidable army. Looking at his vast fighting force, he said out loud, "Not even God can stop me now!"

By this time, Sir Guy de Beauchamp made his way back at his side as was his custom not to finish the day until the king finished his first. Sir Guy said, overhearing the king's statement and trying to remind him of their last conversation, "My king, God is omnipotent and omnipresent over all things in heaven and earth. Over the big things and over the little things like losing a great war over a single person's iniquity."

"I mean, Sir Guy, do you see this victorious and gallant army that we created? I will take all the lands back that they took from my forefathers, all the way from Normandy to the Alps. You will see!"

At this moment, gigantic, dark, ominous clouds started to move in. Thunder could be heard, and dry lighting could be seen at a distance. Light rain started to sweep in waves. Wind also started to hit sporadically. "Hurry, men!" cried the King of England. "You don't want to be out here when this storm hits; you'll want to be in your warm tents tonight!" The temperature drops suddenly, and dark storm clouds started to move in. The file of knights continued slowly, moving in orderly into the campsite. Some of the tents were already set up with their individual colorful banners flapping in the wind, while others were still just stakes on the ground. Still, King Edward watched, sitting on his horse.

"This weather is getting rather unsettling," said Sir Guy de Beauchamp, looking up at the sky and rubbing his left elbow underneath his chainmail with his right hand.

"Now, after all your knight's training and battles you told me about, you don't mean to tell me that you're scared of a little rain. Are you?"

"Not at all, my king."

Just then, a cold, freezing rain started, and lightning started to strike close. About three quarters of the tents were already set up. The rain started hitting hard. Men were in tents already, most likely cleaning their equipment and harnesses from the mud in order for rust not to settle in, or even some laying down already for the night. Most of the unmounted horses were caroused together. But the king still watched; he still had men coming in. His tent was already arranged for him and soon he planned to be there. Lightning started to strike at the center of the camp. The lightning made explosive noises that shattered the men's ears and caused vision to sparkle. The wind picked up so hard that it started to rip tents to shreds. The horses snickered and men were panicking.

"Pardon, my king, it looks like my first battle in these foreign shores will be with nature's tempest." Sir Guy motioned to his squire. "Stay with the king. Protect him with your life. I will ride up ahead to see if I can get the men to control the horses before it gets any worst." Then, Sir Guy rode off into the ranks, yelling his orders as if in command of some fierce battle. Men half-naked were running in the field, trying to control their horses. Others were trying to seek shelter by bracing the tents together. Freezing rain started to produce hail. It was plain that this was no ordinary hailstorm. Huge hail started to hit the ground, hitting a tent here and a tent there. Shouts and screams of men and horses could be heard. Then, the sound of something hard hitting horses and unsuspecting men. Even hitting knights still on horseback. When the hail stopped, King Edward, still on his horse, repented on what he had said a few moments ago. He kept hearing his own words that he had just uttered. "Not even God can stop me now… Not even God…" He turned to look for Sir Guy de Beauchamp, but he was nowhere in sight.

"Sir Guy! Sir Guy!" cried King Edward. Then, he looked at the ground, and there was Sir Guy Squire's lifeless body. The king got off his horse and looked at the poor lifeless body. He then looked around and staggered forward and beheld hundreds of shattered tents and hundreds of dead and wounded men and horses. In an effort to find Sir Guy, he started to move forward, a fog encroaching all around him, making visibility next to impossible. He staggered through the debris field yelling, "Sir Guy! Sir Guy!" Now, the king could not see anyone around him. He heard men sobbing and groaning and horses snorting and whining in pain, but the fog became ever denser. He then heard a voice. "My king… My king…" It was Sir Guy's voice. Finally, he saw a horse with Sir Guy's heraldry. The horse's head was down, licking at Sir Guy's hair. His golden, blond hair was colored crimson with blood.

The king reached the body. "Sir Guy!" The horse was startled and trotted off. The king thought that the horse had almost a human expression of shame just before it trotted off. Sir Guy was lying on the ground, badly bleeding and hurt. A large hailstone was on the ground, that must have hit him on the head and side of his body. The king knelt next to Sir Guy to comfort and tend to his wounds. Sir Guy grabbed a hold of the king's arm, asking, "Sire, my horse… my horse?"

"Don't worry about that now. My good and faithful knight." The king embraced him as if he was his own son. A son he hadn't seen for a very long time. In turn, Sir Guy melted in the king's arms like a child. Sir Guy, gazing toward the king's face and said, "I have failed you. I couldn't defeat nature's tempest for thee."

"No. No one can. Worry not… this was not your fault but mine alone."

"I beseeched thee, send a message to my wife and children that all is well." Sir Guy's voice quivered as he clenched the king's solid right arm. "Aye. I will arrange it…my lad." Then the king wrestle in his mind, *"How could a benevolent God cast such a calamity on all of us."*

Chapter I

In the name of God, the most gracious, the most merciful.

To His Holiness, Pope Urban V of the Blessed Holy Roman Catholic Church.

This is the sworn testimony of the events that took place that ultimately led to the excommunication of the entire mercenary company of men, better known as the White Company. Dear Blessed and Holy Father, please find patience and fortitude to glance down at these humble parchment pages, where you will find the actual true events that transpired between the much-lamented Pope Innocent VI and the White Company. The testimony was written in a way that the writer is not identified in order to protect the innocent. The testimony also has events that appear to take place at the same time at various locations including the very place where you reside – the papal palace itself! Rest assured that this was achieved, due in part, through a humble and harmless agent acting in our behalf. As a result, you will find that the sworn testimony may appear sometimes as omniscient and omnipresent.

Holy Father, you will also notice that there are no beautiful sonnets or poems intermingled for you to read as is the custom; this is mainly because neither the clandestine agent nor I are poets or bards. So, I do apologize in advance if you were expecting such work. Nevertheless, once you have read this entire true account, I feel confident that you will reconsider the matter and make peace with us, like the White Company endeavors to do likewise with your holiness.

The sound, smell, and sight of the blood and guts coming out of an old woman's stomach was too disturbing so early in the morning. It was Richard Romsey. A young squire in our company. He broke one of the rules of swordsmanship to always look first before executing a cut. It was a shame. The old hag was just trying to protect her daughter. How did it all come to this?

No, sorry, this is not a good place to start. This is too disturbing for the sensitive eyes of his Holy Blessedness to start reading. I am wasting good parchment. Let me start over from the very beginning of that terrible day instead...

The calmness of the early morning was broken by the sound of hoof beats hitting on the ground, and the hypnotic, bell-like sounds of metal hitting against metal. It was a small band of mercenaries making their way through a seldom-used road. They traveled on the roadway, forming a somewhat disorganized formation of two files of riders. The band itself consisted of seventy-seven men-at-arms, eighteen archers, forty-five squires and ten pages. In the rear were the baggage carts, a couple of wagons and at the front their elected leader – Sir Riis Ruffin. He had un-kept brown hair, a hefty mustache, and a large, overgrown beard. His face looked dark with dirt and grime. The only thing on his face that looked clean was the white of his blue eyes. He had on, like most of his men, plain plate armor, supplemented by chainmail underneath. His body build was tall and muscular – even on horseback, it was easy to tell. He often wondered why they had elected him as the leader, but he did not need to ponder this at this moment; his immediate goal was to meet up with an English Lord who was gathering a large company of mercenaries in Champagne France.

As far as he could tell, everyone was in high spirit of joining this great English company. They all seem to have had enough of struggling in the countryside lately. The pickings had been slim. Over two decades of war had caused much barrenness over this land. The countryside had been stripped by bands of looters, marauders, and robbers like never before. This was compounded by the king's chevauchée, the noble's oppression of the peasants and the pestilence, the 'Black Death'. Mercenaries are always needed and desired in time of war; but in time of peace, they are as wanted as the plague. King Edward made peace with France; but he signed the truce way too late in the year for most men, too late to go back home to prepare the soil and plant for harvest season, and mercenaries from distant lands had nothing to show for their troubles and expenses. Moreover, the king cannot pay for a peace time army, so, he ordered most of his troops back to England. Is there any wonder why routiers stayed behind to pillage, ransom and hold villages hostage?

Sir Ruffin's mercenary band came upon a small village – if one could even call it that. The village had no name that one could tell; but one thing was certain, its residence must have called it something. The village was no more than twenty- to thirty-odd buildings located on the side of this seldom-used road. The buildings all appeared to have been attacked and had black fire residue, and some were still smoldering. From a distance, Sir Riis thought, *its inhabitants all appear to be dead, but the only way to be sure is to check each building – one by one.* Sir Riis gave the order, "Dismount!"

"Dismount!" could be heard repeated down the file of riders.

"Check each building. Let's see what type of spoils we have for breakfast," shouted Sir Riis as he dismounted. "Everyone with your lance unit." A dismounted lance unit typically consisted of two men-at-arms and an armed squire, or, if you're lucky, another archer. Trained archers were something this band lacked. The dismounted lance units moved in a tight formation, mainly using long pikes or their individual weapons, depending on the threat. A well-trained lance unit could easily dismount armored knights or even face off with a whole charging column of knights.

Sir Riis, handing his horse to a young rosy cheeks leather clad lad, said, "Pages, you know your job… stay with the horses and supply carts." Looking at Sir Godwine, he said, "Sir Godwine, take six mounted lances and do a survey of the area and circle back – just in case this is some sort of trap." Sir Godwine Quatreton was the second in command and the best swordsmen of the mercenaries. He was clean cut and had a well-trimmed beard. His armor shone like a mirror. His red and yellow heraldry was complete and tailored for his steed and himself. He put on his war helm, mounted his gray colored spirited steed, and got busy with his orders picking six lance units to follow him.

Sir Riis went with his squire – Richard Romsey. Sir Riis decided to make him his squire a while back at Bruges. Squire Richard lacked experience, mainly because of his youth, but could hold his own in riding, archery and even some lancing. But he lacked certain instructions, one of them being true swordsmanship. And that was understandable, being that swordsmanship was historically reserved for the noble class. Sir Riis decided on his battle axe for the task at hand. The battle axe would help him in close combat, and there might have been a door or two to break down. Swords were no real help when it came to breaking down doors. The rest of the lance unit consisted of Sir Lajos, a veteran of many campaigns. He said he was a great lord from a faraway kingdom where they only spoke Magyar. He was very tall, built like an ox, and had broad shoulders. One could see his experience on his face with his multiple scars and his huge, gray mustache.

When Sir Riis' lance unit came closer to the village, one could smell smoke and death. Birds of opportunity filled the air and their songs of ad hoc could be loudly heard. The stench of death, at moments, was overpowering, but the unit needed to ignore it. Sounds of mourning, crying, weeping, struggle, and even of laughter soon became clear. Apparently, this village was not completely ransacked and dead; it was still being looted and apparently being raped! Sir Lajos acted on instinct, kicking down the door and digging his sword deep into the first intruder he found. A young girl was being raped by three French marauders. One could tell they were French by the dialect that they were spitting out. Sir Riis took his axe and buried it into the skull of the next-closest enemy. Squire Richard was going for the last one; the one who was doing the coitus crime. Squire Richard employed a short, curved sword that had been brought back from one of the crusades. Such foreign blades were extremely sharp. At this moment, someone rushed from behind Richard; he turned and cut. In a fraction, the stomach of the assailant was cut nearly in half. By this time, Sir Riis dislodged his axe from his opponent by placing a foot high on the wall for leverage and, for that moment, there was a pause. A moment in time, where time seems to move slower than usual. Before Sir Riis could make his next movement, Sir Lajos already took care of the rapist by cutting his head clean off. Unfortunately, the head had no place to go but on the chest of the young lady. Everyone watched as the blood rushed out of the neck of the body like a bottle of wine when accidentally spilled over on a dining table.

The girl was petrified with the decapitated head resting on her bare chest and his blood all over her. Sir Lajos grabbed the head, made a face of disgust, and tossed it to the corner of the room. The head rolled and landed face-up with its eyes wide open in a surprised expression and now it was staring back at the scene unfolding in the room. Sir Riis tried to calm the young girl and cover her with a blanket that he found on the floor. She frantically refused and went straight to the old lady on the floor. She was still alive.

"Maman, maman, tu vas bien maman?" The girl, sobbing, went over to hold her mother's hand.

The mother, looking at her daughter's face, said, "*J'ai mal! J'ai mal!* I don't think I'm going to be *bien* after this… you mustn't worry about me… my love. Don't be afraid… you must carry on… Don't worry, I'm a believer… I'm going to a better place now… it's all God will—"

"Don't say that… How… How can I… ever live without you?"

"He will take care of you now…" Her blue eyes rolled up as if to see heaven, but at that very last moment turned and gazed at Sir Riis' face and died. The girl collapsed and wept.

Sir Riis reached over and closed the old lady's eyes. Richard, leaning over, said, "It was all for the best that that she didn't last too long; those type of wounds are very painful." At this moment, the girl leapt from the ground and turned to attack Richard.

"Idiot! You killed her! You killed my maman! You men are no better than our countrymen! Men! Men! Men! I had enough. Robbing! Stealing! Looting! I want to kill every one of you!"

"I didn't mean it. She slithered on me from behind like that. I'm sorry! I'm sorry this ever happened!" Richard sounded genuinely upset.

"Sorry will not bring her back! Now I'm here all alone, an orphan!"

"The plague killed lots of innocent people, some of them my very own clan." Richard felt like he had to have the last word. There was no need. She went off to a corner of the room, crying and moaning. The girl had long, dark hair, and her mother's blue eyes. She had on what little was left of her torn-up peasant dress.

"What is your name?" Sir Riis asked, trying to comfort her.

"Janet…Janet Festu," she answered, trembling and sobbing.

Just then, another knight came to the room and stared around. "All the other structures are clear, Sir; nothing to be found but death. They sure destroyed this place and picked it clean." He was still shaking his head back and forth, ascertaining the events that must have occurred in this room.

Sir Lajos, cleaning his sword, said, "French, by these bastards."

"Their own countrymen?" The knight did a double take when he noticed the decapitated head at the corner of the room, staring at him.

"Thank you. Let's get ready to move out. The day is still young," Sir Riis ordered.

Richard asked, "What about the girl?"

"What about her? I guess. If she wants to, she can be in our supply wagon and help cook or something. If she cares too. If not, I don't care. You heard what she said, she wants us all killed."

"I'm sure she said that because she was upset."

Just then, it was like she became alive again. She stopped crying. Got up. Got the blanket that Sir Riis tried to offer her, and she placed it over her dead mother's body. She opened a trap door underneath the floor to reveal a stash of ham, vegetables and five bottles of wine. And she went to another room in the house. The lance unit helped themselves to the provisions and made themselves comfortable by starting a fire in the fireplace to warm up the house. They used some of the parchments and letters that were lying around in the house to start a large fire. They walked around, looking for any items of value that they could take with them.

Janet could still hear the invaders rampaging through the rest of the house. She locked the door and rapidly went to her bed headfirst. She dug deep in between the frame and mattress until she found what she was looking for. She pulls out a long sharp dagger and quickly draws it close to her body with the blade pointing into empty space. She stops to hear the invaders talking, laughing and then, her own overpowering heavy breathing. After a little while, she notices that it looks like they will not burst into her room, at least, not for the very moment. She starts to wonder what to do next. She certainly can't stay home. The village is obliterated. If she dared to travel to another village; it would probably be the same. The only family she has left is her older brother who left to serve as an archer for the Dauphin. She gleans the walls and spots her father's crossbow. She has a flash memory of her father hung from a tree starring down at her. Hung by French knights acting on the noble's request to quash a peasant uprising. These French knights killed more than just peasants; they also killed commoners. And then she thought, *they also killed a lot more than that, the role of the French nobles as protectors of the innocent*. She further thought *how ironic and cruel this world could be*. Then, she thinks there is still another way.

When Janet came back, she was wearing a men's shirt and leather pants. She also had on her back the crossbow and the dagger at her side.

She said, "These belong to my papa and brother. And believe me, I know how to use them both. Take me with you. You owe me that much. I have nothing here now. I want to be in your service."

"You are welcome as long as you swear you are not going to kill anyone of us."

"I swear by all that is holy; God the Father, Christ and the Holy Virgin."

"Do you want to bury your mother?" Sir Riis asked, pointing

at the body.

"No. I think she would understand. She said she was going to a better place." She took some flowers that were knocked over from a vase and placed them on top of her body. She reflected for a moment on how happy she was when she and her mother placed the flowers in the vase to enjoy them.

Sir Riis said in a loud, commanding voice, "Well then, let's get moving."

She looked over the mantel at the carving that her father made of their surname for the last time. Before leaving the house, Janet took a stake from the fireplace and started a fire in the house. The house was engulfed in flames by the time the mercenary band came out of the village. Sir Riis tried to look back, but a suppressed incendiary memory was too much to handle; so, he quickly looked away and forward. Squire Richard looked back, sensing that the events that took place were going to change the rest of his life and wondering why he cared so much for a young girl that he had just met. He thought, *maybe the lack of female companionship in a band of male mercenaries?* And Janet: well, she never looked back.

Chapter II

In Champagne, France, the mercenary band continued their journey west. Janet tagged along with Richard and Sir Riis Ruffin on a spare mule. It wasn't long until Squire Richard started to complain about his hunger. Sir Riis asked him, "Now remind me again – why did I decided to take you as my squire?"

"Sir, to instruct me in the use of arms and chivalry in order to complete my education as a knight."

"Ah, right. Squire Richard, I want you to become a true knight, not just a man-at-arms. Any cut-throat, thug, brute or devil can become a man-at-arms. I want something better of you." Sir Riis said, leaning on his saddle and hanging on to the cantle, "You are truly fortunate that you live in an age that you may be able to this at all. It used to be only reserved for the nobles. By my right arm, I became a squire and later a man-at-arm and then a true knight. Now, a true knight is something more… something dealing with honor… something dealing with courage… something dealing with loyalty… something dealing with bravery, something, something more. It's hard to explain with words, but when you have it, you will recognize it. And once you have it no one can take it away from you. Once you achieve this, you will need no Black Prince to kiss you and then slap your face to achieved knighthood. If you truly learn chivalry and place it in your heart; then, no one will take this from you; you will make it your very own."

Squire Richard said, "Make it my own. I heard it, Sir. I think

I understand but my stomach hurts and is making so much noise." Richard also thought that since he had known Sir Riis, he had noticed that there was something odd about his memory, especially for his age. He often repeated himself and his past was often a mystery, even to himself. These were thoughts that he would never say out loud or to anyone, not even at confession. At this moment, he glanced back at Janet, and he noticed that she seemed to be drifting to one side of her saddle. He slowed down his mount to come beside her.

Janet's world was no more, and a new world was just beginning. Her mind was spinning like a whirlwind. She could not make her thoughts stop. She was thinking of a million thoughts and, at times, none at all. She was thinking of her lost mother, father, family, friends, and village. Thoughts of the brutal death of her father and now her mother's death. She questioned in her mind, *what happened to her brother who left to serve the Dauphin. The attack on the village, the rape, the pain on her body and soul. And ironically, happy thoughts of the village's celebrations* all clouded her mind at once. Then she stopped thinking, and just thought of the scenery unfolding in front of her, felt the mule between her legs and heard the English conversation between the two knights. Her thoughts then drifted to the last time she slept: *Was it the night of the attack? No,* she chuckles to herself. *Was it the night before the attack?* She didn't sleep that night either; but why? She couldn't remember why; it seemed like another world now. She remembered; her mother was sick and had trouble falling asleep so she couldn't fall asleep, either. She so looked forward to having a good night's sleep that fateful night.

She was dosing off and leaning away to one side of her mule. Squire Richard reached over with his arm, grab her by her shoulder and pulled her back onto her saddle. She woke up and heard the two knights conversing again.

"Bravery, loyalty, and honor is chivalry. Honor of all kinds; to your Lord, honor to women. Are you listening, Squire Romsey?"

"Aye, Sir Riis. Honor to the ladies. Please continue – Sir," Richard answered as he urged his mount forward to come along even with Sir Riis mount.

Sir Riis looked back, ascertaining what had occurred just a moment ago, and looked back at his Squire. "Oh, there are chivalric qualities like bravery, courage, discipline. Ah, yes, one of those chivalric qualities is discipline." Sir Riis made a motion of his fist from his heart to his stomach. "You have to train your stomach like you train your body to fight." Sir Riis said these things while holding the reigns of his horse with one hand and stroking his overgrown beard with the other.

"What do you mean?"

"Discipline: You train your body to ignore the cold, or harsh conditions from time to time when battle conditions dictate it. Don't you? When holding a bow and aiming to hit an enemy and a fly buzz on your arm or face do you stop what you're doing to slap it? If the life of a brother is at stake? I would hope not! You will ignore the fly! You will learn to ignore ants, spiders and bees. This is discipline. Likewise, imagine your stomach like a puppy dog. You tell it to sit and wait for a while for that well deserve meal."

"I think I understand what you are saying, but it looks like we are coming up to a tavern. Can we just stop and get something to eat?"

"Well… yes, but I wish we wouldn't have come to this tavern just right now so you would have learned your lesson a little better; but the fact of the matter is that I'm hungry too."

Squire Richard took a hold of his crusader cross that he wore around his neck and kissed it. He says that his grandfather took it into one of the crusades and it brought him lots of luck. He kissed it, again, and again, and then gave thanks to almighty God. "At last, a decent meal!"

"Not so loud. This is just for our lance group."

They let the file of men go by. Sir Riis motioned at Sir Godwine. "I will be here for the night to try to get more information about this English Lord and this great company. Keep moving and camp until I return. You know the routine and what is expected from everyone. Also, please let me borrow your Damascus blade." Sir Godwine looked at Janet and then gave Sir Riis a strange look. Then, he gave Sir Riis a small shiny blade. There were four horses tied outside the tavern.

"Squire Richard, do you see the horses tied outside?" Sir Riis said, pointing at the horses.

"Yes," Richard raised himself on the saddle and straining to see, "we are still at some distance, though."

"From here I can tell that three are charger horses for light war use; but one is for heavy cavalry and awfully expensive. Make mine look like a prow horse."

"I can't tell."

"It is the strong muscle definition. It's a destrier horse, I would say, a nobleman's horse. It's the second from the right."

"Do you see it now?"

"Yes. I think so."

After the last supply wagon went by, Sir Riis' lance unit went into the inn's tavern Sir Lajos with his page, Janet, and Squire Richard. Entering the drinking hall of the inn, it was easy to spot the group who had to have the horses. Besides them lined up in a uniform row were four longbows. These had to be English longbowmen. One looked at Sir Riis and one of them said, "Was that your brigade that went by?"

"Aye. And greetings, fellow free soldiers."

"What is that?" he said, pointing at Janet. "A bow-women? What type of brigade has women archers? Ha, I will love to fight this company."

Janet responded, "I bet I can shoot that little thing you call your manhood right off at a hundred paces!"

The English man got up and made a thrusting motioned with his hips and pelvis as he said, "Oh yeah, I think you can at one to two paces, back and forth with your mouth!" Laughter ensued. Janet got flushed and just sat on a chair. They started to laugh, but not just them – other people in the tavern as well.

"Women have no place in the battlefield. They either belong cooking or on a marriage bed."

"Well, that's quite enough," Sir Riis said, "I want no problems. We are all free soldiers here. All forming free companies at will. Look here, we are trying to meet up with an English Lord. One of your very own."

By this time the innkeeper came over and asked, "What do you care for, my good sir?"

"Do you have any rooms?"

"Aye."

"We'll take one room. My friend here," he said, pointing to Richard, "Will sleep at the stables. What do you have to eat?"

"Meat pie or umble pie."

"I would pick the umble pie, if I were you, at least you know what meat it is," mentioned a voice from another table.

"I'll take three umble pies with mugs of ale."

"Can I have milk?" Janet asked.

"No, milk is only for babies and cooking. Besides, it will rot your stomach when you get underneath the sun. Learn to drink ale."

At this moment, there was a loud commotion at the bar. "Francs! What the hell are Francs?" shouted Sir Lajos, grabbing the innkeeper by his neck.

"I'm just telling you that's the new French coins that the king has issued… Of course, your gold sous are good here," said the innkeeper, handing ale mugs to Sir Lajos and his Page. Sir Lajos' Page was young but not much younger than Squire Richard. He had dark eyes with dark hair and was very skinny. Then, one of the English longbowmen who seemed to have awaken from his drunkenness. He was well-built, thin, young with short, straw-colored hair; but the most striking physical feature was that he had one blue eye and the other green.

"My friend, are you trying to join the great English free company amassing?"

"Do you know where they are?"

"Yes. Just keep on this road west until you encounter a town that was devoured by the plague some years back and then go north toward Reims. Then, you will run into them."

"If you are interested, your group can join us. We're in need of more trained longbowmen."

"Thank you kindly for the offer. But I'm not in charge. Let me present to you Sir Thomas Marshal."

Just then, Sir Marshal looks like someone had kicked him underneath the table.

"Yes, yes, yes…" He looks at the last person who spoke. "What am I agreeing to, anyway?"

"That, to thank the good knight and that it is best that we be going on our way."

"Ah, aye. Aye… we have been here far too long."

"Wait, before you go. Is it true? Who is this, Lord? I hate to lead my men into a great disappointment."

"Oh, yes, it's all true. The lord's name is Lord John Hawkwood. He is, *milites nobiles*. Knighted by the Black Prince himself at the Battle of Poitiers."

"Milites nobiles?" Squire Richard asked.

"That is Latin for a true knight. My young friend. But pay me no heed. We were part of King Edward's grand army. But now I'm just in a heraldry pursuit with Sir Marshal here before we head back to England. We need to reach an Officer-of-Arms for a formal marshaling. One of his descendants on his mother's side... I believe. This will aid his sons in future tournaments since he's too old to compete any more. So, we must be going."

"Can I have the honor of your name, Sir Knight?"

"I'm Sir Albert Sterz of Swabia, which is why I'm hard to understand sometimes. But now I'm surrounded by all these Englishmen these days. Nonetheless, at your service."

"I understood you just fine. I'm originally from a small kingdom in Bavaria myself, so, I know of the Duchy of Swabia. Either way, lots of people here are from other areas like my friend and colleague here. Sir Lajos is further east–"

"...And south." Sir Lajos turned to the conversation with a large mug of ale.

"I think I recognize the accent. Magyar? Jó estét kívánok!" Sir Sterz said in Magyar.

"Ah... *Örülök, hogy megismertem! Hogy van?*" Sir Lajos responded in his native tongue.

"Well, I don't speak too much, just a little. Nice to meet your acquaintance." He picked up his longbow and left. Sir Thomas and the rest of the group followed. Sir Riis noticed that Sir Sterz got on the second horse from the right.

Richard turned to Sir Riis. "Why do I have to sleep in the stables? Why doesn't she?" He turned to Janet, who was rocking on her chair, back and forth. At this time, Janet noticed that the room was moving, like being on a boat. She thought it must be the awful-tasting ale. She scoffed and pushed the ale away onto the table.

"Squire Richard, you need to stay with the horses and look after them. They are the most important and most expensive equipment we possess. Now, do what I tell you and go take care of the horses." Richard gave Sir Riis very strange look especially when he figured out that Janet was going with him. Sir Riis grabbed Janet by her hand. "Come with me." They walked and entered the rented room. It was a comfortably sized room, but for a person like Sir Riis who was used to sleeping underneath the stars or in a large tent it felt like a tomb for him. Janet was trembling with fear.

"Don't worry, girl. I'm not going to take anything that you won't give freely. I just want to talk to you," Sir Riis said. Janet was shaking and looked really scared. She was just looking down on the floor and started to cry. Sir Riis started to think that this was going to take longer than he anticipated. "Janet, if you are serious about joining us, you are better off in a more traditional role of support, like cooking or something else."

"Like one of your *putains*… how you say it… whores? That's it. You want me to be one of your whores!" she snapped back.

"No, Janet. Calm down. Do you really know how to use that crossbow?"

"You don't need to worry about that, sir! The first time I get a chance, I will prove it to you. I'm also good with other weapons as well. And I can read and write, too. My papa taught me."

"All right, all right then. But you are still a girl. There is a reason we are called men-at-arms and not ladies-at-arms. And if you really want to be with us you will need to blend in. I need you to cut your hair to look like a man."

"My hair." She took a hold of her long hair and looked at it.

"Oh, yes – your hair." Sir Riis took out Sir Godwine's Damascus blade and tried to grab her, but she gave him the slip. But then Sir Riis faked a move, grabbed her, and started to cut her hair, saying, "Do you want to be part of this company?"

"Oui…Oui!"

"Then stop resisting." Janet stopped resisting and crying. Sir Riis finished cutting her hair and put the blade away. It was a bad haircut job, but at least she looked more like a young lad now, Sir Riis thought. "There is a bucket of water there at the corner of the room to wash yourself."

"I don't need a bath."

"You need a bath. Your face is still covered with soot and there is still dried blood all over your chest."

"I don't need a bath. Do you treat all your men this way? I want to be treated like a man."

"But Janet, you are not a man. I'm going downstairs to the stables now to sleep with Richard. We are leaving at dawn with or without you."

Sir Riis found Squire Richard at the horse stables. "I want to talk to you a little about swordsmanship before we finish for the night."

"Aye, Sir," said Richard, getting his sword on.

"Next time you're in a situation like we experienced at the village; I want you to do this."

"I feel really bad about what happened today." He looked down, shaking his head in discontent.

"Like you said, you need to get over it and just move on with life and learn from the experience. Janet's mother came at you from out of nowhere, but you still had an enemy in front of you. You're lucky he didn't pull out his cock and stab you with a dagger. You must turn your headfirst, that's it, leaving the sword pointing at the first opponent." Sir Riis started demonstrating the technique with his sword and body. "Then, if there is another attacker, you go straight to a cut. If there is no attacker, you don't cut. You got it? Now let me see you do it." Richard got his sword and repeated the moves several times until he got it right. Sir Riis laid down on the hay and drifted off to sleep still watching Richard repeating the same move and some other sword moves that Sir Riis taught him in the past.

Later, when Sir Riis slowly opened his eyes, he saw an attractive young lady staring at him. She had very short hair, a tight shirt, tight leather pants and a crossbow tied across her back. It was Janet. Sir Riis also noticed an arm around his neck and shoulders – it was Richard's. Sir Riis politely picked Richard's arm and moved it off from him. By this time, Richard woke up as well. Janet said, "Well, it's dawn – let's get moving."

"Hey, I give the orders around here... your hair?" Sir Riis said, sitting up and rubbing his eyes.

"What about my hair? Oh... you mean what happened after you butchered it? The inn keeper's wife. That's what happened. She helped me with it and also helped me tailor my garments to fit better. What do you think?" She turned around so they would see the entire outfit.

Richard said, "I like it." Janet responded via a small curtsy.

"It looks very nice – Janet. But the idea is to blend in. And... your... your chest?" Sir Riis said, rubbing his own chest area.

"What about it?"

"You'll were supposed to hide–"

"...What?" Janet said, putting her hands on her hips.

"You enhanced... them... you brought more attention to them, not less."

"Oh," she said, looking down at her cleavage, "I got a cloak that will cover them and will do the job nicely."

"How did you pay for all of this, anyway?" Sir Riis said, standing up.

Janet took a step back. "I got it from the innkeeper's wife. She gave it to me. It was a family member of hers who died years ago from the plague."

"I didn't know?" Sir Riis said, rubbing his head.

"I did everything you told me; so, what's the problem now?"

By this time, Sir Lajos was waking up from all the commotion. He looked up and half his face was covered with horse manure which came from the improvised pillow. He staggered to his feet and walked to a pail of water. "I like the new look. And you're clean and smell nice. Joanna is a miracle worker."

Sir Riis walked over to Janet. "Who is Joanna?"

"The innkeeper's wife!"

"She looks pretty!" Lajos' Page shouted out of nowhere. This was very unusual, for no one had heard him speak before. Everyone thought the boy was either a mute or didn't understand English.

"I don't know about all of this; it's just not… natural," Sir Riis said, putting his hands on his head and rubbing it again.

"Natural for who? If anyone ever gives us a hard time, we'll just say he's French!" Sir Lajos laughed, cleaning his face.

"I don't know. I'm beginning to think all of this is a very bad idea," Sir Riis said, thoroughly cleaning himself as well.

Chapter III

Pope Innocent the Sixth reigned as the fifth Catholic Pope at Avignon. Avignon is an estate in France located adjacent to the Rhone River. Pope Innocent himself was very old and in bad health. Sleeping a whole night was less frequent than it used to be. At his bed chambers, the Pope woke up on his oversized bed, gasping for breath and holding his chest. He pulled on a gilded rope at his bedside in order to alert for his priest attendants. But no one came at his call. "What the hell! Where are these cock suckers? These sons of bitches?" He struggled to get out of his sheets and off his bed. This caused him to fall hard on the ground, making a loud thump. He had on a very light white robe to sleep in, which one could see through to his feeble, misshapen body. The Pope had very short legs and an oversized stomach with hardly any trace of hair on his balding head. He left his chambers, walking awkwardly and staggering down the dark hallways. Bishop Gilles Aycelin de Montagu overheard the commotion that was outside his door. Came out of his room noticed it was the Pope and came to his aid.

"Fire and brimstone, fire and brimstone falling from heaven! Just like in the scriptures, it is written… It's the end of the world!" The Pope stumbled and fell again on the cold stone floor.

"Holy Father, please let me help you." Bishop Aycelin tried to get a hold of his arm to lift him up.

The Pope rejected his gesture. "Who are you? I don't recognize you! You are not familiar to me; go away!"

Two priest attendants finally arrived. "What's wrong, Holy Father?" They helped the Pope get back to his chambers and into bed. One of the priests turned to Bishop Aycelin. "Your Excellency, please go back to your chambers now; we have everything at hand."

"Fire and brimstones... killing everyone. All the king's knights... fire and brimstone! Punishment from the almighty," continued repeating the Pope.

The priest got the other priest attendant. "Get Cardinal Gil de Albornoz quickly!" The second priest attendant ran off. The other priest was trying to get him in bed, but the Pope was fighting with him so he could stand up on the bed.

"Damn it! Get me my pot; you idiot; I have to urinate!" The priest rushed to get the pot. The Pope finally got up again and pulled his night shirt, waited, but nothing. The priest held the pot at the correct height and distance and looked away. The Pope tried and tried but urinated only a few drops. Finally, he gave up. And laid back down again on the bed. Cardinal Albornoz finally walked in very quickly with a glass of his elixir that he had especially mixed for the pontiff. He had on a sleeping robe and an open coat that were flapping in the wind like wings on an enormous red bird as he walked by.

"I had a nightmare – no... a vision from God! Albornoz," the Pope said, pulling up at his sheets, trying to get them to his face.

"I see. Drink this for now; it will calm you and help you go back to sleep."

"Aye." The Pope drank it right away with some of the elixir dripping from both sides of his mouth.

"Go ahead, tell me all about it."

"I've seen His power of fire and brimstones coming down

from heaven to destroy an evil army."

"Holy Father, what evil army?"

"King Edward's, of course!"

"King Edward the Third!"

"Who else? His men have been chevauchée, looting, robbing, and raping the French countryside. And he won't stop until he is king of all France. The carnage... the bodies. I've never seen anything like it before. But was it real? Could it be just a dream, a nightmare, or a vision from God?" By this time, the elixir was starting to take effect.

"Cardinal Albornoz, what time is it?"

"It's very early in the morning... too early. You have dignitaries and a papal report in your itinerary tomorrow. Do you want me to cancel it?"

"No, you Castilian cocksucker. And before you go, can you check behind the curtains for me?"

Cardinal Albornoz walked to the curtains of the pontiff windows. "There is nothing behind the curtains, Holy Father." The Pope, looking hard at that side of his large bed chambers to ensure the Cardinal's assessment, then asked, "No one is there?"

"I assure you, my Holy Father. No. No one. Did you see someone? If there's an intruder, we must alert the guards." The Cardinal closed the curtains.

"No one was there?"

"I assure you, My Holy Father. What was it exactly that you saw?" Cardinal Albornoz crept to his bedside.

"A dark figure. I couldn't see his face. I didn't recognize him either!" said the Pope, still pulling at his sheets.

"What? If someone got in the pontiff bed chamber, we must investigate immediately. I will have to get the commander of the guards?"

"Never mind; I don't see him any longer. You Castilian cocksucker. How long till daybreak?" The Pope was showing signs of the elixir working.

"Holy Father, you need to rest, so, I advise you to sleep." Cardinal Albornoz got up to extinguish some of the candles in the room. *They really turned on too many candles for his little outburst tonight,* he thought. While turning off the candles he glanced at the oversize fireplace. *Maybe the pontiff is seeing shadows cast from the fireplace,* he thought to himself. The column and mantle comprised of two, human-sized muscular angels whose arms and wings held up the mantle. *Quite a work of art*, he thought. He had forgotten the master craftsman's name, but he did remember that he was Italian, from a more civilized time and culture. On his way out, he also noticed on top of the pontiff's personal desk the day's itinerary. After a cursory review, he noticed Bishop Gilles Aycelin de Montagu name on the top of the agenda. That French name sounded familiar, and then he left, wondering to himself about that night's event.

Later in the morning, at the Pope's palace's central courtyard. This was the place where the Pope liked to have breakfast and conduct most of his papal business, especially when it was a nice day.

"Introducing Bishop Gilles Aycelin de Montagu back from papal legate duties," the Papal Priest attendant announced.

"Holy Father, it is a pleasure to finally meet you," he said, bowing and kissing the Papal ring.

"There, there, my son no need to pretend; I recognize you right away. I may be old but I'm not crazy. I was just indisposed last night. My customary attendants didn't come on time. But thank you in trying to give me aid."

"I didn't do anything that my Christian nature wouldn't allow me to pursue. I guess it comes from my childhood. My brother when I was very young was ran over in a horrible accident by a rich nobleman. The rich nobleman didn't care or take any responsibility for his actions. It was up to me to take care of my injured brother. Which I did for a few months until he finally died. I knew then I wanted to take care of the less fortunate than myself. The Priesthood was a logical progression for me since my other brother and uncle are both in the clergy. After I became a Priest, the plague hit my parish hard. I would go out every day to tend to the people that were sick with the plague. I was warned that it was dangerous and that I could die, but I trusted in Christ's blood to shield me. And, as you can see, I never became sick." Bishop Aycelin's eyes started watering and he grabbed his silver cross that was around his neck. "Well, I guess I talked too much. Holy Father."

"Nonsense – please go on."

"Oh, where was I? Oh, yes, the plague. Those were dark days. I saw so much death with the plague and recently at the Battle of Poitiers." Bishop Aycelin adjusted his scrolls in his hands and continued. "This time I was there not as a Priest but now a Bishop, acting as the king's chancellor. The French authorities didn't want me to go out and administer viaticum to the fallen soldiers; but I could not do that. I disguised myself as a local parish Priest and went out with some monks that were willing to do the Lord's work. I saw so many bodies that day that were cut to pieces. I saw bodies at different stages of rigor mortis. The most striking thing to me… was the last expression on some of their faces as they entered the gates of Hell. Sometimes one would find a devoted believer and their face would be calm and restful. I saw so much death between the Black Death and the

Battle of Poitiers that I could feel when death was nigh." Bishop Aycelin placed some of his scrolls on the pontiff's breakfast table.

"How so, my son?"

"I could feel a chill down my spine, my hair felt like it was standing, and my skin crawled."

"Ah, these are natural reaction when tending to people so close to death."

"Yes, I thought that way too. But I was always right when someone's spirit was about to depart. On the battlefields, it would be a race. I started to see the shadow of death hovering and going after the fallen and the sick. Judgement for them would soon be over. The righteous a graceful death. The unconfessed a sentence of hell for their sins. One would hurry to a fallen and give him his viaticum. Then one would like to tend for him until they depart, but I would see the shadows of death progressing down the field. It was a race to save souls, my Holy Father. I saw so much death that I learned to feel it, see it, and even recognize it. I became troubled when death turned and recognized me. But I assure you, I stayed faithful to the Church's doctrine. I know it's hard to believe to see the face of death and all that."

"I think this is your true divine gift from God almighty; don't reject it." The Pope continued to eat some of his leftover breakfast and asked, "My son, have you ever been at Avignon before?"

"Once... actually... at your pontiff election. I worked outside at the conclave and later at the presentation mass. In all, it was quite an auspicious occasion. A very fortunate event that will always live in my mind as a fond memory," Bishop Aycelin said, sitting down, getting comfortable in a chair.

"We are at Avignon for a half a century now, ever since Pope Clement the fifth refused to move back to Rome and purchase this estate from Joanna I of Naples. He then moved the entire Roman Catholic Church court into this Papal enclave in France. Since then, only French Popes have been elected to an ancient Roman institution. Well, that is enough pleasantries this beautiful morning. Well, go ahead, tell me about the news from the frontlines with that Devil of a King of England."

"Yes, I do have news of King Edward and his army. As you may know, the king tried to conquer Paris, but the city defenders refused to meet in open combat. He still tried to siege the city, but the breaches of the city held. Finally, the English left the attack of Paris. They have laid waste to the countryside robbing and looting everything they seen."

"Yes… yes, he says, he is the true King of France, that he loves the people, he loves the land, but then he goes around killing, pillaging, attacking, and destroying like the Vikings of old. I know all of this, please continue."

"The English, your grace, arrived at the gates of Chartres. The defenders of the city again refuse to meet him in open combat due to his large army of over ten thousand men. The English made camp just outside Chartres in an open field. Then, there was a lightning and hailstorm, like no one has seen before. It wounded and killed over a thousand men and six thousand horses. Among the injured was Sir Guy de Beauchamp who later died of his injuries. Since England has battle over France, there has been no other recorded battle that has killed so many men in one day. Truly, it was the hand of God. People have coined this day, April 14th, as 'Black Monday'."

"Black Monday! Black Death! The Black Plague! All punishments from almighty God! This was my vision that God granted his servant to see. Fire and brimstone raining down from heaven to punish the king for his evil deeds. This is even clearer to me now since his troops must have been pillaging and raping on the holy time of lent since that Sunday was Easter!"

"But here is the turn of events, it was reported that King Edward kneeled in the direction of Cathedral of Our Lady of Chartres. It is said that he repented on what he has done and seek peace with France."

"I don't think there can be peace with the likes of him."

"Holy Father, this is not all. The very next day, Androuin de La Roche, who is the French commander, arrived at the camp with a peace proposal. King Edward was astonished. He took this as a sign from God. Prompting him to Bretigny and, eventually, signing a truce. Within days, a Peace Treaty was drafted, agreed, and signed. The treaty stops his claim on the French crown in turn for territories that he wanted. I brought a copy for your grace, that is the main purpose of my visit. It lays out the details and describes all the lands that is now granted to the King of England."

"Tell me. Did he release John the rightful King of France?"

"As far as I know, he is still holding him for ransom and at a very high ransom at that."

"How much?"

"Ransom was set at three million crowns."

"Three million crowns! Absurd! How is France going to raise that amount? Ransom! He is the devil incarnated. All he cares about are domains, wealth, and power. If he doesn't change his ways, so help me I will excommunicate him."

"The cost of peace, my grace. But we are also getting disturbing reports from lawlessness from the lack of French ruling. Additionally, now you have thousands of out-of-work mercenaries. There are reports that they are forming large free mercenaries' companies. The fear is that if they amass into large great companies they can hold hostage whole villages, towns or even cities." The bishop put down on the table his last piece of parchment that he was reading from and lean back on his chair.

"Thank you for the documents, your insights, and the

detailed report; all this will be taken into careful consideration. May God bless you and grant you safe passage to your next destination. Have my clerk write an official papal order for you and your men. Where is your next stop?"

"It will be Milan to visit the Visconti family," Bishop Gilles Aycelin responded.

"Be careful, roads are dangerous even for a Bishop with pontiff papers."

"I travel with a small contingent of men that the Dauphin has gracefully lend for my travels. They are brave, faithful and courageous in caring out their duties."

"Tell me, my son, do you like your present duties?"

"I'm more a diplomat than I am a bishop; but I do like the interaction with the monarchs, the French and the English. I like being involve with important decisions that affect the people."

"Ah… my son, you should be more interested in the future of the Church? Our main goal should be for the pope seat to remain French. And for the pontiff to stay here, not in Rome – that ancient, perverse city. My son, do you happen to know Cardinal Gil de Albornoz?"

"I only know him by face and reputation."

"Well, he seems to know you well enough that he has recommended that you remain in this court. I trust his judgement on these matters. Even though he's a cock sucking Castilian. I need someone here to take care of me while he is away. There are certain things that I only trust him to take care off. Likewise, I will need someone to take care of certain things here at Avignon. Can I count on you? What about if I offer you a place here at my court? Would you be willing to stay Gilles?"

"But what about my responsibilities and duties I've been assigned?"

"Don't worry about that, I will have Cardinal Albornoz take care of everything."

"What do you say, *Cardinal* Gilles Aycelin de Montagu?"

Chapter IV

The next day, the clearing of the mercenary camp was not hard to find on the side of the road. The encampment was almost a complete circle with sentries posted at its only entrance. The sentries recognized Sir Riis Ruffin lance unit and entry was granted. "Greetings! Any good news?" Sir Godwine shouted. He was wearing his aketon that he normally wore underneath his plate armor. He did a double take on Janet's new look and gentlemanly helped her dismount. She didn't appreciate his gentleman's curtesy and scurried to the campfire. Squire Richard waited, mounted, for Sir Godwine to help him down and said, "Sir Godwine... I'm waiting?" Sir Godwine slapped the side of Richard's horse which caused the steed to jump to a gallop.

Sir Riis, dismounting his horse, said, "Aye. We are closer to our objective than ever before. We need to continue on this road; heading west until we hit the next town that was consumed by the plague and then north toward Reims."

"The Black Death?" Sir Godwine's eyes widened, and he stood up straighter.

"Oh, it is supposed to be safe by now, especially if we just travel through it and we don't stop. Besides, I was told that it happened a long time ago."

"Should we make ready to leave today?" Sir Godwine found himself a place near their campfire.

"No, it's too late in the day. Let the men and horses rest we have been pushing them hard lately trying to catch up with this

English Lord. Now that we are close, I'm beginning to feel the responsibility of it all; is this really the right decision for all of us?"

Sir Godwine, squatting down and eating some wild berries that were picked earlier, said, "We all decided on this new venture. So, the responsibility really is not all on your shoulders. So don't worry so much. But we have been pushing the men hard. It's a good location and it is kind of late in the day; I think it's a good idea to stay for one more night."

"Sir Godwine, why was I elected? There are a few men here with noble titles that would better fit as commander... yourself included. Besides, I'm not even–"

"... English?" Sir Godwine said while finishing eating his berries. "Aye. But you have mercenary experience, and for most of us this is our first time. So, they expect that you will lead them to fair and honest mercenary contract work. Moreover, most men have seen you in battle already and have seen you lead a lance cavalry charge... not an easy thing to do. Besides, the way you speak, you pass for an Englishman."

Sir Riis replied, "I only hope that I will be able to fulfill my obligations as honorably as possible and not to disappoint you." Sir Riis gave a slight bow and then, leaning a little closer to Sir Godwine, said, "After we eat, can you set up some archery targets for the archers and for the war machine?"

Later, at a clearing near the camp. "Janet, take a hold of your crossbow. Do you see the target underneath the small green banner?"

Janet took her crossbow from her back and at once started reeling the bow for a bolt. She set the bolt in the crossbow rail. "I see it."

"Well, shoot it! What are you waiting for? Move! I need to see if you can shoot or it's going to be the kitchen and greasy spoons for you. Or worst, I'll send you to…"

An arrow bolt hit the mark and made a snapping noise as it hit its target. "Good. Now, do you see the blue banner further out?" An arrow bolt hit the mark and another satisfying snapping sound with a target hit. "Ah… I was going to say the wooden bucket on top of the…" The bucket splattered with the force of the cross bolt. The mercenaries' group of longbowmen are coming over to practice. Sir Riis asked, "The rest of the archers are coming, and we haven't even talked about changing your name to a male name. What do you have in mind?"

"I don't know. I haven't given it much thought. Hum, Liam?"

"That's English. You change gender, not nationality. What about something common, like Lancelot, or Lancelet?"

"Oh, no, I hate those names. But I like a name starting with the letter L."

"How about Louys?"

"Oh, the idea of somebody calling me that name kills me."

"Janet, the archers are fast approaching. You need to decide quickly. What about Lorence?"

"No, no, not that name please." She shook her head and then said, "Oh, I know, Lambert. Yes, introduce me as Lambert, please."

"Ah, what do we have here? A small Frenchman with a crossbow?" The band of archers were with upon them before they noticed.

"Aye. His name is Lambert. He's part of my lance group… the archer. I beckoned to recognize him as one of my own lance group. In other words, don't kill him and be nice to him."

Sir Hugh, walking over with his longbow, said, "An archer? Shooting a crossbow is not archery." Sir Hugh Heton was the commanding knight for the longbowmen. "There is no discipline in it. Takes no training," Sir Hugh said, looking down at Janet. He pushed her out of the way as he walked back to the camp.

"I never shoot with a crossbow – do you mind if I try it?" a young archer asked.

"Now, the only really hard thing is loading it. Once you do that, you aim and fire," Janet said, handing her crossbow already loaded and pointing downrange. She showed the young archer how to aim and shoot.

The younger archer aimed, fired and hit his target. "Wow, you know how long it took me to shoot the bow and hit the target with such force? But this bolt loading sure takes a toll and time," he said, handing back the crossbow back to Janet.

"I would like to try the longbow," Janet said, "can you show me?" Laughter ensued by the group of archers.

The young archer, putting away the bow, said, "Sure, Lambert, I will teach you!" More laughter ensued.

Janet looked around. "What is so funny?"

"Nothing is funny. It's that you don't know what you're asking."

"Here, try my bow. I will show you the best and easiest way to pull it and shoot it." The young archer lifted the bow high and brought it down slowly, pulling at the string. The sound of the bow's wood as it was being stressed by the string pulled on each end could be heard. As the great tension builds, the archer aims and then the snap of the release of the arrow fills the air. Finally, the sound of the hit of the target that landed next to the crossbow bolt that had just been shot.

"Here you go; now, you try it. I will suggest just leaving one end of the bow on the ground due to your height, which is another permissible way of shooting it, as well." When Janet tried, she had an impossible time with the balancing of the bow in one hand and the arrow in the other. She couldn't hold onto the arrow when aiming and pulling. She gave it her best effort but couldn't make the arrow fly any more than a few feet and with no power.

"This almost feels... impossible."

"Don't feel bad. These men train for years and years just to develop the right set of muscles. Look at their right forearms, they have large powerful muscles. You could almost say they look deformed," Sir Riis said.

"Oh, yeah they have huge forearm muscles."

"And their right hand's three index figures are like eagle's claws. It's from years of training. I, myself, have been training for years and I'm not as nearly as good as them. It's hard to be as good as the English. The English train their people in archery from very young. Whole towns will usually come together on Sunday, after worship, I believe, and just practice and train together."

"Can you show me?"

"Oh, I'm not good enough. Maybe you'll find an Englishman who can teach you properly." Just then, there was the sound and dust rising from a wagon coming to their location. "Oh, at last, here comes the surprise I have for you!" Squire Richard rode up with one of the supply wagons. Janet's heart dropped as she felt like this was all some type of sick jest. And the wagon was the kitchen full of greasy spoons waiting for her to clean. Or worst this was the whore wagon waiting for her to be put to good use by them. She almost fainted.

Finally, Squire Richard drove the wagon next to the group of archers. Sir Riis cried, "Squire Richard, pull the tarp!" Richard revealed a gigantic wooden crossbow. She felt so relieved to see a familiar object of her chosen craft and that they had accepted her for what she really was – one of them, a soldier. Even though she was really a *lady pretending to be a man*. Even back home she was not allowed to join the French force because of her gender, and she had to stay home and take care of her mother. A lot of good that did. Those men snuck up and surprised them at night like cowards. She held back tears. She didn't want them to see that she was getting emotional because this might show her true gender. So, she tried to replace that emotion with that of extreme excitement that men are so often known for. "Wow, that's fucken amazing." She knew men usually got excited about things like this, so she would fit right in.

"Yeah, fucken aye, we can kill any asshole at three hundred paces away with this monster."

"Yeah!" Another archer jumped in, waving his fist in the air.

Sir Riis, jumping on top of the wagon and patting the machine like if it was a living animal, said, "The machine itself was designed to fire arrow bolts. Squire Richard and a mercenary rock slinger modified it to also shoot rocks. Richard can you please do the honor?" Richard locked and loaded a rock. "Do you see those banners on the ridge?"

"Yes; but I thought those were for another group of archers since they are so far away."

"What other archers? This is all of us. Those are for the war machine."

"We try to use rocks more than bolts because the bolt shafts come at great expense. Rocks are a little easier to come by. You just to have pick the right sizes and shape them up a little." Richard shot at the target.

"You are too low. Did you seen where it landed?" Janet

asked. Richard grinded his teeth and locked and loaded and fired again. "You're right and low this time. Did you see it?" Janet asked again.

"If you think you can do better, then try it yourself!"

Janet loaded the crossbow and fired the rock – it fell just shy of the first target. "That would have killed or at least injured the enemy!" a voice came from the group of archers. She loaded another – this time it hit the mark. The arches that were spectators were 'oohing' and cheering, "Lambert hit his mark!" and then she hit the next target with no adjustments.

Sir Riis thought, *I need someone that can hit the target the first time under pressure. I'm convinced she is the war machine shooter from now on.*

Squire Richard thought, *why are they cheering and shouting for Lambert? Who the hell is Lambert?*

Later that night, the tents were all set up as custom. Sir Riis' tent was between Sir Godwine and Sir Lajos. Sir Riis Ruffin's tent resided Squire Richard Romsey and now officially archer Lambert. That night, Janet was preparing a place for her to sleep.

"Now, Janet, whenever you have to go…" Richard said.

"Go where?" She looked up with a questioning look.

Richard, setting up his sleeping cot, said, "Your necessities… I can be your lookout to make sure nobody notices."

"Notices what?" Janet said, finishing up on her bed rest area.

"Well, that you're really a girl!" Richard said, walking up to her and raising his hands to remove his aketon.

"Do men really pay that much attention to each other when their doing their… necessities?" Janet stood her ground with her hands on her hips.

"Actually, yes, it may happen."

Sir Riis was getting comfortable in his cot. "Janet, use Squire Richard to protect you. We don't want people to notice the truth. People's ignorance to the whole possibility of a women warrior is beyond me. Have you ever heard of Joanna of Flanders?"

"Oui! Who has not heard of Jeanne la Flamme? She dressed in armor, led men into battle and defended her keep when her husband was imprisoned. She managed to burn the invaders' camp when they were away so that's how she earned her moniker. She also urged fellow country women to do likewise because of lack of men to engage the enemy."

"That's right – until she was told to stop, leave her land, and was sent to England under king's order," Sir Riis interjected as he propped up himself on his sleeping cot.

Janet responded, "Didn't King Edward declare her mentally unstable and lock her away?"

Sir Riis had a faraway look in his eyes. "Oh, he very well did lock her away at Tickhill Castle. She is still there today. And that's my very point. Likewise, my mother was no warrior, but she scared the living daylights out of my father, who was one of the greatest warriors in the whole kingdom. Besides, I've seen the future. You have shown it to me today… Janet."

"I did?"

"Ja, you did. I see a future where it doesn't matter if you are a man or a woman. As long as you can properly aim and hit the enemy. What does it matter what you have between your legs? We tried many men before on that siege machine; it was not just you. You have a natural talent. I really mean that. Richard, do you remember the tall red-headed fellow? He was the one who shot at Sir Godwine thinking he was a practice target."

"Ha, yeah, I remember him. He killed his warhorse instead."

Laughter from the both of them filled the tent.

"Aye. Shot his horse right from underneath him almost killing Sir Godwine in the process. Sir Godwine was so upset, he had that mare since his childhood. Some say, they heard him say, why it couldn't be him that got shot that day. Ha, that guy was so blind thinking he was a target. Whatever happened to him?"

"Oh remember, the Gascon skirmish? He perished there. Curious thing was that he was the only one who died of several stab wounds with a small Damascus dagger found on his neck. All the others were injured from arrows or other projectiles... Hum... interesting."

"And what about that guy who got his right hand caught on the machine's apparatus and when he fired it... cut off his hand!"

"Ha! Aye! Yeah! I remember that."

"Whatever happened to him?"

"Oh, that's Leftie; he is our cook now."

Janet looked at her right hand, leaned over to Richard and said softly at his ear, "Tomorrow, you'll going to take time and explain to me exactly how that happened."

"I will. You can lean on me."

"All right, Richard *Motherslayer*, I guess I will have to lean on you."

"I don't like that title!"

"Well, that's what you are to me."

"Sir Riis, will you teach me swordsmanship?"

"Swordsmanship? I guess...I can teach you that. But we had a long day already... you still have energy?"

"Oui!"

"Young people..." Sir Riis got up and put on his sword. "Actually... this is a good time to practice sword training. Early in the morning or late in the evening that's what my late sword-master use to say." Sir Riis took out his sword and placed it on her throat in one swift seamless move. "Would you like to be able to move like that? Richard, please show her, come to an on-guard position." In one swift move Richard took out his sword and moved his whole body to an on-guard position. Some noise was made when he removed his sword from its scabbard. "Richard, you know better than that. Do it again. Try to make no noise." Richard tried it again, but this time he moved silently, like a cat. "That's better."

"That was very quick. Teach me to do that."

"It's simple… practice, practice, practice. Let me show you what I did very slowly." Sir Riis went through the motions very slowly. "Watch my hands, how my figure tips barely touch the sword blade, so one knows where the sword is at all times, while drawing it in that way you should be able do this without looking. Now you try it."

Sir Riis took off his sword and strapped the belt around her slim waist. The belt's smallest hole was still too loose for her, so he tied the belt around her waist. "There, this should work." She had trouble taking the sword out the scabbard and holding it; so, Sir Riis went into how to properly hold the sword, "You see how the handle is shaped. It is shaped so you know where the sharp sides of the blade are at all times. Again, so you can manage the sword without looking at the blade. The pads of your hands should never leave the handle like they are now." Sir Riis gently kicked the sword off her hands. "Pick up the sword again and hold it properly." This time Sir Riis kicked the sword; Janet almost dropped it but somehow managed to hold on to it. "Feel the difference?"

"Oui. It's also very large, heavy, and, I think, a little too long for me to handle properly."

Sir Riis found himself sweating a little thinking of her choice of words; but decided to ignore them and continue the lesson anyway. "Yes, I believe so. Squire Richard is terrific at acquiring things. I'm sure he will help you get a proper sword for your body size. But I want you to try his first to see if the weight and balance will work for you?"

"I'm tired. Sir Riis, thank you very much for the lesson; but I think the day did get to me. I think I want to go to sleep now," Janet said suddenly.

"Sure. Likewise, I need to sleep as well," said Sir Riis. Then, he thought, *I think I said something wrong. Yes, I forgot Richard's sword nearly sliced her mother in half. That heathen curve blade: a* scimitar *I believe is what they are called. I wish Richard would just have gotten rid of it.*

Squire Richard, putting away his prized sword, said, "I think I will go to sleep as well." Richard thought *he might just have to get rid of his sword that his grandfather brought back from the crusades if he wanted to be on better terms with Janet.*

Chapter V

At the head of the column, Sir Riis Ruffin could see the outline of the village starting to form. Getting closer, he could notice it was deserted with overgrown vegetation. The farm fields were in disarray, overgrown and completely on usable for cultivation. Still closer, Sir Riis noticed the buildings with all the familiar windows and doors nailed closed and marked with painted crosses. This was the mark that the plague; the "Black Death" has visited. Sir Riis lifted his right arm to halt his files of knights.

"Sir Godwine, this must be the village that I was told about."

"Now at the center there supposed to be a main road that turns into a fork..." At this moment, four riders approached from the nearby wood line. They did not appear to be a threat. Their war helms were tied to their saddles' cantle and their crossbows tied to their backs. Soon it became clear that it was Sir Albert Sterz and Sir Thomas Marshal and their two longbowmen.

"Thank God. We have reached you in time," Sir Sterz said, catching his breath.

"What happened?" Sir Godwine said, pulling on his horse toward their direction.

Sir Sterz held his reigns and leaned on his cantle. "It's a trap. Before you reach the fork in the road, a band of French marauders have set a trap. I suggest reversing the trap on them and turning south."

"South? I thought you told me to head north toward Reims?"

"I know. I had to be sure that I could trust you. And that you were not part of King Edward's men."

"King Edward's men?"

"Aye. The fear is the treaty that was signed by King Edward and the King of France. What is the King of England going to do now about the problem of all the free soldiers and free companies amassing? Moreover, some of your knights have colors matching the Earl of Warwick himself. So, we had to be sure you were not part of King Edward's men." Sir Riis and the others turned their heads to look at Sir Godwine's bright red and yellow heraldry tabard and banner.

Sir Godwine shrugged his shoulders and raised his hands, saying, "Aye, the right colors not the right design any English lad could tell you that."

"Now, I'm telling you the truth. You can send a scout up ahead and verify that I'm telling you the truth," Sir Sterz said, sustaining his defense.

"Sir Godwine, send some scouts, but first get with Sterz's men on exactly where they are and send the scouts by themselves. It's not that I don't trust Sir Sterz, but his trust is severely compromised for the time being," Sir Riis ordered.

"I understand. I would do the same thing if I was in your position." Sir Sterz was more relaxed. "Sorry about the whole thing but I just must be careful who we let into our company. Better said, whom I let into my company. I'm the Lord you seek. Or one of them. I'm in charge of the cavalry while Lord Hawkwood oversees the longbowmen. I suggest not to evade the French soldiers they know this is the only way into our camp. If you place the longbowmen on the opposite side of the ridge, we will have the advantage over their crossbowmen. They only think they can win the day because they have the element of surprise, and they have crossbowmen station on the rooftops. The archers are too scared to go inside of the homes fearing the plague. You take those two elements away they will lose the day. Besides, these French marauders are causing a lot of problems around these parts. Towns and villages that were friendly toward us have been destroyed by them. They commit atrocities and the local people think it's my company."

"If you know of their crimes, how come you haven't done anything to stop them?" asked Sir Riis.

"I have my men hunting them but to no avail. They have been slippery moving fast and hiding like rats. My men think that they move fast and under the cover of night. If you help me take care of them here and now you and your men will earn your spot in the company, instant trust in our society. What do you say?"

"Aye, I would still like to hear the report from my men first. Until then make yourself comfortable, my Lord. But here is another question, why would an English company be led by a foreigner from a Germanic duchy?"

"Ja, I could ask you the same question – Sir Riis Ruffin."

After some time, the mercenary scouts came back. "It's all true down to the last men," reported a mercenary scout.

"How many archers do you think we need on the ridge?" Sir Godwine said, removing his war helm.

"All of them including Lord Sterz's men. Are you game, Lord Sterz?" Sir Riis proposed.

"Ja, I'm ready for the hunt. Even though I'm not so good with the longbow."

Sir Riis, putting on his chain mail coif, said, "Get Archer Lambert up there with his crossbow, as well."

The mercenary band went down the deserted street of the dark abandoned village. All the men-at-arms at the ready with their lances straight up to heaven. The doors all nailed closed and marked with crosses. Funny thing, the plague. So many people died and then others found great wealth. To this day, scavengers can still find objects of value if you just know where to look. The sound of the horse hooves echoing on the empty street was disturbing. Then, Sir Riis started to hear a mysterious heavy breathing sound next to him. He turned suddenly at the ready to see who or what was making this sound and then he sees a vision of a large, gigantic crow like creature which startled him. Later, he realized it was only Sir Godwine who put on a physician mast to fend off the plague. Sir Riis glanced behind him to see that lots of the men made improvised fabric masks over their faces to protect themselves from this invisible enemy. He turned the other way to see Sir Lajos who was with no mask laughing without a care in the world. He really loved danger. Sir Riis thanked God that he was on their side. *Besides,* Sir Riis thought, *why would fabric hold back the plague when we have metal war helms?*

Making the turn on the street and turning to the fork on the road, they saw a person with long blond hair laying on the ground, a box opened with gold coins turned over, and a dead horse. A woman was crying and looked up at them, begging for help. *How predictable*, thought Sir Riis, *the telltale signs of an obvious trap. Well, maybe it would have worked if we didn't' know any better.* That was when Sir Riis gave the sign with his arm for the arches to do their duty.

The crossbowmen that were on the rooftops started screaming from the deadly arrows hitting their mark and started falling onto the street below, all around the lady in distress. By now, Sir Riis noticed that the lady was not a lady at all, but a man dressed as a lady. He looked around in panic and started screaming something in a French dialect that sounded somewhat familiar. He ran into the first side street. The marauders came out looking surprised at their comrades dead all around them.

Sir Riis knew the French marauders were still very dangerous. The next expected part of their trap were unmounted knights armed with pikes ready to dismount charging knights. That was when Sir Riis gave the order for his knights to lower their lances. The knights all in unison lowered their lances from lance-rest on their cuirass. Long hours of practice seem to have paid off. The cavalry brigade seemed like a living metallic animal moving all together as one. Sir Riis gave another order instead of what the enemy was expecting – a cavalry charge. He gave an order to split the rank in half in order to let in his own unmounted knights armed with mace, axe, and lance. The lance-bearers typically had two men-at-war running and screaming and pushing and breaking the pitiful French marauder surprise that they had for them. Behind them were the archers that made it back from the ridge. Soon, Sir Riis motioned for a trumpet retreat and all Sir Riis' men did not hesitate to heed the call. When the last of his men made the battle line, he motioned to close the cavalry rank and then he calls for a real cavalry charge. Lances were lowered and the pace of the horses picked up. The marauders awed, soften and beaten were no match for a real cavalry charge. The lances with their long iron tip found their unwilling marks all too easy. Blood ensued and havoc ruled the hour now. Sir Riis victory was assured within a moment's time.

Sir Lajos broke off from the rank and leapt off his horse and went after the men dressed as a lady. He cornered him at the end of an alleyway where their supply wagons were left. The marauder reached into the supply wagon. He pulled out a sword and executed a battle yell. Sir Riis went after them both. He watched from his steed.

Sir Lajos had his sword drawn to the enemy. "So, you like to pretend to be a little girl? Well? Speak!" When he spoke, he spoke with the French dialect tongue. Sir Lajos cut off his head and the hands holding the sword. "You know who these bastards are, don't you?" He looked up at Sir Riis. Sir Riis gave him a questioning look and looked down at the body which now was cut into four parts. Sir Lajos said, "These are the ones who raided Janet's village." They turned around and made their way back to the rest of the men.

Back at the main street, Sir Riis noticed Squire Richard running after a French marauder into another side street. A moment later, he came back to rejoin the mercenaries, but he had a smile and was holding something in his hands.

Ah, the sound of victory; men groaning and screaming, Sir Riis thought. Typically, weapons, when they hit the mark, didn't just kill instantly; the men may lay there wounded for hours. It was the responsibility of the winning side to end the suffering. Sir Riis was convinced that these were the men that attacked Janet's village; he could tell by the French dialect that they were speaking while begging for their lives.

"Janet, do you recognize these men? I think they were the ones that destroyed your village."

"Oui, it is them." Janet had tears running down her eyes. She said, "I volunteer to finish them off."

"If you want to. I will get someone to show you where their weakness of their armor is, that way you can learn from this experience, as well. Bring her one of our pikes the ones we use to dismount other knights!"

Janet was crying when she was doing this duty. Another soldier, who was doing the same task, noticed her. "Oi, it's all right to cry if it's your first time doing this horrible task. I cried when it was my first time too. It's not natural for men to kill other men."

"Such a strange statement coming from a mercenary," Janet said, wiping away her tears.

"Think that you are doing a favor for these poor souls. They would most likely die from these wounds anyway. Besides, think about it this way, we are bringing a balance back to the world."

"How so?"

"If we are not ones doing this; they would certainly be doing this to us. We are part of this great balance. Everything is in balance now, and we should be happy for this. In this moment in time everything is in balance, and we are alive – in Nature's balance," the soldier said.

"These are the bastards who killed my friends, family, my loved ones, and my village. They all deserve to die, each and every one of them. But God granted me my vengeance this auspicious day!" She then thought as she moved between the fallen, *I was actually crying because I was happy and delighted. And I was ashamed about this. But now… I know… I had a part in bringing balance back to my life. And I'm happy because my conscious is… clear and balanced.*

One of the defeated French marauders was on the floor and overheard her words and was trying desperately to reach for a fallen sword. "Oú allez-vous pêcher?" she said, as she thrust her pike right between his chest piece and the unprotected armpit, a weak spot on the knight's armor. She plunged it deep, and a splatter of blood landed across her face.

"Oi, this little Frenchmen learns fast! I'm glad he's on our side," said the soldier with the same task, chuckling. She pulled the lance out and smiled.

Chapter VI

Lord Albert Sterz led the small band right into the great company encampment. The whole encampment was massive and very well organized. The encampment itself was designed with concentric files of tents and colorful banners that signified whose tent it was. All the tents were lined up in orderly straight military fashion. As the band rode by, men from the camp would do small bows of respect to the guides. Here and there Lord Sterz and Sir Marshal wave their hands or would give small nods back. One of the men-at-arms who had a similar armor as Sir Lajos noticed the band entrance and turned and ran up one of the files of tents.

    The band of men reached what appeared to be the center of the camp and dismounted. Sir Riis told Sir Lajos, Janet and Richard to stay behind with the horses. Lord Sterz told Sir Marshal to stay and look after them. Sir Riis and Sir Godwine walked into the large tent that was half open to the camp's rectangular center area. There was a group of chairs and a table with parchments, small wooden boxes, feathers for writing and a balance for weights among other things. In the background, you could see armor propped up on stands to hold until its owners need it for battle. There were two men seating at the table. One was large and had a pair shape body of an older man, even though he was still very young. He had no beard, his hair light blond but was starting already too thin out and blue eyes. The other was muscular, light complexion but with pink sunburn with dark hair and blue eyes. He had no shirt and a series of scars that could be seen across his back. They seem to be in a somber conversation when they turn to look at the incoming party.

"Well, guess who decided to show up?" cried the shirtless gentleman getting up from his chair. "How was the heraldry marshaling?" Then he started to laugh out loud.

"Great! I think, I got the last men we needed to complete the last contingent. Gentlemen, I would like you to meet Sir Riis Ruffin and his second in command, Sir Godwine Quatreton. Gentlemen, this is Sir William Thornton. He is the treasurer for this here great company. And this is Sir John Hawkwood the second in command of this company and in command of the longbowmen."

"Sir John Hawkwood? I thought you were a Lord?" asked Sir Riis, taking off his mail coif. This caused great laughter from the group.

"Lord? There are no real Lords around here. They all packed up their loot and went back to their wives and children. All went back to their citadels and castles over the channel or to Brittany or wherever they came from. We are what's left of the great English army that King Edward disbanded. A free company, not unlike your larger group. Why would you think that it was a real Lord amassing this company of cut throats?" Then, laughter started again. "Well, I guess if I was an English Lord, I would be a piss poor one at that," he said, sitting back down on his chair, putting his feet up. His feet were swollen and abused from traveling in harness. "With that said, since I'm in charge of thousands of men, I would not take it as an insult if someone would call me as, a Lord. The same goes for my German friend here Sir Albert Sterz. But I hear the more correct term for a mercenary commander, or a military commander is, Captain. And in Italy they would call us Condottieri. But with that said, I find no one here is calling us Captains but Lords."

"Sir Riis Ruffin got approximately a hundred lances with some longbowmen. But more than that, the brigade already proved their mettle," Lord Sterz said as he grabbed some wine and poured himself a cup.

"How so? I hope you are not trying to let them in with any special privileges. They will have to earn their way and agree to the same terms just like all the other band of men or brigades we recruited so far."

"No. They helped us to get rid us of the French rat infestation we had lately."

"What? King Charles of Navarre henchmen? They were pillaging and burning and not leaving anything for anyone. Quite a dreadful thing, not good for the common people, the peasants, or us mercenaries," said Sir Hawkwood, sipping on his cup, revealing his gold seal ring with a hawk image.

"Since we are foreigners, we were getting blame for most of the destruction. But are you sure it was them?" asked Sir Thornton.

"Oh, they cover up their heraldry very cleverly, but the dead always give up the truth." At that moment, Lord Sterz pulled out a bag with two dozen or so items of Navarre heraldry.

"This is indeed a great day! "We thank you young lads if you did take care of Charles the Bad henchmen," said Sir Thornton as he poured himself another wine cup. "What do you say, Lord Hawkwood?"

"Brilliant! Just what we needed if you are willing to pledge your men to our cause and make us all rich! He said while putting on an aketon. But first tell me… what is your story?" Lord Hawkwood said this and walked over to him.

"My story?"

"Aye, your story – how you and your men came to be?" Lord Hawkwood walked closer to him.

"There is no knight's tale to tell but the truth, Lord."

"Aye, aye, whatever you call it. Your story."

"I suppose no different than anyone else out here. We got the call that the king needed siege weapons. Before we could reach them at Chartres, King Edward already signed the peace treaty with France. The order came to disband, and most of the nobles left to go back home. The few soldiers that remained were left formed a small mercenary band which elected Sir Godwine and myself as their leaders. We kept one of the siege engines which was light and mobile; the rest we put to fire."

"I meant this kind of life. Mercenaries, my good man? How did you find yourself in this kind of life? Do you like this new kind of life?" Lord Hawkwood again stood very close to Sir Riis – not in a threatening manner, but uncommon and uncomfortable.

"How so?" answered Sir Riis.

"Do you like a life of a mercenary… for you… and your men? No king? No country? No borders?" Hawkwood turned his head as if to hear him better.

"If we are speaking candidly, I'm glad that all those old overweight lords, knights and squires that were obligated to fight for the king are gone. They made me sick. They would complain all the time. And at night they would cry themselves to sleep. When it came to fighting, they would sit back on their steeds and watch, afraid to join the battle. Now I'm in the midst of men that want to fight and want adventure at no cost… well, sometimes, I would say, at a cost. After all, we are mercenaries at the end of the day."

Sir Hawkwood got close to Sir Riis' face and said, "Huh, I like this one." He backed up, drank some more. "Yes, that is one thing that we all have in common: we are young and a sense of adventure; we are all experiencing a sense like something that is not over, yet. A sense that we are making history. Well, I hope you experience what you are looking for… here with us in this Magna Societas." At this time, Sir Riis noticed that either Lord Hawkwood was not acting in his full capacity or was completely sober.

"I'm very appreciative so far, but I would like to go over some details before I commit my men to anything, if that would be all right with you?" Sir Riis got comfortable on one of the chairs. Lord Sterz leaned over the table as he explained, "We are a society of free soldiers in a free company. Free from any obligations from any one country. We serve no king. Working for whoever would pay the most. You and your men are expected to uphold the chivalry code but above all be faithful to our company's cause. In turn, our society is strength in numbers. Not to mention, we have notaries for legal matters, physicians, healers, constables and a treasurer. Sir Thornton can go over the finer details like financial splits, etcetera."

"Yes; but if you don't mind me asking what are our immediate plans? The Champagne countryside is torched due in part to the routiers and the French marauders. There are no rich patrons around here that I'm aware of. To the west, King Edward is still roaming around. He might just decide to function as the royal authority and abolish the free companies that are forming."

"Austere, my newfound friend." Lord Hawkwood rolled out a huge map. "Just before you came in, I was discussing this matter with Sir Thornton. We met with Sir William de Grandson yesterday he acts as the kings' envoy from time to time. And he assures us that if we swear that if we don't raise arms against the King of England, King Edward will let our mercenary enterprise act at its own discretion."

"How are we going to have any assurance of this?" asked Sir Godwine.

"Well, we really don't. But we have faith that he will hold his oath."

"We can write it into our mercenary contracts we make; that way the king knows our intentions," answered Sir Thornton, finishing his wine and pouring himself another.

"Aye! I like that proposal. Sir Thornton please ensure that this is taken care of at the time of contract executions."

"Well, this is all great and good, but what about the here and now? I have over one hundred bellies that I'm responsible for. What's our immediate plans?"

"Yes, Sir Riis Ruffin spoke like a true leader. We are going on a pilgrimage for your men… and for all of us. A pilgrimage for John the Baptist." He tossed down a gold coin on the map and then strategically placed it over the city state of Florence. It was a florin coin with the image of St. John the Baptist on the exposed side. Then, he took his dagger and laid it pointing south on the map toward the Italian peninsula. "There my friends are our destination. There are plenty of rich nobles from rich city states like Pisa, Florence, Siena, Milan, Venice, etcetera. All fighting each other and it will be us in the middle profiting from their war ventures."

"Why not travel west over the Pyrenees? I heard that the Crown of Castile needs good experience mercenaries. The Castile Kingdom wants to turn the whole Iberia peninsula into a Christian nation by driving out all the Moors infidels," asked a new knight that walked into the tent area. He was tall, slim, with red hair, and had bright, shiny armor like Sir Godwine.

"That is not a good idea at all. We would have to travel

through King Edward's established territories. I'm not sure that he would let us just walk on by without some sort of toll. And even if we make it there, it will be a crusade with limited returns on our investment, Sir Nigel Loringe."

"I think there is a nobility to be marked by the cross. Neither my father nor I ever had the opportunity to partake in such a venture."

"I'm not aware of the Holy Father calling for such a crusade, at this time. Presently, I see the southern route as the best for all."

Sir Nigel was hoping that they would travel to the Iberia peninsula. He remembered a fond memory from his youth when he met a young girl from that part of the world. He so hoped and dreamed that he would see her beauty again. Then, he considered that the Italian peninsula would have beautiful ladies as well. "I see, then south it will have to be," Sir Nigel responded.

"Now – getting there, we need to go through the eye of the needle… Pont-Saint-Esprit."

"Pont-Saint-Esprit?" Sir Godwine said while scratching his head.

"Translated in English as the Fort of Saint Esprit. Whatever you call it; it's a massive, fortified bridge the likes of which you haven't seen yet, my untraveled friend. And we must pass through it to go over the mighty Rhone River. This is the gateway to the southern river valley basin where the journey over the Alps is more passable. Some say where Hannibal first forged a trail when he invaded Rome. I have connections there that will guide us right through. But before I go any further, I need to know, are you in or out?"

"Everything I heard so far is acceptable. Florins coins look, sound and taste–" Sir Riis picked it up and bit into it to test if it was real gold. "… A lot more enticing than these new Francs I heard so much of."

"Aye, we are in. Where do I put my mark?" Sir Godwine reached for the coin and pocketed it.

"Splendid. Welcome Cavalier Riis Ruffin, you are now commander of a contingent of men and you will not need to worry about feeding them. That responsibility will fall to me now."

"How many more men I'm responsible for? How many men are in a contingent?"

"Oh, don't worry about that now, just a few more cavalrymen that will be assigned to you later. Accordingly, you'll need to combine your general expense coffers with ours. You can trust Sir Thornton here. He was once the most respected accountant in all London."

"London! What ever happened?" Sir Riis asked.

"The Tower. That's what happened!" Sir Sterz quickly replied, laughing.

Sir Thornton stood up angrily and said, "It was not the Tower! But Marshalsea Prison! Not the Tower but Marshalsea!" He quickly gained his composure and sat back down.

"Don't worry, he wasn't there for illegal accounting practices if that was on your mind. He was there actually for getting caught laying with his patron's wife! Not only that, but he was also courting his daughter at the same time!"

Sir Thornton flew from his chair again. "I told you not to ever tell that story again! You bastard! I told you that in strict personal confidence. I can't help it if I have a weakness for the fairer sex." At that moment, he looks outside the tent to the crowd. "I just can't say no when it comes to–" Thornton was now staring as if in a trance in the direction of Janet who was there with Lajos and Richard! Sir Riis got up and moved himself between them to block them from his view. Sir Thornton came to his senses again. "... Women. At least I don't lay with boys or barn animals – that would be an abomination. Like some of the rumors that men in this company do."

"I think the scriptures say something about coveting a neighbor's wife," Lord Sterz said, pointing out.

"Don't be ridiculous!" Thornton threw his hands up in the air. "I didn't even live near my patron's manor. I had my own abode far away at the center of the city."

"Let's move on to the task at hand. Shall we? What is our total numbers now with our newfound friends?" asked Lord Hawkwood.

"Our entire company consist of approximately 3,500 cavalrymen and 2,000 longbowmen." At this moment, Sir Riis noticed from the corner of his eye that Sir Lajos was gathering quite a crowd. Sir Riis thought that he needed to investigate before things get out of hand.

"One last thing, a minor detail, all of your men. They will need to get a white tabard or surcoat if they don't have one already. A white tabard and banners for all will be our heraldic crests from now on. Tomorrow, I will give the order for all the knights to swap their tent's banners to be all white. For all the knights including you, Sir Godwine."

"What value does my heraldic emblem gives me now? I agree we must be a white company."

"White Company! I like that! A *Tabula Rosa*, a clean slate to start a new," Sir Godwine said, pouring himself the last of a flask of wine.

"We must show that we are a company of mercenaries. A free society of mercenaries," said Sir Sterz, getting up from his chair, holding his wine cup. "... With no king, no pope, no emperor, we are a white company, ready for employment."

"Or you could say we bow down to none," Cavalier Riis said, trying to finish his thoughts.

"… But to John the Baptist," Sir Sterz laughed. "But we have not decided what we are going to officially call ourselves."

"I see, maybe something scary like the Company of the Kill or of Death or Blood?" responded Sir Godwine, finding a chair and seating back down.

"Well, it could be more chivalrous like Company of the Rose or Flower or Escallops or something like that." Lord Sterz removed his surcoat and looked at it with an imaginary look.

"We all know that Sir Sterz wanted it to be the Company of the Star," sneered Sir Thornton.

"One thing for sure, if we don't decide soon, we won't have time for everyone to color or sew in a design," scoffed Sir Hawkwood. "Let's toast to this occasion. Wine for everybody." Pouring wine for everyone, they then toasted this occasion with great jubilee.

Cavalier Ruffin went back outside to join Richard and Janet with Sir Marshal. "Where is Sir Lajos?" Sir Riis asked.

"He's right over there; looks like he found some new friends," Richard answered pointing to the small crowd gathering. They all looked friendly, had the same similar armour, and looked very respectful – a little too respectful toward Sir Lajos. Smiling, giving him small vows and reverent salutes. Sir Riis thought, *if they would have had their families with them, they would have given Sir Lajos their babies for him to kiss and bless, as well.* He then said out loud, "All right, Sir Marshal, can you direct us to where our camp will be setting up?"

Chapter VII

Lord Albert Sterz was not being deceitful or jesting this time. Sir Riis Ruffin's band were the last number of men that he needed for this enterprise. He gave the order the very next day that the great company was to break up camp and start the journey. Bright and early the following day, Lord Sterz gave the order to break up camp, mount up and make formation. Everyone appeared gallant, all uniformed with their shiny armor and white surcoat. All the colorful banners were exchanged for white banners. Apparently, they all had time to shine their armor and get in uniform, except for Sir Riis' contingent since they just joined this great company. Sir Riis' original band looked like misfits because they didn't have time to get ready. All except the cavalrymen that were added to Sir Riis' contingent which were almost half his original numbers.

Most of the leaders in this company already had plate armor and wore it at the formation. Sir Sterz had his shiny decorative plate armor on. In this era only the nobles or men-at-arms that could afford plate armor would wear it for protection. Lord Sterz, Lord Hawkwood, Sir Marshal, and Sir Thornton got together in a small ridge overlooking the rest of the knights. At the very end of the files, as customary, were the supply wagons, the war machine, and a portable catholic altar for mass that Lord Hawkwood insisted on.

"Maybe we should say something to the troops before we depart on our first leg of our journey," said Hawkwood in a low tune voice to Lord Sterz.

"I'm not prepared to give a speech, and I'm not good at giving speeches anyway."

"Just say whatever comes to your mind and keep it short. These are mercenaries, men of action, adventurers, they don't care for any long speech."

"It's too bad we couldn't decide on a majestic company name," scoffed Sir Thornton, looking awkward in his armor.

Lord Sterz spurred his horse to take a few steps forward, "Come on, Titan," and then he cleared his throat and said, "my men, you all look glorious and victorious with your shining armor and dressed in white. You remind me of the tales of the crusaders of old, who left their homelands to liberate the Holy Lands from the infidels. They, too, were dressed in white but marked with a large red cross. While our pursuit maybe different we are still Christian men with Christian values and a chivalry code of conduct that should not be forsaken. From now on we shall be called 'The White Company' and our pursuit will be honor, glory and gold." The men cheered with great anticipation of the adventure to come. Sir Sterz leaned back on his saddle and waved his hand to motion the company to move forward.

"Very good, Lord," Lord Hawkwood said to Lord Sterz.

"The White Company? Because we couldn't decide on a color? White coats with red crosses? I believed those were the Knights Templars who were a subgroup of crusaders... Did anybody notice that?" mocked Sir Thornton.

"Come on, Sir Thornton, we are already on the move." Sir Hawkwood prompted his horse to move forward to the head of the column. Horses and men moved forward in a sea of gray dust.

After some considerable time on this very field, events unfolded unknown to the White Company: Glistening knights came upon the recently vacated field. The band of knights were made up of a small group of longbowmen and a column of plated horsemen. The lead knight, who had a squire holding up a long bright red and gold banner, came forward to inspect the horizon. The lead knight had a stern face and strong physique, a veteran of many battles. They observed the empty field and noticed hundreds of depressions on the ground, mounds of earth, and hundreds of scorch earth from where campfires once blazed. It was obvious that there was a large army on this location at one time. Suddenly, the wind kicked up the dust on the open field so that it hit into their metal armor. As they made their horses trot toward the center of the empty field, they came upon a patchwork of recently erected tents that were currently occupied. They had a few campfires set up to keep their men and horses warm. Soldiers came out of these tents to greet them. One of them exclaimed, "Greetings, honorable knights. I am Sir Robert Briquet at your service."

"Greetings! I'm Sir Seguin Badefol and my second here is Sir Camus Bour. Tell me my fellow knight, was this the site where the English Company amass?"

"Aye! Good Knight. They are all gone now. South, I believe, maybe… searching for warmer weather. You missed them and I don't think you can reach them by now. Even if you and your men would be able to reach them, the word is… that they met the numbers that they were looking for."

"How come you… and your fellow knights didn't leave with them?" Sir Badefol was being very polite. With a realistic look at these men, one could see why they were unwanted. Most had very little armor or any side arms of any value. They were dressed in leather or mail, and others either had no armor or were barely dressed in rags. Some appeared like peasants holding a pike other like bandits others were short in statue and still others were missing an eye, an arm or even a leg.

"We were not considered to their standard, my good knight. Not really fair, when most of us already served loyally to the king for many years. Alas, we are but poor, humble soldiers who fought for the king and now we are discarded and unwanted."

"Well, at least you're honest honorable knights. You and your veteran men rejected and unwanted… leftovers on this cold field. I and my men appear to be too late for this affair. Apparently, the leftovers and latecomers are all in the same boat." He got off his steed, bent down and took a single blade of grass that had survived from the field. He placed it in his mouth and looked around. "South, you said?"

"Aye, my lord toward the Rhone River valley."

"South." He walked back and forth. "South, south…could be Italy to Papal states, or Avignon!"

Finally, his companion knight, Sir Camus Bour said, "Avignon. Where the Pope resides! Ha, do they want absolution from their sins?"

"No, something much, much more precious, the biggest ransom of all! How much will kings pay for their Pope? We will head in that direction as well ravishing everything in our wake. Avignon is a great price, indeed." He looks around and walked back and forth kicking up dust from the ground then answered himself, "Avignon it is, then."

"Impossible! Avignon has never been taken. It is a walled city. How are we going to breach its defenses? Look around – it's just the few of us." Sir Camus Bour's voice was getting angrier and spreading his arms around.

"Our numbers, good knight?" asked Sir Robert Briquet,

looking around at his misfit band.

"Yes, our numbers are few for now but soon they will grow. Besides, we do not have to defeat the city. The great English company that amassed will. They will take the burden of taking the city and its walls. We are just going for the leftovers."

"The leftovers?" asked Sir Camus Bour dismounting from his steed, as well.

"Yes, let them handle the hard task and we will reap its rewards." Turning to Sir Briquet and placing his arm on his shoulder, he said, "And we will not reject none. As long as you have the spirit and can hold an axe or a mace or a pike, we will accept all." At that moment, they noticed a dust cloud as a great number of soldiers walking toward the vacant field. "What a sorry lot we are the Tard and the Venus," Sir Camus Bour finally said looking at the forthcoming knights.

After a long day of travel, the White Company set up for the night. Janet came up to Sir Riis. "Are you going to teach me more swordsmanship?"

"Let me guess… you're not tired." She gave him a grin. "Is all the equipment dusted off and cleaned for the night?"

"Oui."

"All right, then." Sir Riis took off his sword and instructed her to do the same moves as the first time. *She really has to become familiar with the sword and hopefully soon we can acquire one for herself*, thought Sir Riis as he watched her going through the sword moves. Then, she stopped and started looking at the sword. She examined it from top to bottom. "What is this inscription on the handle's pommel?" She was showing it to Sir Riis as if he had never seen it before. Sir Riis took the sword and held it like a defenseless newborn baby. "Oh… it says, *"Wiste I,"* he said with a very soft, pensive voice.

"What does that mean?"

"Oh, it's my old family moniker. It means 'I knew'."

"Old family moniker? You said you were promoted to men-at-arms and then became a knight. But I have a feeling you are a true noble knight, aren't you?"

Sir Riis was staring at the pommel now and using the candlelight that was available in the tent. The reflection off the pommel made a flash of light across Sir Riis' face. "Oh... yes, I lost her forever." Moreover, he started to remember how lovely she was before he lost everything.

"Who did you lose?"

"My wife, lands, position, birth rights... daughter. There is no need to say that I am a true Lord! A Lord of what? And then go to a long explanation on how I lost everything. Hell! I don't even remember how I lost it myself! So, I say, I got promoted like the rest of these bastards out here; then the conversation is short – just how I like it."

"You must have loved her very much."

"You don't know what you're talking about, girl."

Richard enters the tent after finishing his task with the horses. "Sorry, I took so much time. I had trouble with Lucifer."

"Lucifer?" replied Janet.

"Lucifer is Sir Godwine's horse. He bought it after his mare died. It's the big gray one with a black mane and one gray eye. The mean-looking one, Janet."

"I know him, but I didn't know his name. He is a beautiful horse."

"Beautiful?"

"Beautiful, if you know about horses. That horse is magnificent. He has great muscles and a relentless spirit."

"Yes, beautiful and with an awful temper. He scares me whenever I look at him and he looks at me with that eye of his. The name suits him well. He hates me for some reason. It's said he paid over eighteen gold souls. That's over three times as much as a regular horse."

"Ah, but that's not a regular horse. It's a destrier. Meant for heavy cavalry. Well, wealth the money," Sir Riis injected into the ongoing conversation.

"What is going on? Sword training?" asked Richard.

"Yes. Janet is going over some basic sword moves."

"Well, she can't do it with your sword – it's too big and heavy for her. I got her the perfect sword. I got it from our French friends that we met back at the plague village." Richard got the sword from his belongings. It was wrapped up with pieces of cloth. "Go ahead, Janet, unwrap it. It's for you, my gift to you." She grabbed it and unwrapped it. It was actually a very well-made sword. One could tell by just looking at its handle and scabbard. She grabbed it and held it as a newborn baby, not unlike Sir Riis did with his sword. Her face became rose-colored, and she started to tear up.

"It's beautiful so far. Thank you, Richard, for thinking of me. I don't think anybody ever got me something before other than my family members."

"Go ahead, draw the sword. I can't wait for you to see it." The sword blade was impeccable. It was clear that this was an expensive sword to make.

Sir Riis looked at it under close observation. "It has a couple of small chips on one of the sides, but a good swordsmith can easily fix that. It has good weight and balance. This sword looks like it was just made for you. Train with it and it will save your life. Now continue doing the basics with it so you can get familiar with its weight and balance. Each sword has its own soul that you must discover and tame. When I think you're ready, we will move on to different fighting scenarios."

"What do you mean fighting scenarios?"

"It's training as if you had an invisible opponent or an attacker and how you will react and defend yourself and do a counterattack. You will have plenty of chance to practice on our journey. For now, just practice on just drawing the sword and putting the sword away back into its scabbard." Janet did just as she was instructed. "Yes. Yes. That's it. Now do it slowly, very slowly." Janet slowed down as instructed. "At a slower pace. Yes, that's it."

Janet finally said, "I thought the point was to learn to draw the sword fast. How can I learn to draw the sword fast if I'm doing it slow?"

"The question should be how can you do it fast if you can't do it correctly slow? I will teach you to do it correctly. It is better to ensure that you learn the right technique slowly. So then, drawing the sword fast, you will use the right techniques without thinking. Then speed will come by itself. Janet, you will see it like magic. Trust me. That is what my late sword-master would call, the spirit of the dragon."

The next few days. The company kept its pace on its march south to Pont-Saint-Esprit. It almost seemed like the company was on the run or had some type of time scheduled. Sir Riis was not worried about it, but one thing was for sure – the complete plan would not be revealed to all the cavaliers, not yet. After another long day of travel, Sir Riis saw Janet on the ground of the tent. Cleaning her sword, but she looked ill at ease.

"What's the matter?"

"Just sad, I guess. I miss my brother. He is the only family member I have left. I would like to see him again someday. He left to be a crossbowman in the French duchy. I believe he is serving the Dauphin now; I'm not really sure. And my father was killed by noble French knights; he was hung like a peasant. When the French peasants revolted near Paris the French nobles united and killed anyone that looked like a peasant for great distances out of northern France." Janet started to get emotional and teared up. "My father was not a peasant – he was a French commoner. He was schooled and knew how to read and write. And he had a civic roll in our village. It just not fair."

"I know that, Janet. And I'm sorry to hear that; maybe sword training is just what you need now."

"This is why I joined this mercenary company; I hate the French and I do not love the English either but here, here in this magna societas is like a free country, a free society with our own set of rules. We don't have a king to bow down to or belong to any kingdom and we raid rich nobles, and that is why I like it here."

"Free company, a free society, made of freemen. I never really thought of it that way; but, I like it. Sir Godwine is very young, looking for wealth and adventure. Sir Lajos… really loves fighting and is in some sort of knight errant. Mercenaries, soldier-of-fortune they call us. What are we really? Degenerates, misfits-of-society that is what we are. We don't truly fit in. All of us. Not one of us is exempt from this. There are no true Lords and no nobles. The so-called nobles here are not the first born, all have empty coffers back home, little or no birth rights; why else would they leave their homelands? To be always tired, cold, and hungry. I myself have no home to go back to. Janet, we all have our reasons to be here, but I like yours best of all. Now get your sword on!"

"Oui." She shook her head negatively and translated her yes to 'aye'. Janet responded by standing up and getting her sword on.

"Sword training is the best thing you can do right now. If you are practicing with a sharp edge sword, your attention can't be at any other place. Discipline. This is an indispensable access in the battlefield."

Janet, walking to the tent door, said, "It's raining outside." Then, she walked to a clear area of the tent.

"This is perfect, then. I don't really want other people to see what I'm about to instruct you. You fight well as a crossbowman but there will be a time when you will have to cross swords. You will never have the strength of a man because you are a lady, but you can compensate with skill. Great swordsmen have excellent skill in weirding their swords – not strength. A sword fight is typically determined within two to three moves. The first move is a decisive move. For the first move to work it must be either a surprise to the opponent... he didn't know it was coming... did not expect it or it was just so fast that the opponent didn't have enough time to properly react to it. It has to be decisive and fast." Sir Riis said this while making a circle on the ground with his sword.

"Yes, fast like lightning. But since most swordplay will happen when two opponents are readily armed and prepared there will be a counter reaction to the action of the first move that has occurred. Hence, the second movement. The second movement may consist of a parry to the reaction of the attacker's first strike. Or a second sword movement to counter the first movement. The mastery is to read your opponent and see what sword movement he will deploy and counter it before he has a chance to react to it. Else, when you get more advanced, bait the opponent on his move and then counter it. Here let's practice slowly so you can see this in action." Sir Riis and Janet practiced a few times slowly with Sir Riis explaining each movement step by step. "Try to parry with the back or side of your sword deflecting the sword ever just slightly; you let the momentum of the opponent carry him slightly off balance that is all you need."

"Why with the side or back of the sword?"

"So, it will not damage its edge. You need a sharp edge so whenever you want to cut with it. If you practice and make this your custom, it will become like second nature just like riding a horse or eating a meal with a knife."

"Like this." Janet parried Riis' sword movement.

"Yes, yes, that's it; just hit your opponent's sword slightly just enough to redirect their sword with a thrust or a cut. And counter like this." This went on to the late hours of the night.

The White Company continued on the road and the season kept getting colder, transforming into a cold hard winter. Janet was training in different fighting scenarios. Sir Riis was patiently instructing her: "This one, Janet, the opponent is attacking you from your left in an ambush. Take a few normal steps forward; take one step forward with your right foot and then one with your left foot, keeping yourself calm, balanced and facing forward. See your imaginary opponent with your peripheral vision. As you take the third step forward with your right foot, rotate the scabbard and handle around to the front of your abdomen and draw the sword out of its scabbard at a slight horizontal angle with your right hand. Rotate to your left to face your opponent on the balls of your feet, and at the same time use the rotation to power a thrust of the sword forward and slightly upward into your attacker chest area. The angle of the sword should be aiming at the heart of your opponent. When you strike move with intent using your whole body. This will be the force behind your sword thrust. Withdraw the blade quickly with your arm and wrist without changing the angle of the sword. The aim is to insert the sword right between the ribcage not too deep. Insert the sword no more than the width of your palm. Pull out the sword in a slightly steeper angle. At this moment, step back with your left foot and at the same time block overhead with the flat side of your sword. Let him slide off your blocking sword and then you can finish him by making a right-to-left diagonal strike or just get out of his way. Correctly executed, the opponent's heart is pierced; he will surely die…almost instantly. Now keep in mind this technique only works if the opponent is not wearing armor."

"What about if he is?"

"Just practice the moves that were taught to me a long time ago by my late sword-master. Also, remember to breathe properly. Even in this scenario you should be thinking how you should be breathing. Every time you raise your sword; you should take in a breath; when you execute a cut or a thrust, exhale. This pattern of breathing should come naturally to you just as if you were walking. This will help control your fear in a duel. Because dueling is scary. And extremely close and personal. It might just be the two of you underneath the All-seeing Eye. Don't expect a crowd cheering for whoever wins. All it takes is one wrong move, and it could be instant death. Keep that in mind too. And at the same time, when the time comes for fighting don't think."

Janet stopped her practice. "But you just told me to concentrate on my techniques and my breathing! And now you tell me not to think."

"I said in a real battle if you think too much you might die." At this time, Squire Richard burst into the tent and looked around with a wild look. He had blood on his hands and turned around to drag something inside the tent. "I finally found out how Sir Godwine keeps his armor so shiny." Squire Richard proclaimed with a loud, excited voice.

Sir Riis said, "It doesn't matter what you found out. He probably has a professional polisher that does it for him. And what are you doing out there? I hope you didn't kill someone, and you are dragging the corpse in here."

"No," Richard said as he dragged a dead goat into their tent. The goat was freshly killed with its tongue sticking out of its mouth. "Sorry, the recipe calls for a goat."

"Well, we can see that! Go ahead then explain yourself Squire!"

"Well, the recipe calls for cutting off the legs from the beast from the knees downward." Before Sir Riis could say anything, Richard took out his sword and swung to cut off the legs of the goat. Blood ushered into the tent floor. Sir Riis and Janet just watched in amazement as the youth didn't even ask before he started butchering inside the tent. Richard continued saying, "Now, I collect the legs and smoke them for a day and keep them for fifteen to twenty-five days. And that's it. Whenever we have need them, they will be here. All we need to do is break a leg and take out the marrow from the bone and grease the armor with it and they will always keep bright even when wet!"

"The rest of the goat carcass?"

"Huh, I don't know." Richard placed his bloody hand on his head thinking and said, "I guess Lefty can cook the rest of it."

"Why? Did you do your butchering in my tent? Get it out of here! Clean up this mess!"

The next time, when Sir Riis, Richard and Janet practiced, they had a little discussion as well. "The chivalry code needs to be in a knight's heart." Sir Riis placed his right hand over his chest. "It's a lot more than just rescuing maiden in distress or being born a knight with all the fancy titles and lands that come with it. It is also knowing when to act in a martial fashion. Knowing when to draw the sword and kill for the better good. Do you understand?"

"I think I understand. The chivalry code should be written in our hearts, so I know when to kill. Thus, saving another fair person's live," Janet responded, mimicking his movements.

"Not too bad. I must have taught you this before. You learn quickly." Sir Riis continued, "When you are at war it is different. You might not even have to draw your sword. It all depends on circumstances and what is your particular function in the battle. But when you duel it is personal; imperative that you know how to use your sword. The sword is a noble weapon; men will always use swords. It's ordained by God. It is the first weapon mentioned in the scriptures."

"That's right – when Adam and Eve sinned, God placed an angel with a flaming sword to guard the entrance of the Garden of Eden," Richard answered.

"That's right, that is why humanity will always carry swords. At least as a symbol if there's another weapon to render them useless."

"Yes. The things of God are eternal. As above, so below."

"Right now, we have the advantage of the longbow. But I predict, eventually, there be a crossbow system that will shoot further and have faster reloads that will beat our English longbows. And there is a lot of advances with black powder and explosives that eventually will dominate the battlefield. I remember we had five mortars at the Battle of Crécy but they only had limited effect on the enemy; no more than noise makers I would say."

Now let's practice our second fighting scenario an attacker to the right. Richard can act as the attacker so you can understand it a lot clearer." Sir Riis positioned Richard where he would stand in as the attacker and Janet where she would start. "Janet—step with your right foot and at the same time break the collar from the mouth of the scabbard by pushing the handguard with your thumb. Step out with your left foot in the direction of your attacker to your right and push the blade almost horizontally all the way out of the scabbard, holding both it and the blade in a horizontal orientation. Step your right foot and make a horizontal cut from left to right using the hips to drive the cut. Then rotate your left foot on the ball of that foot, cutting the back of the attacker's upper arm. Step forward with your left foot and at the same time bring the sword first over your head into an upper guard position and then diagonally downward from left to right. Step forward with your right foot and bring the sword to a normal guard position." Sir Riis continued instructing them over and over again until they absorbed their sword techniques.

At a sudden moment, a shout from outside the tents was heard. "All cavaliers are called to the commander's tent." A sentry soldier was delivering this message to all the cavaliers and commanders in the field. When Sir Riis made it into the commander's tent, all the cavaliers and commanders were already there.

Lord Sterz stood addressing his men: "I need to explain why we are progressing at such a fast pace. One reason we do not want is for King Edward since he made peace with France to decide to be the peacekeeper and get rid of all the routiers and free soldiers in France. The second is Sir William Thornton. He is not only our treasure; but he is also our logistic strategist. He calculated how many men were needed, how much it will cost to take us to get to Pont-Saint-Esprit and the window of time to be there. And how long we should take it for!"

"Take it?" could be heard resonating in the command tent.

"Yes. This is our first objective. Sir Thornton calculates we can hold it for about three months if we have to."

"Why? I understand looting it if we have to pass through it; but why risk staying there for such a long time and risk the Dauphin on us?" Sir Nigel Loringe inquired.

"I'm going to let Sir Thornton explain. Sir Thornton the floor is yours." Lord Sterz pointed to Sir Thornton.

"I'm going to explain… straight to the point as much as possible. I was at a special asking of nobles, magnates, and commonalty of the realm. On my spare time, I visited a local whorehouse. This particular whorehouse had walls very thin; so, you could hear almost everything that went on the adjacent room. I recognized the voice of the patron next door to me that was receiving services. That is when he started dragging about what an important person he was at Pont-Saint-Esprit trying to impress the little whore he was with. So, he goes on and on about all the taxes collected that must go through his post. Later, I spoke with him and got all the pertinent information that I needed. So, I calculate in two months we should make enough money to travel over the Alps and continue with our plans."

"What about the Dauphin?" Sir Nigel asked.

"Sure, he might make a threat toward us; but I he won't be able to muster an army to take on over five thousand men. For him to muster that type of army it will take him around three to four months."

"What about the Pope? Avignon is just south of Pont-Saint-Esprit," another cavalier inquired.

"What about the Pope? He might threaten us, but he doesn't have an army."

"But he might influence a rich noble to muster an Italian or Germanic mercenary company and that wouldn't take too much time."

"The only one in the Pope side would be the Count of Savoy, Green Count Amadeus VI, and he's at odds with the Dauphin so again by the time they put their difference aside and decide what to do we should be long gone."

Lord Sterz said, "Now when we get there, we want a small vanguard force to infiltrate the bridge fortress and open the gate from within. Any volunteers other than Sir Thornton?" Thornton looked surprised and weak at the same time; he found himself a chair and sat down.

"My lance group will do it if we have first pickings at our first harvest," Sir Riis Ruffin said, raising his arm.

"Done," Lord Sterz agreed proudly.

Chapter VIII

"Outrages! Outrages! Guyenne, Gascony, Poitou, Saintonge, Aunis, Agenais, Limousin, Quercy, Angoumois, Aquitaine, Périgord, Bigorre, Gauré, Rouergue, Montreuil-sur-Mer, Ponthieu, Calais, Sangatte, Ham, the list goes on and on… The terms of this treaty gave King Edward half of France. This is just outrageous!" The Pope threw his large parchment copy on his desk.

"The cost of peace Holy Father," Bishop Gilles Aycelin de Montagu responded.

"Peace! At what cost! He left thousands of mercenary soldiers out of work and even his own men are reluctant to go back. He came up with this treaty too late in the year. It's too late for them to go back and plant and harvest on time. They are right now looting and pillaging the French countryside."

"Lots of them just don't want to go back as well. They got the taste of living in a military live style, and they don't want to go back to peaceful vocations. They were also allowed to extract from local villages. After twenty years of war and extractions of the French countryside, their way-of-life has come to a sudden end. According to our network, they are calling themselves by a new name now: 'Tard-Venus'… meaning the late-comers. And they are amassing into free companies."

"Network? What the hell is a network?" The Pope used his hands to emphasize his questions.

"Your Holiness, the chapels, abbeys, nunneries, priest,

monks, nuns, etcetera." Bishop Aycelin walked back and forth when explaining the term.

"Oh, I just never heard it referred to that way. Please continue…"

"There is also talk of one massive English company. They say it's in the thousands. And their intention is to travel south."

"South! South to where? Are they coming for the Dauphin because of his weakness? If so, we must warn him." The Pope looked uneasy as he sat back on his oversize chair.

"We are not sure yet. Soon we will find out."

"Yes, please find out and quickly! We are also located south from them."

"Did Cardinal Albornoz do all the paperwork and elections for promoting you as a Cardinal?"

"I believe he is working on it."

"Well, good. But I also need him to teach you on how to prepare the elixir that he fixes for me. I'm planning to send the Cardinal flying to do papal legate." The Pope smiled and made his hands like a bird flapping his wings. "And I need you here instead taking care of me."

"If you don't mind me asking, Holy Father, what Papal legate?

"I need Albornoz to talk to the Green Count."

"The Green Count?"

"Amadeus VI, the ruling Count of Savoy. He is known as the Green Count ever since he turned nineteen years old. He started to wear green, his horses and his personal guards. But what matters is his geographic location of his territories north adjacent to the Dauphine territory and Avignon. However, the most important is his wealth. It takes money if we must dance with these so-called mercenaries. They are corsairs. Barbary pirates on land. I tell you! The Catholic Church is here to serve the poor, the needy, and the lost. Not to pay off pirates. We will have to use the rich noblemen, ruling patrons, and the monarchs of this world to pay for this mess that they created."

"Your Holiness." Cardinal Albornoz walked in and lowered himself to kiss the papal ring.

"Here you are, Albornoz! Speaking of my favorite red birdy. Please leave us now Aycelin; I will talk to you later."

"Did you do the work I assigned to you, Cardinal Albornoz?"

"Yes, your Holiness. The Marquis of Montferrat is indeed in conflict with the Visconti family of Milan. According to my sources the Viscontis are looking to hire a great company of mercenary for a battle. A well-established experienced company with a vast number of mercenaries at their disposal. Some say it could be as much as twenty-thousand men. We narrow it down to only one company that has that kind of numbers and reputation that the Visconti family would mostly likely hire; we predict it's the Great Company."

"The Great Company."

"Yes, their commander's name is Sir Konrad von Landau. They say he is a master tactician and strategist on the mastery of war."

"What I'm seeing, Albornoz, is that we are going to have to remind the Green Count that historically he is sworn to protect these lands. He is the one that can afford a professional mercenary army at this time. He has had some differences with the Dauphin before but recently that has all been settled with the help of the good Church. We must get rid of this English pestilence that is creeping into the Holy Roman Empire."

"Now, what's going on with Aycelin's Cardinal proceedings?"

"Your Holiness, the proceedings are slowly advancing, but there are some Cardinal approvals that must first take place."

"Stop speaking in circles, you Castilian cock sucker. I know it's a process. I need you to get this done for me. There is no need for you to be jealous of him if that's the case. I need him and I need you. Have you ever heard of a swordsman that fight using two swords? They are master swordsmen of the highest caliber. You two are my God guided swords. So, teach him about the herbs for the elixirs that you give me and make him a Cardinal, for I have uses for both of you."

"But, your Holiness, I'm having problems with some of the other Cardinals."

"Listen here – you remind them that I am the Vicar of Christ on Earth. Do you know what that really means? Whatever I say is God's articulation on earth. So, you get this done."

"Yes, Holy Father."

"If any of the other Cardinals give you any push back, you remind them. That it was I who remove their power of the Counsel of Cardinals; the power to overrule a Pope and rightly so. I will go down in history as the Pope who took down the Cardinals. This is one of my legacies to the Roman Catholic Church. Is that well understood Cardinal? I want him to be a Cardinal before you go to Milan. Do you hear me you Spanish cocksucker! And I need you to convince the Visconti family to keep the conflict against the Marquis alive by sending mercenaries against his very doorsteps. This ploy, hopefully, shall crush the English pest by placing them in the middle. Eventually, we will destroy these English scums plaguing our land."

Before Cardinal Albornoz left with his appointed pontiff tasks, he had a bird of his own that he needed to attend to. This bird lived in a cage and, like any birdcage; the cage needed to be attended to occasionally. The Cardinal went down a long set of stairs that could only lead to only one place in Avignon… the dungeon. This was where the enemies of the pontiff were held.

Cardinal Albornoz came to visit one inmate in particular, an old comrade called Nicola di Rienzo. Senator Nicola di Rienzo who, at one time, was elevated to Tribune of Rome with the help of no other the Pope Clement VI himself. Until fault was found in him and, like the story of Satan, was cast from power by the same pontiff who elevated him to the very same political position. Pope Clement VI denounced him as a criminal, a pagan, and a heretic. In Avignon, he was tried by three cardinals and sentenced to death. The sentence was never carried out because of the death of the pontiff. Cardinal Albornoz acted quickly before any action was taken and caused a stay in the execution of Rienzo. Moreover, there was a chance on Rienzo actual being release since his politics were more aligned with the new Pope. Since then, the good Cardinal had addressed the matter with Pope Innocent several times.

As expected, the cells were dark, humid and of ancient origins. These cells were constructed at least a century before the papal residency. Soon, the Cardinal was led to the cell that he inquired about at the guard post by the pontiff guard. What he saw was a man chained by both arms above his head. The man was naked but with a loin cloth. His hair was wired and was filthy from top to bottom. Spot of blood and bruises could be seen all over his body. Arms were raised to bring about discomfort and he was half seated on a stone slab. The smell of urine and feces hit a person like another door hitting one's face. Albornoz couldn't even recognize if it was really Rienzo.

"Rienzo, Nicola di Rienzo! Is it really you?" the Cardinal asked from behind the cell doors.

Rienzo, raising his head, said, "Who's there? Is that really you Albornoz? Has the Pope finally granted my freedom?"

"It's I. I but at last my supplications has fallen on deaf ears." To this, Rienzo let out a woe that could only come out deep within his soul. "Have you prayed to God Almighty?"

"Of course, I have!" Rienzo replied.

Cardinal Albornoz motioned to the jailer to open the cell door to let him in. The sound of the metal gate cause Rienzo to raise himself and stretch his neck up to see his friend. This caused lots of pain and he let out another agonizing grown. Albornoz came over and sat next to him to help comfort him. He tried to help lift the weight of the chains and at the same time he examined his wounds. "I will see if I can get these chains off from you. But I will stress to pray as hard as you can to God to get you out."

"I will. I will. Please plead with the Holy Father, as well. I will further his cause. See if you can do something about my conditions here; there is a water that drops on my head and I… I, I fear I'm losing my sanity. Please."

"I will. I will plead your case. And I will beg again to that little fat worm of a man; but have you not already prayed?"

"Yes, my lord. Everyday. I pray to all that is holy."

"Have you not prayed to God?"

"Yes. Everyday!"

"Maybe you need to pray to a higher force?" Albornoz lean closer to Rienzo's ear, "To Satan? Lucifer? Who travels from here to there on this world? Is he not the ruler of this world?" This brought Rienzo into convulsions.

"I can never, never do that. My Eminence. Don't make me do that."

The Cardinal patted him like a dog. "All right, all right, search your inner self then… and pray to highest force you know. Go ahead, pray as hard as you can – Rienzo. Guard! We're done here."

Chapter IX

"First pickings at the first harvest! What the hell does that even mean, anyway?" Sir Godwine angrily asked Sir Riis Ruffin on their way to Pont-Saint-Esprit.

"That means Lord Albert Sterz will be in our debt because he didn't have to choose a lance group." Sir Riis urged his horse forward to keep up with Sir Godwine's Lucifer at a comfortable space between himself and the wagon. "In addition, whatever loot we take we can ask him for it, making us a lot richer than the others in the company. Isn't this right, Sir Thornton?" He looked down as Sir Thornton hung on to the wagon as Richard drove.

"Oh yes, and it might also make us a lot more – dead-er, too," Sir Thornton said, very melancholy, staring into nothingness as if in a trance. He did not like the idea of being in this mission. Yes, he was the mastermind behind it, but he was not one to jeopardize his own life if he didn't have to. A handful of men, this was what Sir Thornton calculated a long time ago in a faraway whorehouse. Included in this team was also Janet and Sir Lajos. New armor was acquired and modified for Sir Lajos larger than normal statue that was contemporary with the French guards. Sir Thornton had in his possession forged treasury papers. Well, according to him, the beauty was that they weren't forged papers at all. They were actual French court papers that would go through Pont-Saint-Esprit. The thing was that they were expired papers. But the guards most likely wouldn't notice. They were only trained to see certain seals, parchment quality, watermarks and signatures. That was all. Read the body, context or dates; unlikely, that would be a role for a scribe or the treasurer of Pont-Saint-Esprit. So, the plan was to just show the papers, walk on in, and request to see the treasurer. Since Sir Thornton knew him already, and they are all part of a big happy French family. The plan was to have him give a tour of the facilities.

The group should have arrived in the early evening hours. Even this time was strategic. People are getting tired of the day thinking about dinner or going to the local tavern to end the day, so their guards would be down. The group would acquire basic knowledge of where the guards are. Then the group would wait for the White Company. They would expect them just before dawn still in darkness, the best time for an attack. Then, the White Company will proceed with a two-prong attack: the vanguard force attacking first in order to get the gate open by all means possible, and another infantry force to scale the fortification in the middle of the night to reach the gatehouse just before sunrise. If the vanguard force didn't reach it first, then the infantry force would have to deal with both.

On December twenty-eighth, 1360, they started to see the outline of the Pont-Saint-Esprit on the horizon, and it did not disappoint. First one sees the lights of the smaller structures that are built separately, around, and adjacent to the main fortress. These were the homes, inns and shops that service this fort. Then the actual bridge starts to be seen. It was the biggest stone bridge that everyone in the vanguard force has ever seen. Beautiful wide stone arches that were a marvel to be seen. It had to be to go over the mighty Rhone River. The exterior of the entire structure was whitewashed with lime, giving it the appearance of having been carved from a single enormous piece of stone which greatly enhanced its already powerful manifestation. The road led to the fortress which was a large structure to itself. It was asymmetric and hugged the coastline. The fort, for some reason, had most of its structure to the north and east of the bridge structure. The closer the vanguard force came the more detail was revealed. The battle ramps and the arrow loops became clearer. Continuing on the path led to the two high towers with a massive gate in the middle. The secured inner courtyard lies within; this was their first objective. The force came upon the guarded area just before the gate. One of the gate guards came out with an oil lamp in one hand. He was big and had two missing front teeth. It was presumed that he was the leader because of his manners and the others were waiting on him for orders. He took our papers and glanced at them really quick and said, "*Bonsoir.* Are you passing through or do you have any other business here?"

"*Oui. S'il vous plaît.* Is the Pont-Saint-Esprit treasurer available? We need to see him on official business."

"Follow me into the inner courtyard and I will see about getting him."

The vanguard group followed the guard's instructions and proceeded right through the gate. The gate that, before the night was over, would get open for the White Company. Not an easy task. They took the opportunity to observe the gate in better detail for the appointed time for the raid. The group stretched their necks as they looked all around the gate and its workings as they went through. Parallel stone arches supported a chamber above the road between the two towers. In this chamber there was the heavy timber grille portcullis which could be lowered to block the opening. The bottom of each vertical piece of the portcullis was pointed and capped with iron clad. The face of the portcullis was also iron clad for additional strength. Past the portcullis was a set of substantial wooden doors also reinforce with iron clad. Immediately behind the doors were two holes opposite each other in the walls. A timber drawbar was pulled from a room inside of a tower through one of the two holes, across the roadway, and set into the other hole to further secure the doors. Arrow loops from inside the towers gave the soldiers thorough control of the entry area. If any part of an enemy force was careless enough to get caught in the space between the towers, it was showered with a variety of arrows and missiles. These would be dropped or fired through murder holes in the floor above.

The treasurer came out with this same toothless guard at his side and came up to our wagon. "Thornton! It's been years... I haven't seen you since the plague, if I remember correctly. How's life treating you all this time?"

"Jean-Luc, just doing the king's duty under God's good blessings," Thornton answered, somewhat elated as he jumped off the wagon and massaged his rear end.

"Come inside so we can talk and also bring what you want to lock up for the night." The group proceeded to go inside, carrying a large chest of gold in order to lock it in the Pont-Saint-Esprit vault. Fittingly, the chest did have the company's wealth of gold coins. Thornton thought it would be more believable if anybody looked inside, and great motivation for the men to come and take the bridge and save the group if something went wrong.

"My man, Olark, can show your men to the dining hall, where they can be taken care off. Olark, make sure you take real good care of them."

"Let's go upstairs and get away from this cold. I have hot wine that I want to share with you. The wine is from good vintage, so I'm sure you will enjoy it. Come! We can go over the old times."

"That is so kind of you. You don't know how hard it is to travel and do this job."

"Ha! You don't think I know! You think I have forgotten how hard it is to collect the king's taxes? My friend, you never forget being a tax collector. It's one of the only professions frowned upon in the scriptures right there with being a prostitute."

"Before we go upstairs, this man has to come with me he is my personal guard so he can't leave my side."

"Very well." When the two walked through the door, Sir Riis followed Sir Thornton. And everything went black for Sir Riis. When Sir Riis opened his eyes again, he had a headache, felt the warm fire of a giant fireplace at his side and was tied to a chair. He also heard the crisp popping sounds of the fire as it burned. Thornton was seated in front of him, and Jean-Luc was behind his work desk. Olark was on the other side of him. Sir Riis guessed that Olark must have hurried to the office chambers and hit his head as he was going through the door. Sir Riis thought, *This is not good, but it could be worse; I could also be dead. I guess, I should be thankful to God for that but why keep me alive? And now that I'm shaking the cloud off my head, I see and hear something more perplexing, they are laughing and seem to be having a good time.*

Jean-Luc, tapping on his desk for attention and pointing at Sir Riis, said, "Oh, look like your friend is coming around."

"Sir Riis Ruffin, are you feeling, okay?" Sir Thornton asked.

"I think so."

"Well, let me explain a little of what we discussed so far. It seems we didn't fool anybody with our papers."

"Yes, Olark may look like a moron, but he knows his job very well. Besides those papers, my worst guard could tell they are from about the time of the plague. What did you do anyway get it from some poor Black Death dead man? I can just see it now, the cadaver holding the papers clenched in a dead man fist!" Jean-Luc said this animating the cadaver. Laughter ensued for Jean-Luc and Olark.

"No matter, the end of the story is my old friend here wants a cut in our venture and he will help us out. But I told him that I need your permission Sir Ruffin since you are in charge of this operation. And he also has the rest of our men in the dungeon."

"How much do you want?" Sir Riis rubbed his eyes, trying to adjust to the light emanating from the fireplace.

"I just want to fill my saddle bags full of gold and what my mule can safely carry out of Pont-Saint-Esprit."

"That is all you want."

"Yes, my Lord."

"Well, that's a lot of gold coins. How much gold will be left?"

"This is why he is saying this, Sir Ruffin. He was so kind to tell me that he was informed by the French crown that to be extra careful with security in these next few months because they are collecting the taxes to pay for the ransom for King John who is still a hostage of King Edward. He heard that the ransom was set at three million gold crowns. In the next few months there will be more gold flowing through here than there was in the past hundred years." Sir Thornton said as he scratched his thin hair.

"Please untie me, set my colleagues free and help us in taking control of Pont-Saint-Esprit. Then, you'll have yourself a deal," Sir Riis said, trying to move on his rope bounded conditioned.

"Done." Olark untie the good knight. "But as for the releasing of the rest of your men, there is no need; I hate the use of violence when there is no need. Your friends were in no real danger, they are exactly where I told you before; they most likely finished dinner and are enjoying some wine by now. Isn't that right, Olark?"

"Aye, my Lord. I do have my best men with his eyes on them though, like you instructed."

"Yes. Olark you always do what I instruct you to. That is why I'm taking you with me, just you and I. I will leave my ugly wife, Marguerite, and won't even know that I've left. We will make our way to Paris, a civilized city, and or maybe we'll visit that whore house again... what do you think, Olark?" Olark just smiled and shook his head in agreement.

"Where's my side arms?" Olark handed Sir Riis his dagger and sword back. Sir Thornton started poking the fire in the fireplace. Are you going to look up that whore that you had back then? What was her name?"

"Her name? Heavens, no... no... I don't think I want to see him again; he is probably too old for me by now." Thornton walked closer to Jean-Luc using the poker as a walking stick. Thornton lifted the poker over his head and slammed it down across Jean-Luc's face. "Die, you damned Sodomite! DIE, YOU FUCKEN DAMNED SODOMITE!" Sir Riis acted instinctively, took out his dagger and plunged it into Olark's neck. He knew that Olark would jump and defend his patron as his duty if he did not kill him first. Sir Riis was done with Olark. He pulled his bloody dagger out and then dragged Olark's large body to the side of the chamber. He turned around to look at Sir Thornton; he was still swinging and beating Jean-Luc over and over, repeatedly. "Thornton, stop! Thornton!" He threw the poker violently across the other side of the room. "Please drag his body here beside Olark."

"Sure. How lovely – so the two lovers can rest together

forever in the afterlife."

"Why did you attack him like that? We made a deal?"

"What?" Thornton answered as if coming out of some type of trance.

"Oh… he deserved it. Trying to extract a deal for himself when he knows he has lost this game. If he was going to beat me, he must win me fair not by ruining my plan!" That's when Sir Riis realized that this person was evil.

"I gave him my word; one of these days, you and I will have to settle this," Sir Riis said, and thought, *Right now might not be the right time – Lord Sterz and Lord Hawkwood rely on him too much. I must be patient and wait for the right opportunity.* Sir Riis found a blanket and covered the bodies, especially Jean-Luc because it was disturbing to look at his face. He also noticed there was a cat in the room. That was leaking the blood off the floor. The cat's paws got blood on them, and the cat started to make prints on the floor. Sir Riis quickly cut a piece of cloth with his dagger from a curtain and started to clean the floor.

A young girl's voice was heard coming from the other side. "Sir, it's your supper! Sir!"

"We need to let her in before she alerts any of the guards." So much.

"We don't need him, anyway. We have all the information we need. Later, go outside follow your nose and ears to this dining and drinking hall. See if you can see Olark's henchmen that's keeping an eye on the rest of our men and take care of him. And continue with the plan. So, all we must do now is wait a while till more fort personnel are in bed asleep for the night."

"So, all we have to do is wait here with the dead?"

"Yes, just wait here. Nothing else will go wrong. I promise." Sir Riis started to feel pain on his head. It felt like thumping pain or like someone knocking on wood. Wait, there was someone knocking on the door. A young girl's voice was heard coming from the other side. "Sir, it's your supper! Sir!"

"We need to let her in before she alerts any guards." So much for just waiting patiently.

Thornton opened the door. It was an attractive young lady bringing a tray with food. "Don't you look so sweet? Come on in. The soup looks tasty." The girl looked like she liked the flattery. The door shut. She took a couple steps into the room, and then she noticed the blood on the floor. It was the cat's paw prints that led to the bodies covered at the corner of the room. She started to shake and look like she was going to faint. Thornton with one hand grad the tray with the bowl of soup and with the other arm grabbed her from falling. "There, there, nothing is going to happen to you, my pretty."

"Is my cat all right? "Where is Jean-Luc?" Thornton hushed her and put the tray on top of Jean-Luc's desk. He then covered her mouth.

"Only good things are going to happen to you from now on. So, don't be afraid. You can relax now soon we are going to be in control of the whole of Pont-Saint-Esprit. So, listen to me. Whatever I say, goes. Is that understood?" She moved her head up and down. He let go of her mouth. "Great! Now let's have some soup!"

Thornton was right; it wasn't hard finding the dining hall or finding Olark's man. Most of the fortress was asleep by now. The lance group were in the hall seating at the tables. Sir Lajos was the only one that seemed like he just got there laughing and jesting with one of the Pont-Saint-Esprit French guard. But that person was passing out already, and when Lajos hit him in the back when he said a punch line of one of his jokes; the man fell face forward onto a big bowl of soup, not to lift his head back up. And Lajos just laughed even harder when this happened. Olark's man was getting comfortable leaning against a wall with his arms crossed, more asleep than awake. Sir Riis got beside him and stabbed him right behind his neck. Sir Riis thought, *This cold steel will sent you straight to the underworld; you will get plenty of sleep there.* He got Sir Lajos and Janet together and the rest of the vanguard group. *We need to take care of the guards and the lookouts first.*

    The vanguard group went through the hallways trying to figure out the best way to the pair of gate towers and to the tower's basements. The lookouts would be at the top of the towers. The basements would have access into the rooms that would open the gate and portcullis. Janet and Richard split up to take care of the lookouts for each tower. The hallways were dark and confusing because there were no windows. Light was by candles or oil lamps that were placed on corbels set into the walls. Finally, Janet found a stone spiral staircase. Janet thought, *judging from the distance of where we came in and the little time we spent in the citadel, this must be it.* She climbed the staircase as silently as possible with her crossbow ready to fire. Then it hit her: she started to get nerves; started sweating; she was wondering if she even had enough strength to pull the trigger. Then she saw the lookout. She got lucky. He did not even notice her at all. She could have walk right up next to him if she wanted to. She took her crossbow aim it center mass and fired.

    She shot him deep inside his chest area penetrating the area of the heart and vital organs. Instant kill. She walked up to him. It was her first hunted kill. The other time that she killed, at the plague village, was more like doing mercy kills to the wounded;

killing caught fish... as some would say. This time it was different. She went up to him and noticed that his appearance was very similar to her brother's. About the same age, the hair, his body built, hell, he would probably even be wearing the same type of armor. Then, she stood up and she felt a point of a bolt at her back as she got pushed to the edge of the battlement.

"L'arrét! Quel allez-vous?" A loud voice from behind her questioned. At this moment, the whining sound of an arrow shaft shot at a long distance was heard and then the impact sound of it hitting its mark. The arrow hit the head of the French guard as it went halfway through his face. Impact from the arrow splatted blood and brain matter on Janet's face. Another instant kill. She quickly looked around to see who did it. Then, she noticed from the direction that the arrow came, outlines of men crawling over the battlement walls. They were storming over the wall using escalade ladders. It was the White Company infantry scaling over the battlements that were facing the Rhone River. Then she noticed, when her eyes adjusted to the night, that it was Sir Hugh who had sent the deadly missile her way. Afterward, she noticed Squire Richard trying desperately to get her attention on the other side on top of the other tower.

Janet finally understood what Richard was trying to tell her. She rushed over to turn off the fire lamps at her tower post. Sir Riis and Sir Lajos took care of the rest of the tower guards and then turned their attention to extinguishing all the lights from the rest of the tower fortifications and along the entry area. This had a twofold affect; it gave the signal for the White Company to advance forward and if for some reason someone couldn't sleep that night, they wouldn't see what is coming over the horizon; the White Company approached being quiet under the cover of darkness of the night. All five thousand-five hundred men and horses. Sir Godwine made his way to the basement room and cranked the pulley system to raise the grille portcullis and then pushed the drawbar to unlock the gates. With the main gate open, the White Company moved on through the entry courtyard. Where the White Company proceeded with its second half of its conquest by turning off all the fire lights that faced the eastern side of the Rhone River. Sir Hugh's men were responsible for the side facing the Rhone River. They killed all the battlements guards first and then turned off all the lights at the time when the White Company entered the inner courtyard.

The second half of Pont-Saint-Esprit conquest was not as articulated as the first half. There were only a small remnant structures and a few defensive positions on the eastern side of the river that were needed to contend with. Infantry troops turned off fire lights all along the bridge. Then the White Company moved forward again, very quietly, all the way to the front of the first gate on the other side the eastern side of the mighty Rhone River. This gate and post were more ceremonial than tactical. No attack was expected to come from the internal side of Pont-Saint-Esprit. Lord Hawkwood, who was at the head of the column, gave the order for one of the men to dismount and politely knock at the last gate. A sleepy, angry voice came from the other side of the gate. "Wait a moment. I'm coming! Bloody hell, wait a moment!" The gate guard came to see who would be causing so much commotion. While yawning, he opened the gate and saw over five thousand mounted soldiers standing on the bridge like a colossal metal caterpillar that almost encompassed the entire length of the bridge. Lord Hawkwood urged his mount forward and pushed him down with his long lance. He recoiled back and fell on the hard ground. Then. A foul smell rouse in the air a sure sign that the guard defecated in his armor.

The next day, the focus was on securing and organizing Pont-Saint-Esprit for military occupation. Most of the White Company camped on the eastern side of the bridge with a smaller detachment force within the fortress on the western side. Lord Sterz decided to be on the western side with his own personal camp site adjacent to the fortress and Lord Hawkwood on the eastern side with the rest of the White Company. The eastern side of Pont-Saint-Esprit adjacent to the fortress had all the other associated structures such as shops, homes, barbers, scribes, taverns, etcetera, all that's needed to service such a facility. That night, all of the taverns and drinking establishments were filled to capacity. The atmosphere was blissful, joyful, and celebratory. "We have just taken this town! Pont-Saint-Esprit is ours!" could be heard echoing through the cobble streets. Unfortunately, sporadic sounds of plundering and ransacking could also be heard. Sir Riis Ruffin staggered into a tavern and found Lord Sterz with Sir Marshal. Lord Sterz motioned for him to sit with them. "So, are you're enjoying yourself tonight?"

"Very much, Lord Sterz." Sir Riis noticed that Sir Thomas Marshal was falling asleep on his chair. He leaned over to him and asked, "Do you want to go rest, Sir Thomas?"

"Aye. I place Lord Sterz in your very capable hands. Do not leave him alone until I come back, or you will answer to me." Sir Riis was drunk but became very sober after he was told this.

"So have you decided your first pickings, yet?" asked Lord Sterz.

"Ja, my Lord, I have it right here, a very heavy bag of florins." Sir Riis held the bag up and showed it to Lord Sterz.

"Very nice, I spent most of mine already. I commissioned

myself a new sword today with a new design with my superfluous of Florins." Lord Sterz pulled out a folded piece of parchment and unfolded it. "This is the design. Please take a gander at it." Sir Riis took the parchment onto his own hands. "Ah, it's a fighting fit design, Lord. I believe they are calling these types of swords, a Bastard Sword."

"Ja, yes, that's it. I ordered it through the Pont-Saint-Esprit swordsmith. He will send the order to a swordsmith in Italy. You seem to know about it. What else can you tell me from this design?"

"Well, the blade is longer than usual. The trick will be to maintain the tempered strength for its length. These swords are supposed to be very good for piercing through plate armor."

"Jawohl. That's why I commissioned it. I hope it arrives before we have a major conflict. This would make me very happy… for once." At this moment, a wine bottle flew across the room, almost hitting them, and the shouts and screams of the crowd's rowdiness got even louder. Lord Sterz leaned closer to Sir Riis. "Remind me tomorrow to have Lord Hawkwood assign one contingent of men to maintain peace at Pont-Saint-Esprit." Then, Lord Sterz ducked as a chair flew by him. "Make that two contingent of men. After all this will be our new home for the time being."

"Aye, My Lord." Then, Sir Riis noticed at the front of the door a commotion started going on. It was a woman with a young girl asking if anybody had seen her husband, the treasurer of Pont-Saint-Esprit. Sir Riis soon realized that Sir Thornton had made her a widow and the daughter an orphan. Sir Riis could now hear that she was asking who was in charge of the White Company and that she wanted to speak with him. People started pointing fingers at Lord Sterz's table.

"I don't mean to be rude, but the widow of the Pont-Saint-Esprit treasurer is heading our way."

"Who? Pont-Saint-Esprit treasurer? Isn't he dead? Killed in the conquest?"

"Well, yes, my Lord, I will try to take care of this discreetly." Sir Riis noticed Sir Godwine was almost next to him, so he motioned for his attention.

"Sir Godwine, I will need you to take care of this lady. I believe her name is Marguerite. She is Jean-Luc's widow. The previous late Pont-Saint-Esprit treasurer."

"I will certainly do that." He took a good look at her, since she was very beautiful.

"Here are my Florins, give it to her as compensation for the death of her husband. Tell her he fought valiantly defending his post, but his death was... inevitable." Sir Godwine grabbed her just before she reached the table of Lord Sterz. "Now, let me introduce myself; I'm Sir Godwine and I'm the official in charge of widows in distress."

She at once started crying. "Widow! No one told me he was dead yet!"

"Let's go outside – the White Company is prepared to compensate for your loss. Besides, this is not a good scene for a young little girl." Sir Riis was glad that Sir Godwine took care of the situation. Besides, he was not supposed to leave Lord Sterz alone. While they were walking outside, Sir William Thornton walked in. He was the cause of this whole nasty situation that was unprovoked, unneeded and just simply beastly. He sat at the table where Lord Hawkwood was enjoying his ale with Sir Hugh Heton.

"Lord Hawkwood, you drinking and celebrating? I thought you would be praying to the holy virgin or something like that."

Sir Thornton humorously inquired.

"Good heavens! Whatever gave you that idea? It's a great cause to celebrate. We have taken this golden cow. And I promoted Sir Hugh Heton as my second in command of the longbowmen. Besides ale is safer to drink than water; everyone knows that."

"Well, my compliments, Sir Hugh, on your promotion."

"Thank you and, likewise, congratulation to the execution of a successful plan."

"You were part of Cavalier Ruffin's mercenary group? Weren't you?"

"Oh, yes. Ever since the Treaty of Brétigny was signed." At this time, Lord Hawkwood stood up. "I will be excusing myself." He let out such a loud burp of air that made everyone in the tavern stop what they were doing and look at Lord Hawkwood. Everyone marveled and laughed as to the loudness and duration of it. Then he said in a loud voice to everyone, "You gentlemen carry on and have a good night." Everyone cheered, making birds and hawk noises.

Sir Thornton said, "Good night to you as well, my Lord." Looking back at Sir Hugh, he said, "I'm glad, to finally meet you. And I'm especially glad that we have this little time to chat… just you and me." He moved in closer to Sir Hugh. "What do you think of Cavalier Ruffin?"

"I think he kept us together the best he could. But it was not a profitable venture. I like the White Company a lot better." He took out a bag that was filled with coins and lifted it up and down to make a jingle noise.

"So, it is safe to say that as long as you get compensated handsomely, I can count on you?"

"If you pay me the right amount, I will kill my father and

prostitute my own mother."

"Ha, you are a man after my own heart. Listen now that I have you here, I need you to keep an eye on Cavalier Ruffin and his personal circle of men. Specifically, Sir Godwine and Sir Lajos just keep an eye on them… any information that you can gather might be of value. I found this out from my experience. Now he has two squires Richard and a new little fellow called—"

"Lambert. A little French man. I will kill him for free."

"Ha. I'm already getting an investment on you already. I want you to keep an eye on them and, yes, I want you to do more. Hurt the squires if you can; but be inconspicuous so that it doesn't come back to me or you. They are low ranking, so I don't really care what happens to them. I want Sir Riis off balance so I can get to him."

"If you don't mind me asking, what did Sir Riis do to you for asking this of me?"

"He threatened my life." Sir Hugh looked very serious for a moment, then laughter arose from them both.

Sir Riis was glad that he stayed at his table with Lord Sterz. "What happened Cavalier?" inquired Lord Sterz.

"My Lieutenant Sir Godwine volunteered to take care of the whole situation. He is a good and just man."

"Your men look up to you; don't they? Well, Good! That's how it should be." Lord Sterz gulped another ale down. "So, tell me more about this war machine that I heard so much about."

"It was designed by a brilliant Italian craftsman. He based it on the design of an ancient Roman crossbow machines. The only problem was the arrow bolts that are used for it. It must be a special wood just like longbows. Yew wood from Iberia, I believe. I heard Ash or maybe Elm wood may work as well. But we haven't had the opportunity to try the craft them. Moreover, we have a limited supply of them. Then Richard got together with a stone slinger and adopted it for rocks. They say they can kill someone at three hundred paces."

"Four hundred paces on a clear day. That's what Lambert thinks anyway. "We never used it in real combat yet," Richard said this while walking by celebrating.

"Oh…" Lord Sterz scratched his head.

"Please, Squire Richard, keep moving and celebrating on your own way." Sir Riis pushed Richard away. Then Sir Riis turned back his attention to Lord Sterz. Sir Riis became suddenly solemn and distant at this moment.

"I heard that you are a tormented soul a contender to even myself… well that's what I heard, anyway. Whatever happened to you, Cavalier Riis?"

"Oh, it's a long, sad story, my Lord."

"Well, we have time, my knight; so, tell me your tale."

I think the core of my demise is that my wife and my child died at childbirth were both taken away and killed on the same night. I mean we did all the holy sacraments, but God decided to take my whole world away…where is the providence in that? Ever since then, I have lost communion with God, and I question God's Holy providence." died at childbirth. Ever since then I have lost communion with God. I mean we did all the holy sacraments, but God decided to take my whole world away… all in just one day. Since then, I question God's providence."

"*Beyond all doubt, intellectual and emotional error about the universals is the cause of all sin that reigns in the world.*" Lord Sterz had a faraway look as he said these words, at which Sir Riis lifted one of his eyebrows. Lord Sterz continued the conversation. "Never mind me; something I learned a long time ago from an English clergy member. But let me continue with an example from the scriptures. Let's take Job. He was obedient to God and God blessed him for it. So, God built a hedge of protection around him and his family. This is God's will. Wouldn't you say?"

"I agree..." Sir Riis said with a questioning look.

"Then, God permitted Satan to touch Job and his family. This is also God's will. It seems that God has two wills. One a holy will and the other a permissible will. Job also had his world taken away in a day. All his family, lands and health would seem lost forever."

"Are you implying that I was like Job? And my world was taken away from me?"

"I didn't say that... you did. Remember the story of Job. Job didn't do anything wrong to cause his calamity and sorrows. Job remained faithful to God. And at the end his rewards were twice fold.

"I add this to the hypothesis that God created men with their own evil free wills. So evil men that don't believe in God do evil things all the time. We also have the original sin of Adam and Eve; hence we are also punished with sickness and death. So, what happened might have been permitted by God for God's grander story; in other words, it was for the greater good."

"For the greater good? These are harsh words. How can you say this to me?" Sir Riis leaned back on his chair.

"His thoughts are higher than our thoughts. I know it is easy for me to say and hard for you to have faith in and live by. But just like Job, in the end God is still God. It is up to us to be obedient to His holy will and thoughts and He will bless us and protect us. Like David versus Goliath. David was going to win because it was ordained by God to do so, and David knew it. This is an example of His holy will."

"If this was true, why did he pick up five stones?" Sir Riis picked up his ale and started drinking again.

"Five stones? Well, I don't know specifically why."

"Well Goliath had four other brothers. He needed the other four stones just in case the brothers wanted to take revenge."

"Ha. That's right." Lord Sterz laughed like he hadn't in a long time. He took another ale and continued drinking as well.

"Trial by combat. You know I have a problem with this concept as well," Sir Riis continued.

"Why so?"

"Mainly, they have sanctioned champions as proxy for accuse or an accuser. And there is a big problem with this. If you are wealthy, you can hire a great champion. What are the chances that a poor man can prove his innocence?"

"Very true. Maybe something that the Crown or Church should look into."

"How do you know so much about the scriptures?"

"I studied to be a priest a long time ago. But I don't like to talk about it any longer. What happened to you? I heard that you are a tormented soul not unlike myself."

"Oh… yes, I lost an individual too. I'm unable to elaborate on it. But the words I gave you are always words that I contemplate in my mind, that is why they were readily available upon my lips. Unfortunately, I must keep all my feelings bottled up inside of me which… I would say come in useful… when I'm fighting in the battlefield." And then Lord Sterz smiled.

The next day, Janet had never seen so many gold coins in her young life. Since she was part of the vanguard force, she got a first picking, a full bag of florins coins. She never had so much wealth and she bet her late parents had never seen so much wealth in their entire life. So, she decided to go buy a few things at the few Pont-Saint-Esprit shops available. "Richard, will you go to Pont-Saint-Esprit with me? I must buy a few things."

"Yes, I want to buy a new sword; I need a new one." So, they went together to the few shops that Pont-Saint-Esprit had available. The main shops were lined up on the main street leading toward the bridge and on the street off the main roadway parallel to the river. The shops also typically functioned as the shopkeepers' homes. All the shops were of half-timber construction. This meant that the main structure consisted of wooden beams, usually oak, and the spaces between the wooden beams were filled with daub and wattle. The roofs were covered with either wooden shingles or slate tiles. Their workrooms and shops were located at the front of their shop structures on the ground floor. During the daytime, horizontal wooden shutters were opened out toward the street. The top shutter swung upwards and served as an awning, while the bottom one dropped down to serve as a counter on which items could be displayed.

They went down the street as she got items that she always wanted like fragrant ointments, things she can use for makeup, creams, fabric, etc. When they were walking on the streets of Pont-Saint-Esprit, they went by Sir Hugh Heton. They tried to ignore him, but he went out of his way by crossing the street and pushing his way through the Spiripontain street crowd.

"What are all these things you are carrying? And I see you have Squire Richard here carrying your stuff, too." He reached over and started looking through her stuff. "All this stuff is something a woman would like. Are you buying something for a girl? You have a girl, Lambert? What about you Richard, do you have a girl? I thought not; you two probably play with each other and dream about girls." Janet was upset and about to go into action. Richard motioned to Janet to calm down. "Pay him no heed. He is just trying to get a reaction out of us and disrespect us. Remember the White Company rule of not to disrespect a higher-ranking knight. And he is way up there, now. He is second in command of all the longbowmen. Be careful, with your skill they keep casting you with the archers. You might end up under him taking orders."

"Please let us leave in peace, we don't want any trouble!" Richard said, defiantly.

"I have no time to waste with the likes of squires. No matter, one of these days' you squires will have to answer to me." Sir Hugh kept walking away.

"Sir Ruffin will not allow it. Anyway, don't worry, I'm too happy for him to put me down," Janet said.

"Ah here is the swordsmith shop. I want to go inside."

"What do you want? I'm very busy," the Spiripontain swordsmith asked.

"I was thinking of making a commission for a sword for myself if you don't have anything I like." Squire Richard said.

"Well, against this wall are all those swords that are available. Pick your pick." The swordsmith seemed like an average-built man with his only noticeable facial feature being that his right ear was grossly larger than the left. Richard went over to look through the sword racks. Janet walked over and asked, "My sword has a couple of chips on the blade. I heard it would be easy to fix."

"Let me see what you have." Janet showed him her sword. "Hah, this is a nice one." He then unsheathed it from its scabbard. "Yes, I can sharpen, polish and resurface the blade to get those chips out. You would never know they were there in the first place."

"How much it will cost?"

"It will be between two to three gold sous coins."

Squire Richard jumped into the conversation. "Three sous – you can buy a new sword for that."

"Yes, lad, but you're not talking about an ordinary sword, here. So, the cost is proportionate to the caliber of the sword." Richard and Janet looked confused at what he was saying. The swordsmith continued. "The entire shape of this sword is a lot harder to work with, lads. In other words, the precise work on this one is not the same as the one on the wall that you are looking at, Sir Richard."

"Oh, I'm not a knight."

"Oh, but you will, my Lord, you will."

"No problem in my end. I believe you will take gold florins instead," Janet said while pulling her sword and giving it to the swordsmith. "When can I pick it up?"

"Florins are not a problem, and in about a week's time. Come by, and I will tell you where I am on it," Smith said.

"That long?" Richard asked.

"Oh yes, I'm very busy with the White Company."

"What about you? Have you made up your mind?"

"Well, I'm still confused. Are any of these swords on the wall any good?"

"Sure, they're good to hack, or for a tournament. But do you want your sword not to bend easily? Or if you want something more dependable? Or something special?"

"I have this one now." He showed his scimitar. Janet walked away when he drew his sword out.

"Oh, this one is nice. Why would you want to get rid of it?"

"I need to replace it," Richard said looking very awkward.

"Trade that sword in with your purchase and I will make you a sword that you will carry proudly through the rest of the world. "After they see the high craftsmanship of the blade, people will question if the swordsmith had communion with the Devil. "And you will say, proudly, I got it at Pont-Saint-Esprit when the White Company was there."

"How much?" Richard asked.

"Three sous for the blade and four sous for the sheath." Then he heard a voice from behind him that said, "Take it. I just paid that much just for only my scabbard. Is it ready yet, Smith? I've been without a sword for nearly two weeks."

"I told you what I had to do to it and that was going to take time. I will have it for you next week – Cavalier Andrew de Belmonte."

"How about you, Lord Richard?"

"I guess I will commission my first sword."

"All right, then, don't leave until I have your measurements to design and forge you the perfect sword. And what style sword you like?"

Cavalier Andrew de Belmonte hated waiting for anything. It was such a lack of respect. This brought memories to him of his youth. When he was still merely a child not yet a man, he had to learn horsemanship. A knight had to learn horsemanship at a very young age. Growing up at his father's citadel, he never felt any difference with the other young knights in training. Until they started or maybe they found out that he was the bastard child of the Earl. His mother would slip into his room late at night after the first sleep and comfort him as a mother would. Until she found him crying because of the teasing of the other young knights. He still remembered her words like it was yesterday. "The sooner you realize who you are the better. Learn as much as you can now. I'm sure that with your sword arm you will carve out for yourself your own kingdom." Then he pleaded with her not to let him go out again. That was when she slapped him hard on his face. That slap hurt more than anything in the world. She rushed out of the chamber. He followed her, unannounced. He stopped short of the door, and he could hear his mother crying on the other side. After this episode, his mom stops coming to his bedroom at night. His mom still watched him from afar growing up into a fine house knight. Because of this, he made himself a promise to leave and not come back until he made his own riches.

After, he saw Squire Richard leave with that odd French soldier. He went back to the swordsmith shop. When the swordsmith saw him – "I said next week!" – Sir Andrew rushed to where he was at and grabbed him with one hand by the neck. He pulled his dagger with the other hand and placed it on the neck as well.

"I heard what you said the first time. I don't like your jesting. It's so unrespectable. Do you understand me?" From the point of the dagger, one can see blood starting to drip down the sweaty chest of the swordsmith. All that the swordsmith could do was nod in acknowledgement. At this precise moment, Sir Godwine entered the shop and said, "Problem with your order, my lord? If you really want to kill him, Sir Andrew, we will not have a swordsmith to take care of our equipment. I'm sure he will make it right whatever he has done. Please remember that you are a White Company Cavalier and should act as such." Sir Andrew pushed the swordsmith away and immediately the swordsmith grasped for air. As Sir Andrew walked pass Sir Godwine, as if two alpha wolves had to pass each other in the night. As he went by, as he was leaving the shop, Sir Godwine felt a feeling and a sensation on his sensory nerves that he has not felt in this company of men before.

"Thank you, Sir—" The swordsmith was still trying to relax and gain his composure from the encounter.

"It's Sir Godwine, my good friend. I came here to see your wares that I heard so much about."

"Aye, thank you anyway. Please have a look around." The swordsmith was still rubbing his neck.

"Anywhere in the shop?"

"Yes, anywhere."

Sir Godwine looked around, and mostly on the workshop side of things. That was where he noticed an unusually long piece of steel being forged. "What is this long steel for?"

"Well, that's for Lord Sterz's special commission."

"Is this the new sword he ordered?" But the swordsmith was silent on the matter. "I thought he told me that it was going to be created by an Italian swordsmith. Last I knew you are Spiripontain, are you not? And this time do not stay silent, speak!"

"Aye, I said it would be done by an Italian because of the higher price I can charge. Simple – I can forge a sword just as well as any Italian swordsmith or even better. Besides, the actual design is from a Castilian swordsmith not Italian. Look, I will give you some coins to be quiet about all of this, or maybe some swordsmith service?"

Walking back to the White Company's camp, Janet asked, "Richard, what does it mean when a man winks at another man?"

"I don't know. I never had that happen to me. Why do you ask, anyway?" Richard was struggling with the packages as they walked.

"The handsome knight that was behind you winked at me."

"So, you think Sir Andrew is handsome?"

"Well, forget I said that. What does that even mean?"

"I don't think it means anything. Other than that, he is friendly, I would hope. Besides, there is nothing wrong thinking that he is handsome. Because he really is. He has almost female features, but still very male. It would be good to have him as a friend; I have heard only good things about him so far."

"Oh, like what?"

"His men say he is fair and just toward them. He is also one of the cavaliers of the White Company. The swordsmith was not making up that title or he just doesn't know. Sir Andrew is always hanging around cavaliers William Boson, Adam Scoto and Rubino de Pingo whenever the cavaliers are gathered together."

"How do you know so much?"

"Oh, I try to spy into the command tent whenever I get the chance just to keep my ears open and see what type of information I can pick up."

"What? What type of information would you need?"

"Janet, what type of information, I don't need? Information is power. To be at the right time at the right place is crucial for a knight or for a commoner. Your life might depend on it."

"Who are you? Don't you just want to complete your training to become a knight?"

"Janet – I still want to do that. But I also want to become a baron and I need information to settle lands back at Bruges, like the price of the lands, the best crops to plant, the taxes, finding out the lord in charge, the cost of passageway? And the most important the quantity of wealth I will need to save."

"All right! I got it. But still, Richard, if they find you lurking around a command tent when you shouldn't be there it might get you in trouble."

"Janet if I ever did get caught, all I would say is that I'm getting something for Cavalier Riis Ruffin. Or I was discussing a matter with Lord Hawkwood. Who is going to go back to Lord Hawkwood and ask him anything? And who would look up Sir Ruffin? Half the Company is scared of him already, and the other half don't want anything to do with him. And if they do have the balls to ask Sir Ruffin, he would say something like, 'Oh, Richard, yeah, he is my squire. He is probably getting something for my horse… now get out of my way'." Richard said this while walking and avoiding water puddles.

"Why would you say that about Sir Riis?"

"Because it's true. We don't experience it because he looks after us. So, we have a different impression of him. But other people are plain scared of him. I think he gives a bad impression, most likely because he hardly smiles. I don't know. It's hard to explain. I asked people the same question before. I guess there is no real answer."

"Oui, but I still don't understand how you managed sneaking around with so many work responsibilities that we have?"

"Janet, do you think I needed to do so much work with the horses? Or the war machine? How much maintenance do you think a giant wooden crossbow takes anyway?"

"Hum, that explains why you weren't around when they asked a bunch of squires to build up some of our defensive mounds. I need to learn from you. I see, tell me more, my squire. We still have a little while till we reach our camp. So, how many cavaliers are there in the White Company, anyway?"

"I counted at least seventeen cavaliers. Sir Nigel Loringe is the most powerful of the cavaliers. He is very tall, lean and a redhead. He is similar to Sir Andrew – he commands an air about him that people gravitate to. He seems to command a total of five contingents. So, he orders around his other four cavaliers like a pack of hunting dogs. I don't know their names just by faces. I don't know their names just by faces. I also found out that day that they reassigned Sir Lagos with the Hungarian contingent. And that the Hungarian men elected Sir Lagos as their cavalier to lead them."

"I like Sir Lajos. He is like a gentle giant. He saved my life once."

"When did this happen?"

"One unlucky day, I snuck away when we first joined the White Company. I was foolish. I saw so many men, I thought I could find my brother in this multitude. I wandered into a corner of the camp where they were not friendly and wanted to fight and beat me up. I was afraid of being discovered as who I really was. Out of nowhere comes Sir Lajos. He said something like, 'you don't want this little one.' And then he picked up the biggest of the group by the neck and threw him across the campfire. After that, everybody backed up and left us alone and then he escorted me back to Sir Riis tent."

"Well, I will certainly miss him. The next time we see him will need to celebrate his promotion."

Squire Richard, bringing in the packages into the tent, said, "Talking about our tent, and here we are."

From time to time, Lord Albert Sterz would do company business at the Green Boar. Mostly all the cases were personal commotions of different men. Usually, men not getting along with others. The solution, simple, the reassigning of the men to different lance group or even to a different contingent.

"Any other grievances before we adjourn? This is cutting into my ale time," Lord Sterz said, sitting with Lord Hawkwood and Sir Thornton.

Sir Nigel Loringe brought in front of them his young squire. "I caught this squire stealing from me and I want satisfaction."

"Come forward, squire. Did you steal from your appointed knight?" asked Sir Sterz.

"No. I did not Lord. He is gravely mistaken. I have nothing."

"I don't mistake anything. He stole from me, and I want satisfaction."

"What was stolen, Sir Nigel Loringe?"

"Some of my personal equipment."

"What exactly?"

"I noticed personal items missing. Most notable a dagger that was pass down from my father and his father's father."

"I see. Where is the dagger now?" asked Sir Sterz.

"I don't have it, ask him! Ask the little thief!"

"Is it possible that you may have misplaced it?"

"No. I want satisfaction."

"Sir Thornton. What would be the punishment for such a petty crime?"

"Petty crime! I want satisfaction!"

"It is supposed to be twenty lashes. But you can reduce the sentence per your discretion," Sir Thornton finally responded.

"Since I don't see any good evidence of a crime, I will reduce the lashes to ten. I also will allow reassignment of the squire after he gets punished. Take him to the public post for his punishment."

"Do not worry, little one. Did you do this crime?" Lord Hawkwood asked, getting up from his chair and walking to the lad.

"No, Sir. I am innocent."

"I will be your proxy, then. Come, Sir Nigel have your

satisfaction with me."

The crowd was already gathered at the public post. Sir Hawkwood took off his aketon and grabbed the iron rings. Everyone witnessed his back which bared marks of previous lashings. "Go ahead, Sir Nigel, get your satisfaction."

"I don't want to inflict pain on you!" Sir Nigel looked back and forth as he examined the crowd. He quickly thought that he would lose face if he didn't go through with it. "But you leave me no choice!" He said this while picking up the lash. The Cavalier proceeded with the lashing. Sir Hawkwood did not cry; he didn't even flinch. When it got to number ten, he grabbed the lash, without looking, twisted off his grasp and looped it around Sir Nigel's neck and knocked him off his feet. Lord Hawkwood got on top of him and began choking him with the lash. Sir Nigel's face got to a color of an unnatural red. Sir Hawkwood continued strangling him. "I beg that you learn your lesson. You must be respectful for the men that will save or maybe not save your life some day!" At this, he released his hold to let him breathe. Sir Nigel started breathing heavily to regain oxygen into his lungs. "Get up and go about your business!" He slowly got up and staggered to his feet and walked away. The crowd parted to let him go. Then, the crowd started to make hawk cries in admiration to Lord Hawkwood. They picked him up on their shoulders and carried him to the tavern for lots of ale.

"Where are we going to assign the young lad?" asked Lord Sterz.

"I will... I need a squire." Sir Godwine volunteered. "Come get your things. I will show you to your new tent."

Chapter X

"Routiers! Routiers! Routiers are a pest to France, to the Crown and to the Blessed Holy Church. I received a dispatch from the Dauphin, yesterday. He wants the Church to do something about this pestilence, at once! Thousands of out-of-work soldiers pillaging and rampaging all over the French countryside. Ha! Thanks to that fucken' King Edward's peace treaty. We'll need every weapon from our arsenal to get rid of these rodents! It won't be easy." Pope Innocent rubbed his chin. He turned and motioned at Cardinal Aycelin. "Come, come, and sit down at my desk, make yourself comfortable." Cardinal Aycelin de Montagu did as he was tasked. This was the pontiff's personal desk at his massive bed chamber where sometimes he would conduct Church business as well as personal business. There were two other priest attendants and two pages sitting quietly along the chamber's walls. The Pope walked to his chamber's window, moved the curtains, opened the stained-glass windows, and let in a cold breeze of freezing air. "What will be our first shot, our first edit?"

"Aye, Holy Father. Let's offer some kind of reward or benefit to deal with the problem at hand. This will foster good godly knights against the evil doers."

"Yes, I like that. First, let's issue indulgences to those who opposed these routiers." After a few minutes of Cardinal Aycelin writing, he said, "Yes, yes write so the words stay on the parchment." He waited a few more minutes. "Let me see it. Yes, well done." He turned to one of the priest attendants. "Here witness it and send it to put a pontiff bull." Then, he turned back again to Cardinal Aycelin. "I don't think I could have done it on a first draft with these other assistants which I had in the past, not even with Cardinal Albornoz, that Castilian cock sucker."

"Oh, Holy Father you are too kind." Cardinal Aycelin sat on the chair, holding his hands together.

"No, I mean it others write… like if they had two left hands. Next, we need to order the mercenaries to disband their companies, leave the area they had taken, and repair the damage they had done."

"Yes, Holy Father shall we give them a time frame in which for them to do this? Like three months or maybe six months? Cardinal Aycelin picked up his long feather in order to write again.

"Heavens, no! They will need to do this within a month or suffer excommunication! Additionally, clerics and laymen will also be forbidden to join, employ, or to even favor any of these routiers companies or brigades; anyone supplying them with food would be anathematized to the extent that only papal absolution could release them. I think this would be fine for now, but other crossbow fire bolts that the Church will get ready to shoot are: All towns, villages, and individuals found guilty of negotiating with routiers will have their privileges, liberties, and fiefs withdrawn; routiers and their descendants will be ineligible for public office for maybe… hum… maybe two… no, three generations; and their vassals would be released from their oaths of loyalty. You have all that, Cardinal Aycelin?"

"Aye, Holy Father."

"Additionally, any church or cemetery where a routier had been buried would be placed under interdict until the corpse is exhumed and removed. You have all of that?"

"Aye, these are very strong edits, if you don't mind me saying. Holy Father."

"Yes, I do mind you saying! This scourge must be brought under control, or it will come to our very doorsteps. We must fight fire bolt with fire bolt! If these routiers are not brought under control soon these bolts will have pontiff bulls on them." The Pope walked to his bed and sat on it. On his bed he grad his head with two hands and starts robbing his forehead and temples.

"Are you all right, Holy Father?"

"Yes, quite well. I think we did enough for one day. Once I have my elixir, I think I will finally have a good night sleep."

The Pope woke up; finally, he had had a night where he slept the whole night. Had his breakfast at one of his favorite courtyards. He loved to listen to the morning birds bringing in the songs of a new day. He had a hard-boiled egg with bread, butter, and a small glass of wine. A priest attendant made his way to his table and made his presence known. He was perspiring unusually for this time in the morning.

"Holy Father, there is some important news I must convey. Pont-Saint-Esprit has been overtaken by English mercenaries."

"What did you just say?" The Pope cut through the egg and spilled his wine on the table.

"Holy Father, an enormous company of free soldiers have overtaken Pont-Saint-Esprit." Priest stepped back and shook a little.

"What do you mean... overtaken Pont-Saint-Esprit?" the Pope said, yelling and slamming his first on the table. "How many are they?"

"I have been told in the thousands."

"What?"

"That is all we know." He continued to back away as the Pope got up from his chair.

"Well, get me someone that really knows what is going on. And get me Cardinal Aycelin de Montagu!" The Pope pushed the priest with his fist. "Right now, move!"

"Your Holiness," Cardinal Aycelin said, arriving at the breakfast table of the Pope.

"Did you bring me the elixir? I'm not feeling well today. You will need to go to Pont-Saint-Esprit and legate for me. You have to tell the mercenaries to leave from Pont-Saint-Esprit, peacefully. As you may know it's only a day's ride from here. It's only twenty-five Roman miles north from here. You will have to get rid of them. Where is Cardinal Albornoz?"

"Holy Father, he should be close to Milan by now to deliberate with the Visconti family."

"I can't believe that this happened without him here with me. The Castilian cocksucker is a great military commander and fighter. I always depended on him for situations such as these. Now, I will need you to go out there and convince the mercenaries to leave the area and fight for the Green Count, or the Marquis, or the King of Castile… for all I care, anywhere but convince them to leave away from here. Find out their intentions. How long they plan to be there. Their exact numbers. There make up. You may need the help of one of the French escorts that the Dauphin lent at your disposal to ascertain the force they have. Write a letter put my Papal seal and ask for peace but they can't be at my doorstep," the Pope said, exhausted and holding his heart.

"Your Holiness, you need to go to your bed chamber and

rest. All of this seems to be too much for you."

"Yes, yes. Bring my elixir there. And bring me the Papal treasurer I need to know how much is available if I must pay them off. One last thing, send a message to Cardinal Albornoz to come back as soon as possible. Tell him, the wolf is at the gate."

After the Pope settled down with his elixir, Cardinal Gilles Aycelin de Montagu made preparations for his journey to Pont-Saint-Esprit. He also left word with the Papal physician that the Pope was not feeling well. His skin color, his manners, the way he conducted himself reminded him of someone very ill. He had the Papal letter drafted and addressed to Sir John Hawkwood as he heard he was the leader of this English free company. The destination of Pont-Saint-Esprit could be reached in one day, but it took a good day's ride. He calculated when they got there it would be in the cover of night. Cardinal Aycelin informed his detachment of French soldiers to get ready to leave at dawn.

Cardinal Aycelin made it to the part of the pontiff palace where his French detachment was instructed to stay and to wait till further orders. The commander of the regiment was called Sir Remon.

"Hello Sir Remon. How are you and your men holding up?"

"We have been in worst places my Cardinal. So compared to them, this is like a holiday."

"Have you heard what happened to Pont-Saint-Esprit, yet?"

"I've only heard that English mercenaries have taken it over. Nothing else."

"That's right. His Holiness wants me to go there and find out what their true intentions are and to influence them to leave."

"Do we have any idea how many they are?" Sir Remon asked.

"No. Just that the numbers could be in the thousands. That is one of the reasons why we are going there. I need your help for a true estimate on numbers and composition of the company. I, of course, don't know anything of military matters, so I will have to rely on you."

"*Oui*. It'll be a big task; I will trust also on my right-hand man, Sir Lorens. Sir Lorens is young but very resourceful, has good vision and is very skillful at his profession. He will be a great help for us."

Nicola di Rienzo woke up by the gable hitting the table of the red hooded tribunal. Their faces obscured from Rienzo's view. A voice came from the tribunal. "Bring forth the witness." It was a young, beautiful girl with long dark hair covered only with a tattered cloak and completely naked underneath. This was evident because the cloak was open for all to see. Bruises and scratches could be seen all over her body. Clear marks that she was interrogated by the Holy Church. "Speak witness," a voice from the cardinal tribunal was heard.

"I saw him with the Devil… he was speaking to him… plotting to control Rome… to control people… to have orgies and mass fornications like in ancient times." She said this while she was shaking and moaning.

The voice came closer. "Good, good little one." It was one of the red-hooded cardinals. He walked over to her and grabbed her face.

"Can I go now?" she asked, trembling.

"No, tell them more." She started to shake her head no, but he stopped it. He grabbed the back of her head which made her cloak drop to the floor. Her eyes rolled to the back of her head which made only the whites of her eyes visible, and she said, "Rienzo, you were blessed from among many until hubris was found in your heart. Now, purgatory must come to you first before redemption."

"I didn't tell you to say that!" he said very angrily. He desperately and violently threw her to the ground and kicked her over and over.

"Can I go now?" she asked, whimpering and trembling. "I did what you told me."

"No, no one leaves here… until I say so!" He laughed and turned to see Rienzo. Finally, Rienzo saw the hooded person's face, and the face was Cardinal Albornoz. Then, Cardinal Albornoz pulled out a sword that looked like the one he used to wield, and he beheaded her. Her head flew from her shoulders and rolled almost to his feet. That was when he noticed that in her long hair was a snake. No, multiple snakes were in the hair. No, they were the hair, then the head started to move with the effort of the snakes and the face turned toward his direction. He shuts his eyes; thinking to himself that it couldn't be real. Then, he heard the gable hitting on the table over, over, and over again.

He finally woke up to water dropping on his head. He heard a soft voice saying, "Rienzo, Rienzo!" He opened his eyes and saw a small head with long hair floating in from the other side of the cell. He thought it was the head from the dream floating in the air. He shut his eyes again and screamed. There was no one in his cell but darkness. "I'm going insane… in this place. God, please get me out of here. Albornoz! Get me out of here!" Rienzo then heard the metallic sound of the gate opening and a voice from the guard. "Be quiet and make it quick." Rienzo saw a small figure walking into the cell. He almost thought it was the young girl in the dream; but it was a young catholic page instead. He scurried to where he was and put a piece of bread in his mouth and said, "Cardinal Albornoz hears your supplications. He sends his blessings and is trying to get you out of here, with God speed." Rienzo quickly swallowed the bread. Then the boy had a flask of water and gave him something to drink. He also put ointment on the wounds around his hands. Rienzo cried and said, "Thank you, Cardinal Albornoz, for hearing my prayers."

Chapter XI

It was Sir Riis Ruffin's task to tell Sir William Thornton that the Papal legate was requesting a council, and the meeting was going to take place at his office chamber which was the previous Pont-Saint-Esprit treasurer. The previous treasurer was not lying about one thing – he was like a king at Pont-Saint-Esprit, because he had the biggest, nicest office chamber in the whole outpost. Sir Riis knocked on the chamber's doors and the girl, from when he was there with Sir Thornton on the night of Pont-Saint-Esprit conquest, opened the door. She was barely dressed. "Can I help you, Lord Riis?"

Sir Riis thought, *Nobody ever calls me that but, technically, I guess she is correct. Should I correct her? No, it makes no difference.* The chambers stank of fornication, libations, and spoiled food. "Girl... please open the windows to let some air in. The pontiff legate is here, and they want to parley." Thornton was laying on his field cot that he brought into the chamber in order to make this his sleeping quarters. "Sir Thornton, Thornton! Please wake up, man!" Nothing. "Sir William Thornton!" He couldn't wake up. "Girl, what is wrong with him?"

"Nothing, he is just very tired from working so hard."

"From drinking and fornicating, I bet!"

"No, my Lord. He works very hard into the late hours of the night. He spends a long time working going over Pont-Saint-Esprit official documents. He just doesn't spend time, for-ni-ca-ting or drinking or anything like that. He set up his sleeping cot here for those long hours he spent here going over these parchments." Sir Riis took a basin that was full of water and poured it on top of Sir Thornton. Sir Thornton waved his arms as if he was swimming in water. That surely woke him up. "Wake up, man! Lord Albert Sterz, Lord John Hawkwood and a representative of the Pope will be here any moment!"

"I'm awake. I'm awake! Nicole, please get my sleeping cot out of here, get some logs on for the fireplace and get me an ale from the tavern next door and help me get dressed." Nicole just stood there paused, processing what to do first. "Don't just stand there. Get some of the servants or pages to help you, in order to help me… now, move!" In a few seconds everything was coming together and starting to look and smell presentable. The pages came up with fire logs and got the fire started. It was badly needed since the windows were open, and a rush of cold winter air came in. It was a clear day, and this was the first time that Sir Riis had a chance to see the view from these windows. One could see the bridge, inner courtyard and a few of the adjacent buildings that were built overtime to service the fortress facilities. The tavern and a new structure that had just recently been erected, the portable Catholic chapel that Lord Hawkwood insisted on bringing. Between both structures there was a large decorative stone post with permanent metal rings that was used for public announcements or other public spectacles. For instance, if the punishment of a condemned soul was to be hung and quartered, one of his quartered pieces might hang there for the public to view. Sir Thornton came beside me, Sir Riis finishing off his outfit and said, "All the things I learn by just staring out these windows."

"How so?" asked Sir Riis, imagining him like a big, gigantic vulture, staring out these windows.

"From the window you can see Sir Sterz going to the tavern and staying there for days and nights. Sir Thomas Marshal always at his side with ever a watchful eye that nothing bad should happen on his watch. Kind of sad if you think about it. He will drink until he passes out. Then, sleep at the table wake up and then will start drinking again and then repeat again with a cycle of going back to his field tent for a little while. That is why he has it close by and not on the eastern side of the bridge. He probably just takes a rest to his tent just for Sir Thomas sakes rather than for his very own sakes. The discipline of Sir Thomas; he must love him a lot. Sir Thomas is a lot older than Lord Sterz. I wonder what the whole story of those two really is. Do you happen to know?"

"As you described, is how I first met them both. Lord Sterz passed out on a tavern table and Sir Marshal by his side. I can only imagine that it is the love of a father toward his son," Sir Riis said, shrugging his shoulders.

"Now, Sir John Hawkwood, on the other hand. In the mornings he will go to the chapel and give thanks to God and in the evenings as well. Then, he will have dinner at the tavern with a good mug of ale. He will not stay there too late, and later he will go back to his tent catch up on reading materials, practice his swordsmanship, inspect the troops, inspect the sentries, do a perimeter inspection, go back to his tent, write a letter, read some more but this time for his amusement, pray and then he will sleep for about four to five hours. And then start everything all over again."

"I see you like to analyze people, don't you?"

"Well, I don't have great fighting skills. I know this… so I have to substitute that disability with knowledge."

"I'm curious – what do you think about me?"

"About you! You really do want to know?"

"Yes. After the experience we had together. I rather do."

"Without needing to say it, you are an excellent cavalier and a master swordsman. You were formally trained so I suspect you are not what you let people believe. For instance, that you are merely a man-at-arms. And the way you speak."

"The way I speak?"

"Yes, you try to hide it. But there is something in the way you pronounce your words. You, my friend can't hide it. You are from the other side." Sir Thomson got his sword belt on.

Sir Riis scoffed at this. "The other side?"

"A high born. That is why you can hide your accent and your English sounds… fitting. You are of noble birth, but something seems to have happened to you and now you are in this predicament. You like to be in control of the people around you but not be in charge of the entire game. But Sir Riis, you have a huge flaw… you wear your heart outside your armor. And you don't notice this weakness… until it's too late."

"Ha, that sounds nothing like me." Sir Riis thought, *Damn, he must have dialog and tea with the devil himself. I must get him on to another topic before he has me talking about how my mother didn't love me, and how my father made me feel inadequate and how I lost my true love.* Sir Riis continued in an audible conversation, "Sir Thornton, what is the White Company's next prudent move?"

"Let's see what the Pope presents to us first. And our goal will be to stall for time–"

"…Time. I need more time." Lord Sterz walked in, putting on his armor and trying to look presentable. "So, where is he?"

"No one is here yet, my Lord." Looking out the window, Sir Riis saw the Cardinal escort coming into the inner courtyard. One can always tell a Cardinal with their traditional red hats that they wear. Those wide-rim red hats had been a traditional institution for over a century now. It's very rare to see a Cardinal, especially after the plague. Some said their numbers had dwindled to less than twenty with the Black Death. Moreover, they usually would send a clergy member or a bishop to legate, but since the White Company was almost at the Pope's doorsteps, the old pontiff must be panicking.

The Cardinal and his escort made their way into the chamber. It was the Cardinal and the French commander Sir Remon and his right-hand man Sir Lorens. When the Cardinal finally entered the chamber, the white cat ran out between his legs, almost causing him to trip. He started to fall and wave his arms about to hang on to something or someone. Sir Lorens quickly grasps on to his eminence, but both of them almost fell due to the Cardinal's weight. Sir Remon finally assisted in stabilizing the both of them. The Cardinal finally regained his composure and seated himself.

"Let me introduce myself – I am Cardinal Gilles Aycelin and I speak for Pope Innocent VI. I also bear a letter from his Holiness himself with his Holy seal bearing greetings and a plea for your company to release Pont-Saint-Esprit to the appropriate authorities so passage and commerce can resume. I am prepared to facilitate a reply to his Holiness at the earliest hour."

"Before we go any further, we are missing, as you say, a *Condotiero* to join us," Sir Sterz said taking the head seat of Thornton's massive desk. "I am Lord Sterz and this Sir Thornton, and we are waiting for Lord Hawkwood."

"Ah… Lord Hawkwood. He is the *Condotiero* of this enterprise, is he not? I have the letter addressed to him. I do hope I got it right?" Cardinal Aycelin inquired with honest concern in his voice.

"Not technically; I am. But I do take his advisements, very seriously," Lord Sterz said, sounding a little irritated. Lord Hawkwood walked in, escorted by Janet. Sir Riis thought, *What was she doing here? I try to keep her away, so she won't get noticed. If I remember correctly, I sent Richard to fetch Lord Hawkwood. Something must have happened to him, and in Squire Richard's wisdom he decided to send Janet.*

Janet seemed to be in good humor with Lord Hawkwood till she saw the French guards. Her demeanor changed and the color of her face became pale.

"Your Eminence. Lord John Hawkwood, at your service."

"Now that we are all here, let's get started." Sir Thornton went by the fireplace and rubbed his hands together. He picked up the fireplace poker and started poking at the logs to get the fire warmer.

"Like I said before, let me formally introduce myself; I am Cardinal Gilles Aycelin de Montagu, and I speak for Pope Innocent VI. I also bear a letter from his Holiness himself, bearing greetings and a plea for your company to release Pont-Saint-Esprit so free passage and commerce can resume. I am also prepared to facilitate a respond to his Holiness at this very hour." Lord Sterz looked at Lord Hawkwood and Sir Thornton. "Let us converse in private for a moment. Just a moment your, Eminence." They went to a corner of the room. Sir Thornton said, "We need to stall for time as much as possible. The more time we spend here the more wealth we will accumulate."

"So, what will be our reply? What are we going to write down as our terms and conditions for us to leave Pont-Saint-Esprit?" Lord Hawkwood inquired.

"We do not need to write anything back."

"What? That might be seen as a slap on the face to his

Holiness!" recoiled Lord Hawkwood.

"I say we don't need to write anything. Next time we will respond. At this moment, we will buy more time. Plus, maybe he will throw out a number for us to leave," Sir Thornton said with his arms crossed.

"I like this course of action. I didn't like that he didn't even recognize me as the leader," Lord Sterz said.

"How do you know this?" Lord Hawkwood asked.

"He addressed the letter to you. Lord Hawkwood."

"Are we in agreement, then?" Lord Sterz said as he came closer to the Cardinal so he could hear their answer. "We heard your message. We will consider the matter. Your Eminence can go back to your Pope. Thanks for the visit."

"But your reply, I have clerks if you want to dictate your conditions."

"Our message is that there is no formal reply at this time."

"But I need to bring a message back to his Holiness!"

"A message? Reply to him like this: We are mercenaries; we bow to no man or king, and not to your GOD! We bow only to St. John the Baptist! Relay this message to your Holy Pope!"

"This is blasphemy!" The good Cardinal recoiled back.

"Now, now, let's not let things get out of hand." Lord Hawkwood tried to calm the situation.

"Tell him that! Lord Hawkwood will show you the way to your men," Lord Sterz said, irritably.

"This way, your Eminence. I hope this little outburst will be overlooked."

"Well, if this is what you want – Lord Hawkwood." Cardinal Aycelin looked beat, standing up from his chair.

"Your Eminence, it will mean so much to my men if you can visit our chapel. Can you spend a few minutes and stop by before your leave?"

"Of course, what type of man of God would I be if I don't take time to feed the flock? Bless you, my son." Looking at Hawkwood, then, turning to the rest of the command staff, he said, "I bless all of you, even though I believe you are sending the wrong message by sending no reply." They left the room with Lord Hawkwood and Janet in tow.

From the window, Sir Riis could see Lord Hawkwood leading the Cardinal to his temporary Chapel structure. A crowd was already gathered for the Cardinal's blessing. Sir Riis could recognize a few faces in the crowd such as Sir Thomas and Sir Lajos – even Sir Hugh was there. He could even see Janet lingering also in the background as if waiting for an opportunity, like a lioness waiting for its prey. Sir Riis thought that he might be overthinking the situation at hand.

"What is our next move, gentlemen? Do you have anything yet, Sir Thornton?" Lord Sterz asked.

"I'm working on it. But I think stalling for time is the best move for now."

"Well, I'm going back to my business." Lord Sterz looked at Sir Thornton.

"Going to the local tavern?"

"Jawohl. The Green Boar. You know where to find me. I only stay there so I'm available for my men at any giving moment." Lord Sterz said, leaving the room, "Till next time."

"What is our next move, then?" asked Sir Riis.

"I usually don't discuss my recommendations to subordinates. But I can give you some facts that I have discovered, and you are smart so you will most likely will figure it out; our next step all by yourself. The Catholic Church will stop at nothing to see Pont-Saint-Esprit open again. Not only do they need commerce over the bridge but also the commerce that travels underneath it on the Rhone River as well. Pont-Saint-Esprit is a critical transportation center where taxes and important notary work is transfer and recorded. I have been analyzing all the ledgers of the counts and lords of the region. I discovered that the Dauphine kingdom is not going to attack us, at least not at this moment. Their sole purpose is to defend Charles V, the Dauphin. We can be at the Dauphine doorsteps, and they will let us walk on by if we don't raise a sword," Sir Thornton answered the question, getting up and closing his large windows.

"What about the Green Count of Savoy?" Sir Riis inquired. "Oh. He is noble; he is very brave and sworn to defend the Dauphine territories. The Green Count has quite a reputation as a warrior and technician, a real master-of-war. And I would hate to fight him in the open field of battle or any tournament for that matter. He is also at odds with the Marquis of Montferrat. Either way Savoy or Dauphine lie in our path of our objective. A battle may be inevitable with the noble Green Count." Sir Thornton answered as he started to walk Sir Riis toward the door.

"Can we just pay a toll to go through his lands? The White Company has amassed a lot of wealth lately with all the taxes we collected so far and not counting the ransom that the Church will ultimately pay. We may have enough to offer a good ransom to the Green Count," Sir Riis asked walking next to Thornton.

"The good count is sworn to protect his ancestral lands– he will never do that. According to my research, his word means more than gold. Likewise, Cavalier Riis Ruffin, your word means everything to you, too." At this point, Sir Thornton led Sir Riis out the chambers and closed the doors in his face. Sir Riis thought, *I hate him. Whenever the chance presents it selves, I will have a fair and honest duel of honor with him under God's eyes.*

Janet finally found her opportunity. She waited patiently and kept her eye on one of the French soldiers – the one in particular who caught her interest. She had found him very interesting ever since she saw him upstairs with the Cardinal. She followed him as he started walking as to urinate but then he took a sharp turn to the company's main camp. Looking very suspicious, he turned and looked around. He had a string of beads tied to his right hand. She waited until he was on the other side of the berm where no one would see them.

She came up behind him and grasped with a strong hold his right shoulder at the same time she kicked his inside left knee. He was taken off balance and fell on the ground, taking Janet with him as well. "I got you. You French spy!" He went for his dagger since that was the only weapon, he had on him. "What, don't you recognize me, big brother Sir Lorens Festu? Is that how you treat your dear little sister?" Janet took her helmet and cloak off.

"Janet? Janet is it really you?" He tried to embrace her as he helped her to her feet.

"Not so loud. I am known as Archer Lambert around here," she said as she dusted off grass and dirt.

"I miss you so much. But how are you here or, better yet, why are you here?"

"The French marauders attack our village and killed our maman."

"Are you sure?"

"What do you mean? That maman is really dead or that they were our countrymen?"

"I guess if they were French."

"Believe me – one of them raped me."

"I'm so sorry."

"I may be young, but I'm not stupid. Maybe you haven't noticed since you were with the Dauphin, and I guess now in the service of this Catholic Cardinal, but the rest of France is in chaos. The English, French marauders, and routiers are looting, pillaging and destroying the French countryside."

"I'm quite aware of the leftover mercenaries; they are even calling themselves by a new name, the Tard-Venus."

"All right. But the problem is even bigger. It's from within our country; it's within the monarchy; the class structure itself. It's not uncommon for peasants to rebel because of the heavy burden placed upon them by monarchs. Higher taxes or if they can't pay them; they must work without pay. And all of this with half the number of people due to the plague. If the peasants' revolt like the Jacquerie did, they are quickly killed by French nobles likes Charles the Bad."

"It was a band of his knights, acting on his edicts that hung our father."

"King Charles of Navarre? He is at odds with the Dauphin; he only wants to usurp the Dauphin since John is a prisoner of the King of England."

"Well, not when it comes to putting down the peasants or commoners."

"Charles the Bad sent scores of his knights in suppression of the peasants after the Jacquerie uprising. He made them look like marauders. And they have killed tens of thousands of peasants and commoners alike. The second time they hit our village they killed everyone and left nothing. That's when mother died. And I decided to join this English Company thinking that maybe they will end up fighting them later and maybe I can find you too. And

I was right on both accounts. But don't worry, I extracted my vengeance on the Navarre's marauders. This company ran into them again and we killed them, all of them," Janet said, half smiling. "And I ran into you this God-blessed day." Janet tied her hair so she could get her helmet back on.

Sir Lorens was taken back with the gravity of all this news. "Come with me," Sir Lorens said, putting his hand on her shoulder to imply, '*stop dressing*'. "I will take care of you. I can talk to the Cardinal myself; he is a reasonable man."

"Why should I go back? For what? To have some type of normal life? Get married, have children and then have a husband that beats me up whenever he is angry or wants to hump me whenever he wants? No… I was taught to fly with these men, and now you want to clip my wings. And where should I go – back to France? French monarchs treat the peasant people as if they are expendable. If I go to the English side, it most likely be the same thing. I like it here with this group of freemen. We are like our own free country here, traveling wherever we want. A free society with our own set of rules.

"But you only have one leader; what happens if he does atrocities to you and your fellow soldiers?"

"According to our bylaws, in such case we can elect a new leader. Face it – this is God's undiscovered country. Come and join us."

"I can't, I owe too much to the crown already. I can't betray it now. Besides this society still sounds like Vikings or sea corsairs but on land. Janet, I fear that this is not going to end well for you."

"We might be Vikings, but we don't promote atrocities on innocent peasants. We go after the rich nobles. And we aim right at their throats…" She took out her sword and in one swift move had it right at his throat. "If this was what you are going to offer me big brother, get the hell out of here."

"No matter what, I'm glad to see that you are all right and healthy. Stronger than ever I expected; you are not the little girl that I remember. All I can say is that if my luck runs out with the Dauphin, I will take you up on your offer."

"Tell me – what were you really doing? What are the beads on a string? Is that to keep count? Are you counting our numbers?" Janet inquired.

"Well, I guess I don't make a good spy after all."

"It will be best for me to be on my way back to my people." Janet kissed her brother on the cheek and left. Unbeknownst to the two, Sir Hugh was on the other side of the berm, spying on them. He didn't hear the whole conversation, but he heard enough to come up to some conclusions of his own.

Janet was worried about Richard. She hadn't seen him since he was supposed to take Lord Hawkwood to the Cardinal parley. She went up and down the camp and the berms that acted as fighting positions if it called for it. Finally, in one of the open tents where the company physicians were, she saw a familiar silhouette of Richard. She rushed over to his side. There was a physician that came over near Richard's bedside. "He was found on the east side of the berm, unconscious with a serious head injury. Do you recognize him?"

"Oui. He is Richard… Squire of Sir Riis Ruffin. Sir Ruffin is Cavalier for our contingent. Together we are part of Sir Riis personal lance group."

"I'm sorry; I didn't know. That's what happens when it's a company of over five thousand men who are gathered together. He will need to come out of it soon; the longer it takes for him to come out of it the more chances of losing his life."

"I will stay next to him until he comes out of it then. Can you send word to Cavalier Riis Ruffin?"

"Aye. I will right away."

Janet took a wet cloth that was on a bowl on top of the side table. She rinsed it out well and placed it on his forehead. Richard started to move his head from side to side and started to mumble. After a few hours, Richard opened his eyes and said, "There's my beautiful angel." Janet looked from side to side to see that there was no one around. "I think you hit your head a little too hard." Then, she whispered, "It's me, Janet."

"I never thought I would see my angel again. I thought I had died," Richard said with a silly smile. "Oh, my head!" Richard grabbed his head.

"I'm glad that you are awake. Try not to move. Oh, Sir Riis came by, but you were still unconscious. I stayed behind until this moment."

"Ah, so you care about me?"

"Richard, whatever happened to you?"

"I'm not too sure. Someone must have hit me. I can't remember anything. But I suspect it was Sir Hugh. And the reason I say that because you know we never got along with each other, and he was the last face that I recognized before everything went blank."

"So, you seen him hit you?"

"No, but I did see him about just before this happened to me."

"Oui. We can't trust him, and I never liked him."

"Why live afraid of people that can hurt us. Janet, let's run away together and make a life together away from the White Company."

"What? I can't believe what you are saying. You know I love the White Company. I will not just leave just like that. Besides, I can't believe you are the second man who ask me to run away."

"What? Another man? Who was that? Do you have a secret lover?"

"No. I found my brother. He is part of the Cardinal's French escort."

"Unbelievable! I thought you told me you didn't know where he was, other than he was serving the French King."

"I didn't, but now I found out he was appointed to the Dauphin. And the Dauphin has appointed him as an escort to a Catholic Cardinal. He told me they are staying at Avignon."

Richard, moving around on the cot, said, "I think I'm in love with you."

"You have a serious head injury!" Then, she whispered again, "Lower your stupid voice, people might be listening." She said, looking around, "People have died of such injuries! I think the physician said something of making a hole on your head." Then, she leaned over to him and at a lower voice said, "How do you know you are in love, anyway?"

"Because I only think of you all the time."

"I don't think that is love but maybe the beginning of love."

"Be that as it may. I have it."

"Where is that physician? I'm going to make that hole on your head myself that way thoughts of love will just leak out. Richard, you're too young for me, and you are still delirious from your injury."

"Too young? Janet, we are the same age!"

"Oui. But females mature faster than men. In female years, I would say I'm about Sir Riis' age."

"Sir Riis? Are you in love with him? He is a tormented soul

he will never make you happy. He lives with ghosts. I can't believe that he will ever make you happy. I can make you happy. We can find some land and farm it and have babies."

"I'm too young to have any children."

"So, now you're too young to have any babies?"

"Oui. Can you get up so we can go to our tent?" Richard tried to sit up and move out but couldn't. "Don't move, then. I will get either Sir Godwine or Sir Lajos for help." Janet rushed out of the physician tent to look for help. She ran out so fast that she didn't really notice her surroundings or who was around her. She slipped a little and ran right into Sir Hugh, hitting his massive body.

"Where do you think you're running to, little Frenchman?" Sir Hugh inquired.

"I have no time to talk to you." She noticed he was on the downside of a pathway that was slippery due to the occasional rains that were falling lately. She knew he would be off balance if she pushed him out of the way. So, she did. It had more of a result than she expected. Sir Hugh fell backwards at a mud pond with a large splashing sound. All this spectacle resulted in great laughter from all who witnessed it. Sir Hugh sat up in the middle of the pond and felt very embarrassed about the whole incident. But she didn't have time to even enjoy it. She was thinking of getting Richard back to their communal tent. *Is this love?* she asked herself as she ran to find help.

Chapter XII

The Pope hated lying in bed, even for his own good health, but his personal physician recommended bed rest. Hearing a light knock at the door, he responded to announce himself.

"It's Cardinal Aycelin de Montagu."

"Ah. I hope you have some good news for me, like that those sons of whores from England are all long gone from Pont-Saint-Esprit."

"I hoped I had such good news as such your Holiness." Cardinal Aycelin came to the side of the bed to kiss the papal ring, but the Pope pulled it away at the last instance. "What? What happened? Are they still there? How long do they plan to stay there?"

"It's a formable force, my Holy Father. In the thousands. The French commander and I branched out and did our own survey and we estimate more than five thousand but less than six. They call themselves The White Company and their leader is Lord Albert Sterz. I delivered the letter as per your instructions and requested a reply. No – I demanded a reply. But there was none. I believe that they are simply stalling for time."

"My God! You are the dumbest Cardinal I ever promoted to a red bird. Of course, they are stalling for time. They want as much gold as they can carry away from the taxes collected for King John's ransom! I will excommunicate them. Excommunicates the whole lot! Who do they think they are? Get the Papal scribes in here. This will get their attention."

"Excommunication, my Holy Father? To condemn over five thousand souls, that's… unheard of. There are Christian men in that company. They have a Christian Chapel. I myself had a mass and blessed them when I was there. To go back and excommunicate them all? This is all too hard for me contemplate."

"You must be the dumbest, soft-hearted Cardinal ever! You are supposed to be one of my holy angels doing God's will on earth. What do you think the Death Angel of God had to do when he had to do God's will over Egypt? Oh, those poor little first-born children; I can't kill them! I swear if Gil de Albornoz is not back here on time, you will go and do my holy work." The Pope held his hand over his heart. "Please leave now. I'm getting very, very upset."

"Should I get the papal physician?"

"No. Just leave me!"

Cardinal Aycelin found himself at his chambers that evening. He couldn't eat because his thoughts were all over the place and he just didn't know what to do. The thought of going back to the group of men that he recently met, blessed, had communion with, and to tell them that the Pope has excommunicated the whole lot was too much for him to bear. He started to pray to God for comfort and a solution; prayer was something that he often relied on for answers in the past.

There was a soft knock at his door. It was Sir Lorens Festu. He made his way into Cardinal Aycelin private room. It was a small modest room not what he expected from a Cardinal.

"Cardinal Aycelin, remember me?"

"Yes. What can I do for you, Sir Lorens?"

"I have a few things that have been bothering me."

"Ask my son."

"Did you know about the persecution of King Charles of Navarre toward the French peasants and commoners? Not only around Paris but far and wide on the countryside. They have killed tens of thousands of peasants and commoners alike. And committed hideous atrocities... even reaching my childhood village."

"There have been some reports of atrocities by his knights and by other noble knights. But atrocities have been conducted on both sides, my son. It has been reported that the peasants conducted atrocities, as well. You can read it yourself; there lies the report on my desk. The report explains how peasants killed a certain noble knight, put him on a spit, and roasted him with his wife and children looking on. After ten or twelve of them raped the lady, they wished to force feed them the roasted flesh of their father and husband and made them then die by a miserable death. Reports such as this spurred for the sanctioning of putting down this peasant revolt."

"But this quenching of the peasants reached my peaceful village. I was told that my father died... hung on a tree by these so-called knights. And later my mother died when my village was raised to the ground by them. Did the Church sanction King Charles to pursue and punish peasants well after the Jacquerie peasant revolt? The Church should condemn his actions and stop this madness. The Church can't stop a noble knight from performing his duty! Charles of Navarre is a noble acting accordingly to the French Crown. Just like the Church can't stop clergy members from doing carnal sins. Christ as our Savior who forgives all. It is all part of God's providence."

"God's providence? French soldiers looting, pillaging and destroying the country's countryside?"

"As you know, France does not have a standing army. The

French crown relies on the French nobles to fight and bring peace. To create a standing army, taxes will need to be increased and allocated for this standing army. The peasants were rebelling because of the heavy burden placed on them. So how are they going to pay higher taxes? Besides King Charles of Navarre wants to usurp the Dauphin since John is still held hostage by the King of England. Mark my words, Charles the Bad, will eventually reap what he sows."

Then, there was a hard knock at the door. It was one of the Priest attendants this time.

"Please come. The Pope's condition has gotten worst. He is asking for his elixir."

"I will be right there. Sir Lorens, my sympathy for your lost. Don't give up hope on the Holy Church. We must continue this conversation at a later date. But for now, I must attend the Holy Father." When he reached the Papal bed chambers the papal physician was still there. Aycelin had the mixture in his hand.

"What do you have there?" asked the physician with his hand outstretched. He took the small bottle, sniffed, and kept it.

"It's the pontiff's elixir that Cardinal Albornoz showed me how to mix." Aycelin's composure was uneven with this question. "I hope this is not harming him. I was just instructed to mix it and give it to him at night so he can rest."

"If this is what I gave Cardinal Albornoz a while back and it is properly mixed, it should be all right. The Pope is asleep now. But I suspect that he had a serious heart computation. He needs to remain in bed – don't give this to him from now on. I will go over other herbs; I would like for you to give him in the morning because it is getting late." There was a soft knock on the door and Cardinal Albornoz walked in, still wearing his journey clothes. "How is the Holy Father? I came as soon as I was able to."

"His condition is stable for now. But I must check on him tomorrow morning," the physician said, putting his equipment away.

The next day, Cardinal Albornoz got word that the Pope wanted to see him. "Holy Father?" Albornoz knelt at the side of the bed and kissed the Papal ring. "Cardinal Albornoz, I want you to excommunicate the White Company... all of them."

"Yes, Holy Father. I completely agree. There have been additional reports that ever since the news of the capture of Pont-Saint-Esprit is out, many other bands of mercenaries have been moving into the Rhone River valley. Excommunicating them will send the message that this type of behavior will not be tolerated." Cardinal Aycelin walks beside the bed. Apparently Aycelin was also called for, as well.

"Please, please, your Holiness, don't do that. I beg of you."

"Now that's enough from you, Cardinal Aycelin. I need you here at my side. I will dictate my pontiff opinions for the next elected. The edicts that we worked on so hard need to be enacted against these insurgent mercenaries, if not by my hand... then by the new pontiff. I also want you to stay by my side and pray for my soul. I feel that the end is near."

"Please, Your Holiness, don't speak like that."

"Cardinal Aycelin please leave us. Cardinal Albornoz has some reporting to do for me." Aycelin left the room.

"Cardinal Albornoz, it is imperative to get Pont-Saint-Esprit open again the fate of France depends on it. If the excommunication doesn't work on those English bastards, try one hundred thousand florins to flush them out. Try to negotiate first, but no more than one hundred fifty thousand is available according to the papal treasurer."

"Understood. Where should I influence them to go?

"I don't care; across the Pyrenees or over the Alps, anywhere away from here!"

"Albornoz, tell me what happened at Milan with the Visconti family?"

"The die has been cast, your Holiness – the Visconti family have a Great Company on move to battle against Marquis of Montferrat."

"Great! Great! Maybe you can influence the White Company to fight on the side of the Marquis; so, both companies will annihilate each other." The Pope finally laughed. "Tell me, Cardinal, what about Senator Rienzo – when is he going to go south and further our cause?"

"Soon, when he is ready, Holy Father."

"When he is ready? I granted his released months ago. You would think he would have recruited enough men and horses by now? I would think he would look forward to taking on his old foes. What is he waiting for?

"Well, after the dungeon his body must get well enough to ride. I will have a talk with him. If I must, I will lead him out of here like we did a long time ago. Don't worry, I will get this done, Holy Father."

"Well, I will hope so. I am dying, you know!"

Rienzo was woken up by the metallic sound of the keys hitting the cell door and swinging wide open. Cardinal Albornoz told the guard, "I will call you when we're done." The Cardinal walked into the cell and asked, "Senator Rienzo, how are you doing?"

"Albornoz, my good friend, did the Pope release me?" Rienzo lifted his head to see his cardinal friend.

"Did you pray? Rienzo?"

"Yes! Your Eminence."

"Rienzo... Rienzo, to whom did you prayed to?" Rienzo started moving around and struggling like a trapped rat.

"I don't want to lose my eternal soul. I had awful nightmares. I don't want to die, your Eminence." He stopped moving around, looking around rapidly, and started crying. Albornoz came to his side and started to comfort him. "Do not be scared, this is not an inquisition. I am your friend of old." Cardinal Albornoz reached into his robes and pulled out a piece of bread. He started to feed it to Rienzo like one does a bird. "Listen to me very carefully: I will not kill you, just answer truthfully. Did you pray to God or the Devil?"

"I prayed to God! I couldn't pray to the Devil."

"Did God get you out? I see you're still here. I have no orders to release you. I suggest for you to pray to a higher vicar."

"No! I couldn't," Rienzo answered, looking around like someone else was in the room.

"That's all right, Rienzo, for you see there is no Devil or Lucifer – that's something that the Church made up to scare little children. But I have taken upon myself to be responsible for you, my little child. I will take care of you. Pray in my name and I will make sure that you are release and taken care off. But you must earnestly pray in my name. Will you do that, Rienzo? Can I count on you? If you do that, I promise we will be back together in the battlefield doing what we do best. Bringing balance and order back to this world!"

"Yes, I promise. But why can I see the Holy Father? I'm sure I can convince him on my release."

"Pope Innocent is the biggest idiot ever elected as Holy Father. He has taken what we have built and destroyed it overnight. Under his watch, he made the right conditions for separations of all the pontiff states. You and I made an alliance of all the city state to be under a pontiff banner. I wrote the Constitutions of the Holy Mother Church in order to regulate the pontiff alliance. Rienzo, don't worry about that fat little worm. I have taken care of him."

"What do you mean, your Eminence?"

"Rienzo, you may soon have to call me soon the Popemaker." Albornoz chuckled a little when he said this. "Soon the Pope will pass away due to my elixir. It looks like it finally has run its course. I didn't even have to give my terrible recipe to my new chess piece, there was no need. I gave him enough already these many pass months for it to do its function. I just gave Aycelin the recipe of the tonic that the old physician gave me a very long time ago. No doubt, the old physician must be analyzing it right now as we speak, that old bird. Soon the concave will start, and all my pieces are in position. Do you know why Aycelin de Montagu is such an important chess piece to me? I wonder if he even knows how much I value him. Do you know why, Rienzo?"

"No, your eminence." Rienzo chewed on the small piece of bread in his mouth.

"He is brother to Cardinal Pierre Aycelin de Montagu and nephew of Cardinal Gilles I Aycelin de Montagu. No wonder when I saw his name on the Pope's itinerary it sounded so familiar. I have leverage over the other two Montagu; but this one I made him a Cardinal. Their votes will be critical since there are such a small number of cardinals since the plague. Everything is set for the new Pope that I selected. This will fix our stage for a new era of conquest. Guard, we are done here!"

Chapter XIII

At Sir Thornton's chamber Lord Albert Sterz and Lord John Hawkwood are taking the news of the White Company being excommunicated by Pope Innocent VI. As is customary, the windows were wide open to let the stench Sir Thornton's fornication with his wench out. A comfortable roaring fire was a blaze at the fireplace. Sir Thornton was poking the fire and Lord Sterz was sitting down on the desk. Lord Hawkwood was standing in the middle of the room with both hands resting on his belt.

Lord Hawkwood asked, "the whole company?" Taken aback, he almost fell onto a chair.

"The whole stinking company! What do you think of your precious Church now?" Lord Sterz said with a sadistic voice pointing at Lord Hawkwood. Lord Hawkwood found himself on the chair and pulled himself to the side of the table.

"I can't believe it. Once they see the pontiff postings, the men's moral will be distraught and heartbroken." Lord Hawkwood put his head down on the table and his hands on top of his head.

"Settle down, Lord Hawkwood, only a small portion of the men out there know how to read." Thornton came over and interjected.

"That doesn't matter. The ones that do will certainly tell the others!"

"This only tells me that the good Pope is getting ready to

pay. You just watch, and see? The Holy Father is getting very desperate. He wants us out of here no matter the cost to his reputation." Then Thornton started laughing like if someone said the funniest tale he has ever heard. Went over to the fireplace and started poking the fire again.

"If he does pay what then?" Lord Hawkwood raised his head.

"We can seek Amadeus, the Count of Savoy; he may need mercenaries. I hear that he is at odds with Marquis of Montferrat and the Dauphin." Lord Sterz got up from his seat to look out the window.

"The Green Count is a true knight, of noble birth and a true strategist. He is trained in knightly combat and according to my research has been educated as a master of war. It is reported that he has being educated on the ancient Roman military works of De Re Militari and De Regimine Principum. But he is lacking wealth according to my research. But I do believe we have no choice but to travel to Savoy," said Sir Thornton. At this moment, there is a soft knock at the door. "It is I, Sir Godwine Quatreton; I was sent for?"

"Oh, yes, come in, you don't need to worry you're not in any trouble or anything like that. I was the one who sent for you," informed Lord Hawkwood calmly, "I just wanted to ask you a few questions about your charger?"

"My steed? What about my stallion?"

"Aye, what do you call him?"

"Lucifer, Sir."

"How did you acquire your great horse? Or I should say how did you acquire Lucifer?"

"I purchased Lucifer from a horse dealer that said it was from a nobleman's horse who didn't want to pay to ship it over the channel." Looking at Lord Sterz, he said, "Please, Lord Sterz where is all this inquisition leading to." Sir Godwine was standing in the room with one hand resting comfortably on his sword handle and the other on his belt.

"There, there, Lord Hawkwood; when I acquire my own stallion, *Titan,* I myself purchased him in a similar fashion," said Lord Sterz walking from the windowsill.

Sir Godwine added, "I didn't even find out his true name till later when I found it engraved on his bit."

"Nevertheless, I'm prepared to offer you three time the amount you paid for him." There was an awkward moment in time, and then Sir Hawkwood said, "Well, what do you say, Sir?"

"I say, I've rather have a good steed under my ass than gold weighting down my ass in a battle. Why are you even asking, Lord Hawkwood? As far as I know you have a fine stallion yourself."

"Well, to be honest, Sir William de Grandson, while he was visiting, mentioned that the Earl of Warrick was looking for this particular steed. A large gray horse with one gray eye. It meets your horse's description, even the very name."

"Do I have to give up my stallion then?"

"No, not at all. We bow down to none. Just realize this; the story of this steed is not what you thought. It apparently was the Earl's son and, sadly, the son died at Chartres. The Earl may claim it someday so be aware of it."

"Do you need me for anything else?"

"No, you're free to return to your men."

"Thank you." Sir Godwine turned to leave out the door.

"Hum, just one more thing Sir Godwine, how is your new squire working for you?"

"What? My squire? Oh yes. It turned out, that he was an

ordinary thief, after all. I caught him doing the very sinful act myself."

"What! I can't believe it. After I inflicted punishment for him. He sounded and looked so sincere and convincing."

Lord Sterz said, "I told you acting as a proxy is very unwise."

"Aye, sir very unwise indeed. From now on, if a punishment is sentenced out by our court, then a proxy will not be allowed. You got that Thornton? Thornton? Can you get the notaries to transcribe that on our legal ledgers? Thornton!" Thornton was finishing up urinating into the fireplace. "I got it, I got it."

"Never again." Sir Hawkwood wondered very pensively to himself as Sir Godwine left the chambers.

Later, Cavalier Riis Ruffin walked into his tent to see Janet tending to Richard. "How is the patient today?"

"Much better Sir. I think; I will be able to help around here soon," Richard said, smiling.

"Good. But concentrate in recovering first." Then, he looked at Janet, "do you want to do some sword training?"

"I don't know if I will have the mind for it, today. Excommunicated… I need to go to a clergy and pray for my forgiveness of my soul, so I won't burn in hell."

"You don't need to go to no clergy. And I will recommend that you stay away from any clergy members. If they ever find out that you are a lady and not a man, I'm sure they will accuse you of having intercourse with the Devil himself and burn you at the stake. Besides because it was a Pope who excommunicated us, it will have to be at least his equal rank. And as far as I know, there is only one Pope in the entire blessed Catholic Church."

"So, are we doomed, then?" Janet looked down toward the ground.

"We are not doomed. The Pope is just one man. He just wants us out of Pont-Saint-Esprit to further the cause of the French Crown. And he doesn't have the power to condemn us to hell. There were plenty of strange things when the plague was rampant that I witness. I observed whole congregation dead on their pews; all gathered together to pray to almighty God. Then, I witness rich nobles that cursed God and left the cities, villages, and towns to live in their country estates and survived. Now tell me – where is God's providence in that?"

At Thornton's chambers the White Company leadership met again with the Papal legate. But this time, the deliberations were with Cardinal Gil de Albornoz and his reputation preceded him. The Cardinal had a reputation of presenting a treaty first; and, if the treaty was rejected, he will come back with an army. This strategy was done until the Italian peninsula was united into the Papal States. First, the proposal then the sword. Everyone in the chamber knew his reputation. No wonder, the atmosphere in the chamber took on an unwanted sinister atmosphere very unlike the first encounter with Cardinal Aycelin de Montagu. "I have a proposal that I think you gentlemen will find acceptable." The Cardinal continued, "I suggest you take the one hundred thousand florins; it's the best and final offer."

"There is also the issue of excommunication," Lord Hawkwood injected.

"Ahh, excommunication. Oh, yes. I will see if the Holy Father will be kind enough to rescind the bull. I'm also going to give you some friendly advice or you may consider it more like useful information."

"Information? Like what information, your eminence?" Thornton inquired.

"Such as the Visconti family of Milan are attacking the Marquis of Montferrat. The Marquis of Montferrat is very wealthy and can afford a great company like what you have amass. So, take your company to the Marquis and offer your services; he will most likely take you up on the offer; he will need valuable soldiers like yourselves."

"Sounds like a sensible plan of action," said Lord Sterz, leaning on his chair.

"Wait, what mercenary company did the Visconti hired to battle the Marquis?"

"The mercenary company? Oh, yes… I think they go by the name of the Great Company."

"How large is this company?"

"I'm not too certain on that."

"Any idea your, Eminence?"

"I would have to say no more than a few hundred…perhaps a thousand."

"Your Eminence, deliver the hundred-thousand florins to our treasurer and you will see the White Company mobilized," Lord Sterz said with a smile.

"I'm glad we came to a happy resolution in this matter. I will inform the Holy Father. He will also be elated." The Cardinal and his French guards left the room.

"I think we should take some time to really think our next move," Lord Hawkwood said in a very pensive tone.

"Yes… no matter what… I think it's about time we move out. We don't want to overstay our hospitality with the Pope. If you gentlemen require my presence you know where I will be," Lord Sterz said jumping from his chair heading to the Green Boar.

Chapter XIV

Janet was tied with her two hands over her head facing the public stone-post that was between the tavern and Lord Hawkwood's portable chapel. Most of the company was gathered around it already by now. "The charges are treason and fraternizing with the enemy." Sir William Thornton recited the charges from a table that they brought out to the courtyard.

"I saw him myself," said Sir Hugh Heton as he addressed the arbitrators and mostly the gathered crowd.

"Other charges include striking and being disrespectful to a higher-ranking knight," Thornton continued. This scene was playing before Sir Riis eyes, and he did not like how it was playing out. No not at all. He had to do something and fast.

"I did nothing wrong; I only pushed him out of my way; I'm sure I can get someone that witness it; I am innocent. And about fraternizing with the enemy, I only went to see my brother – that was all," Janet pleaded from the post.

"Yeah, his French brother-in-arms! I bet. To give all type of secret information about us."

Sir Riis rushed over and pleaded to the White Company courtyard court. "Look, I take responsibility for the young lad. Lambert always told me he had a brother that he was seeking."

"But did you know that he found him? Do you know his name? Have you ever seen him before?" Sir Thornton held papers on the table.

"I have to say no to all accounts; but it does not mean he is not saying the truth."

"Since no one will believe me and no unjust will win in the sight of God, I want a *Trial by Combat*!" Janet declared.

"If a fight is what you want, little French man, a fight is what you will get. But first I want satisfaction for the insult that you did to me."

"Sir. Isn't it enough to fight the young lad?" Lord Hawkwood asked.

"I want satisfaction. There is a rank structure that he violated he needs to be punished according to our rules."

"What does the punishment call for?" Lord Hawkwood turned his head toward Sir Thornton.

"Ah, let me see… twenty lashes, sir."

"Twenty lashes! Oh dear, I hardly believe that he will survive that, being that he is such a scrawny little guy."

"Go ahead, Sir Hugh Heton, get your satisfaction," Lord Sterz announced, standing up and walking over to oversee the punishment. Everything was happening so fast – a little too fast. Sir Riis ran over to where Lord Hawkwood and Sir Thornton were residing. "I will be the proxy for the lad's punishment!"

"Unfortunately, Cavalier Ruffin, a proxy for punishment is no longer an option in the White Company." Sir Riis had to think of something else, but just then he realized that the custom was to take the shirt off in order to administer the punishment. And before he could think of something to stop this, the deed was done and there she was with her breasts out so the whole crowd could see them. And there was no denying that nature has created her as a woman. There were gasps and howls in the crowd and questions and statements abound: "he is a she?", "is he a boy with breast?" "a lady dressed like a man, I've never… do all Frenchmen have breast? I knew it all along!"

Sir Hugh grad the whip. This sight seemed to have make him even angrier at himself and this in turn made him angrier at her. The insult was somehow even greater. "Wench, I'm going to tear your pretty back off!" He took to flocking her and did not hold back not even once. He was getting exhausted from the punishment as he was inflicting it, staggering and sweating profusely. He took off his surcoat and swung a few more times. He took off his chain mail and a few more strikes.

"Why don't you take off your aketon, fat ass? Are you scared to show of your fat-girl chest?" Janet said defiantly. People from the crowd started to laugh. A voice from the audience said, "Yeah, show us your manly chest, Sir Hugh!" He looked around, getting angrier, and took off his shirt showing off his oversize fat chest. It started to rain which made her back look even worse with the blood mixing with the rainwater.

"Nineteen, twenty!" screamed Lord Sterz. "Stop, Sir Hugh…" He kept striking her. Lord Sterz leap from where he was and grab the lash from his hand. "That's enough! It's over."

"Now, let's do this great trial by combat together under God's sight so everyone can see what a lying whore you really are! Lying all this time that you were a man. You lied to us too, didn't you! You are a traitor! You were going to sell us out to the Dauphin! Wasn't you! Admit it, so your life can be spared."

"Wait! You can't expect her to fight like this! Fight at a later day when she has time to get better. She can't hardly stand on her own. Look at her. What kind of fair fight would it be?" Sir Riis screamed.

"Yes. We will consider this. This will also give us a chance to further investigate the truth about these charges. Maybe we can find this brother of hers and get to the bottom of this." Lord Hawkwood turned to Lord Sterz.

Squire Richard ran up to her. She was barely whispering when she spoke. "I will fight… I will fight. Tell them," She whispered to Richard.

"No, Janet. I can't let you do that; I love you too much. I can't lose you. Now that you are in the open, we can be together in the open and no one can say anything about it. I will fight for you. I will be your proxy. I will be your champion. That's in the decrees of Trial by Combat. I will argue with Lord Hawkwood. They will have to let me fight for you." Richard carefully untied her from the post and slowly brought her to her knees. He knelt with her so he could comfort her and to continue the conversation.

"If you really love me, you will shout from the top of your lungs that I will fight."

"No. No. Don't make me do that, I beg you. I said I will fight for you."

"If you really love me just do it. Your shout will show that you really love me."

Richard with tears running down his cheeks stood up and cleared his throat and yelled at the crowd, "She will fight by trial by combat!" Richard then turned and looked at Sir Hugh straight in his eyes. "For verify I tell you, if she doesn't win, I will kill you myself!"

"We are still considering the matter," said Lord Sterz turning to Lord Hawkwood.

Janet looked at the ground, trying to find the energy to stand. "Ask them if it would be any different if I was a man?"

"Janet, in your condition, not even a man would stand up given a chance," Richard replied. Janet stayed there in silence, not moving a muscle. She looked at Richard in his eyes and said, "I am no man! Get my sword. I will fight; this ends today!"

"Oh God, it looks like she made the decision for us." Lord Hawkwood overheard Janet's cries.

"Help me get a cloth to wrap it around my chest and tie it tightly." She turned to Richard. "It isn't out of modesty because everyone has already seen what I have. It's that I need to keep my breast out of the way of the sword fight that is about to come."

Janet kept looking at the ground holding her sword like a small cross. "God, I pray to give me victory this day because you know that I'm innocent of these charges. And that you delight in showing your strength and power on the little things of this world. He is bigger stronger more experience than me; if I win it will be a miracle. Let it be for your glory… then… amen." She thought *Sir Hugh is off balanced. His anger made him this way*.

Janet started to get up and remove the sword from its scabbard. She could see Sir Hugh from the corner of her eye. *That bastard is not even waiting for me to turn at him so we can face each other.* She was ready for a frontal attack but if he was going to attack her from the left, that would be all right by her, even better, she thought. *He has no aketon*, she thought. Janet would be able to aim just right between the ribs where the heart is. Just like she trained with Sir Riis and Richard. She brought the sword in to a slight horizontal angle with her right hand on the handle and on top of her right thigh. Sir Hugh was coming in on a straight down sword cut. Screaming at the top of his lungs. She did not move but waited for him to come to her. She kept her proper breathing. She kept her discipline. Why waste energy that she didn't even have? She did her side trust while rotating her body. The sword entered right between his rib cage – not too deep, just about a palm width, and then she pulled it out on a slightly steeper angle.

She raised the flat of the sword to parry Sir Hugh's sword to protect herself from his incoming sword, however, the momentum of the mass of his body fell on top of her. Sir Hugh was dead. His carcass was pinning her to the ground, half her body underneath his. When people realized that Sir Hugh Heton was dead, there was a moment of stillness and silence and then an explosion of crazy shouting. Squire Richard came over to pull her out.

Sir Riis rushed over to congratulate her. "You did well, my Lady! You did very well, Janet! "

Lord Sterz came over joining the celebration. "Janet! I knew Lambert didn't fit you well! Whatever your name, you are the first recognize women knight in a mercenary company! You are a man-at-arms... my Lady."

"A man-at-arms?" she said, trying to regain her composure.

"Yes. Congratulations... Dame Janet." Lord Hawkwood said.

"Do you know what this means, Janet?" Sir Riis said.

"I think so... No, not really."

"You have now all the rank and privileges of a Knight. Dame Janet," Lord Hawkwood said proudly, turning to Sir Riis. "Cavalier Ruffin is Squire Richard also ready to become a Knight?" Immediately, Richard knelt on the ground. Sir Riis looked at him and paused for a moment. "No, not yet, my Lord, he is not. He will be soon."

"Squire Richard, you listen to this knight – he knows what he is talking about. He sees something in your training that you still lack. That is all." Lord Hawkwood then came to help him up and said close to his ear, "We all don't need to be slap in the face to then realize that we were a knight all along." He chuckled a little. "Don't be resentful toward Cavalier Riis. He will make you into a knight, and it's only up to you to become a true knight.

That's the key and let no one tell you any different." Lord Hawkwood then turned back at Sir Riis, and they shared a few words together, looked back at Richard, and acted as if they had agreed to a secret pact concerning the young squire.

The White Company finally mobilized and left Port-Saint-Esprit. There was no fanfare, no crowds to cheer them goodbye that day when they left, just a decapitated Spiripontain's head on a pike that had one ear larger than the other.

Chapter XV

Lord Konrad von Landau was seated on his black steed flank by his lieutenant and his personal guards. His armor was plated, decorative and dark metal, and his helmet had a large gold-colored visor with a large, golden nose piece. His helmet was decorated with feathers of a colorful exotic bird. Konrad's men all wear dark tempered plated armor and black colors. The Great Company's banners were fields of black and gold. Sir Konrad made his preparation well. He knew that the English company would have to travel on this certain pathway that will lead to Montferrat. The mastery-of-war teaches him to pick his ground for the decisive battle in order to be victorious. The valley is the perfect area for an ambush. The two opposing ridge lines are spaced perfectly a part, and the wood line can conceal troops on either side. He maneuvered a brigade of heavy cavalry to make them stop on a certain area of the path. Right where he wanted them to. He also ordered his crossbowmen on both sides with reserves to do a bounding over to the rear once they passed the highest peak of the pass. This maneuver would block any retreat of the company. After that it would be like shooting fish in a bucket.

"Here they come, Lord Konrad," shouted one of his men who was perched on a tree.

"I see them. They all look so nice with their shiny armor and surcoats. Let them all in. They are all welcome into this valley of death. Remember crossbowmen, stay out of sight and only shoot when I give the orders. Lieutenant, can you account for all their longbowmen yet?"

"Nay, just cavalry."

"This worries me," said Sir Landau, half to himself while scratching his chin.

"Should I take a scouting lance group to see if they out flank us?"

"Yes; but make it fast. We don't want any English coming up our ass when we least expected them." The lieutenant ordered a small patrol to scout the rear. Lord Konrad and his lieutenant kept watching the long train of men and equipment until. "I see the last of the supply wagons over the pass. The time to spring the trap is now. Give the order to light them up." The lieutenant followed with a few hand signals to order his men. Buckets of fire were used to light up the cross-bolts. Each crossbowman was responsible for getting their bolts tarred and lighted with fire. They moved as stealthily as possible covering the glow of the fire as much as possible from the direction of the enemy.

"Light them up," could be heard repeated down the wood line.

The White Company moved along the pathway and a formation of mounted heavy cavalry knights appeared in front of them. Lord Albert Sterz could smell a trap; this terrain feature of a valley was what he would consider a danger area, and he never would have proceeded without taking proper precautions. Lord Sterz was relying on Lord John Hawkwood to move his longbowmen around and into position in time. Moving the mighty longbowmen into range is critical. All he had to do now was to time everything just right. Calculating the time in his head. It should have been about the time that was agreed upon with

Lord Hawkwood. Lord Hawkwood's men made their way through the thick wood line as silently as possible. Lord Sterz saw a lone arrow from the wood line hitting near to him; this was the signal that they were in position. He moved his arm down; this was the signal for the longbowmen to release their deadly arrows.

A rain of the Great Company's fire cross bolts filled the heavens. The supply wagons became engulfed in flames first. The wagons also blocked the rear of the company column blocking any chance for any escape. Men-at-arms began dropping from their horses with a loud crash of metallic clunk of mud and armor. Horses and men screaming in pain and death. The company commanders and cavaliers shouted orders to the rest of the men to do a frontal charge but to no avail.

A rain of deadly English arrows were hitting their marks. Amadeus, the Count of Savoy, was distressed as his men were falling all around him. He did not anticipate two thousand longbowmen out flanking him on the adjacent wood line. Not only longbow arrows were making their marks but also large crossbolts which would take out a knight or sometimes even two at the same time. The Green Count wondered where these bolts were coming from and who would dream of such a devilish machine.

At the uppermost ridge, Dame Janet was on top of the war machine, handling the gigantic crossbow. "Richard, give me another bolt – they are really cutting down the enemy!" Sir Riis and Sir Godwine were both mounted, watching the spectacle.

"Ha, ha, did you see that? The crossbolt bounces off the armor of the first poor soul and then it imbedded into the man-at-arm behind him. Ha, Janet is finally earning her keep," Sir Godwine said, trying to control Lucifer. The chargers jumped, frightened whenever the giant crossbow released a new bolt. "I tell you, Sir Riis, if you were not right about her, I was going to kill her this very day."

Sir Riis looked at Sir Godwine closely and said, "You must be jesting, my good knight."

"Ha, am I, Cavalier Ruffin?"

"Janet, that was the last bolt we can use. We need to keep at least one to make more. Let's exchange it to shoot stones," Squire Richard said as he quickly swapped out a part to modify the machine. "Here you go. You are ready to shoot." Dame Janet sent her deadly rock right into the mist and kills a knight. Sir Riis said, "Janet, that's enough. The archers seem to be finishing their arrows. Sir Sterz will call to stop the archers at any moment." Janet shot another and the gallant knight went down with his steed. "I said STOP!"

Janet defiantly said, "The Green Count is coming into range. Shall I take a shot at him... Sir Riis?"

"No! Janet, he is a noble knight. His men are loyal and will fight to the last man. We need someone to stop this slaughter. The Green Count is expected to do the right thing when the time comes." Janet waited for a few more moments and then fired. The rock flew straight to the Green Count. Unknown to the Green Count, he lowered himself on his mount to retrieve his sword that was implanted in a combatant. The rock flew over him and jumped onto the wagon killed one of the personal green guards. Sir Riis got on top of his steed and jumped to get hold of Janet. He flew in the air and landed on her, pinning her down on the wagon floor. "I said that's enough!"

Janet laid there with a half-smile and said, "Ha, if that's what it took for you to lay your hands on me; I would have done it a long time ago. Besides, I'm glad. I did it; all those noblemen deserve death."

Sir Riis, turning to Sir Godwine, said, "Ready our men. After this next volley of arrows, I anticipate that Sir Sterz will call for us."

"Aye. I really love this task! We will be on the second wave going down the hill." Sir Godwine unmounted and grabbed his war mace. Sir Riis contingent was task with running after the dismounted knights to finish them off. He moved his men into position to wait for Lord Sterz signal.

After the last round of death from above, Lord Sterz gave the command for the cavalry to move into position. The Green Count thought, *Finally, we can meet on the open field like men with a cavalry charge.* Moreover, the Green Count also thought that there was a chance for him to save the day. A cavalry charge was what he was used to and made his reputation on. He motioned to his men to get prepare for a cavalry charge. The White Company's cavalry moved into formation. Two ranks off set with each other. Their lances pointing up toward heaven. The Green Count gave the orders, "Lower your lances, commence the trotting and keep the line!" Lord Sterz and Sir Nigel Loringe, at front of the ranks looking very gallant stood their ground. Their ranks lances didn't level off but stayed pointing toward the heavenly sky. Lord Sterz looked to the side of the wood line and gave another signal with his arm. This time, the rest of the White Company came out of both sides of the wood lines. These were unmounted knights in tight formation armed with pikes, spears, and halberd. These spears were all specially designed to dismount knights off their warhorse with sharp iron tips and flat bladed hooks. These men would run in formation as a unit and when they reach the intended rider, they would snag him with a pike-hook and pull the rider down. They would leave the dismount knight right where he fell and move on toward the next knight. Then, they let the second wave of men do their task. The next wave of men moved quickly armed with battle axes and maces. They would swing and beat to kill the fallen knights without mercy.

The company's Lord received a deadly crossbolt on his neck. The lieutenant in charge took the company banner which was a Crucified Christ above a large set of stag horns behind a white field. He rode up and tipped it down, signaling an unconditional surrender. Lord Konrad accepted the surrender and rejoiced in his victory, but he soon realized that his adversaries did not have the large contingent of longbowmen that he has heard so much about. He asked the defeated lieutenant, "What is the name of your company?"
"The Company of Saint George." Lord Konrad has heard of this company before. They have been doing mercenary work in the Italian Papa states. *These are not the ones that came from the remnant of King Edward's invasion force*, he thought.

Lord Sterz gave another order via trumpet to be heard over the noise of battle. This time a White Company brigade moved quickly and formed a rank in front of the Green Count's charging cavalry and formed an impregnable wall of shields and spikes. The other brigades moved in tight formations on the adjacent sides and began to make short work of the mounted knights. They were grabbing them off their horses and spiking and killing them where they landed. The fighting dismounted White Company Knights were getting ever so closer to reaching the Green Count himself. The Green Count's world was falling all around him – if he did not act soon, not only would he lose the day; he will lose his own life! One of the count's personal knights fought his way out, carrying the count's green banner. He rode up to where Lord Sterz and Sir Loringe were in the field. He lifted his visor. Lord Sterz said, "Well, who do we have here? If it isn't William de Grandson himself."

"Aye, the one and only."

"What are you doing here all dressed in green?"

"Like my good Lord Sterz, where there is honest mercenary work and pure gold, I will follow."

"I see. Does your count yield to end the bloodshed of his men?"

"Sirs, I marvel that you who all your lives sought honor, should now without cause, without quarrel, without right, wage war on one of the most good, noble, valiant lords of the whole world. He agrees to end the bloodshed. He is a proud knight. He is *milites nobiles*... I only encounter a few like him in my lifetime. If you would only have met him under a separate circumstance, you would know about his noble chivalry and hospitality. Please let him save face from one knight to another. And let us pick up the wounded and go on our way. You have the day, good knights!"

"Give word to the Count that he can gather his men and wounded. And that he is free to leave the battlefield unchallenged. Also tell him that if we get a chance, I would like to joust against him at a tournament one of these days." Sir Grandson rode back to relay the message. The count could be seen at a distance raising his visor and acknowledging the acceptance to a future tournament challenge.

"How dare you give up our ransom that our men fought so

hard for!" Sir Nigel Loringe angrily protested.

"Gold and ransom are not all. The White Company won a great victory this day against a gallant knight that has a great reputation in this part of the world. At this moment, this is more important than wealth."

"You just better hope that none of my men and horses got killed or wounded, or I will need compensation for this day!" Sir Nigel angrily spurred his horse on to check on his men.

Lord Konrad walked through the devastated battlefield with the defeated Lieutenant in tow. The sounds of the wounded filled the air. The mourning of men and horses was mixed with the cry of crows like an unholy melody. When they arrived at the body of the fallen commander. The body was almost in a kneeling position due in part to him falling on a spear after the bolt went through the neck. Lord Konrad said, "He's in the perfect position. The defeated Lieutenant interrupted by defiantly asking, "Condottiero, extend to us the courtesy of collecting our dead." Lord Konrad drew his sword and immediately raised it to a high position and executed a straight down swift cut. The head flew off the ex-commander's body and blood oozed out like crimson snow. "Ja, collect that for me and wrap it up."

Chapter XVI

At the Castle of Malgrà in the territory of Rivarolo, Sir Konrad von Landau brought the decapitated head of the company commander to the Marquis of Montferrat. The head was wrapped with the Crucified Christ above a Stag company banner now stained with human blood. The second in command lieutenant of the ill-fated company was forced to carry the war trophy himself. This was at the Marquis' grand room where he receives his guest and sometimes his enemies. The Marquis was seating against a wall on an elevated chair. He was slightly older than the rest of the surrounding knights. He had long, dark hair and was clean shaven. Was dressed in his noble clothes with a large metal bracelet on each arm. He had in his right hand a battle mace with a long handle. This type of battle mace was typically used for mounted warfare.

"This was the company of mercenary you hired. I think you need to give us their tribute and an official apology to the Visconti Family," Sir Landau said with his war helm under his arm.

"Don't worry, I will settle my account with the Visconti Family myself."

"We also would like to be compensated," the ill-fated lieutenant shouted.

"Compensation! But you lost. However, I will compensate something for you and your men that I think is fair considering the damages."

"And you Sir Konrad von Landau take your gold and leave

to wherever level of hell you came from."

Sir Konrad laughed, turned around, and left, unescorted. While he was leaving, he ran into Cardinal Aycelin de Montagu. "Running into the likes of you. I notice were ever there death surely a crimson Cardinal will follow."

"My business is with Marquis of Montferrat. I have never met you and I have nothing to converse with the likes of you."

"There, there, Cardinal. The other Cardinal I met was nothing but pleasant and delighted with my profession." Cardinal Aycelin kept walking away to meet the Marquis. "Give my best to Cardinal Gil de Albornoz," Sir Konrad said, turning his head over his shoulder as he walked away. Cardinal Aycelin didn't say anything else to Sir Konrad, but he was perplexed with the idea that the Pope was behind, encouraging Italian mercenary involvement and ushering them into France. And now encouraged another mercenary company into another bloody battle.

The Marquis' attendant announced, "Cardinal Gilles Aycelin de Montagu, the pontiff legate to his Holiness Pope Innocent VI." Cardinal Aycelin noticed that the Marquis' grand room was covered with painted cloth hangings, and banners from exotic brigades and other military companies. There were different helmets, shields, war helms, weapons, and various other types of armor that he never had seen before. Some of these armors, and shields appeared from another age, maybe ancient. There were also human body parts: heads, hands, and arms at various stages of decomposition or treated for mummification. There were complete prop-up armors at various poses at the corner of the grand room, as well. As the Cardinal got closer to talk to the Marquis, he noticed that the owners of the armors were still wearing them in various states of rigor mortis.

"Welcome your Eminence to Rivarolo. I wish it would be in a happier time. Lieutenant, please take your compensation and leave; it is more than fair." The Marquis was swinging his mace back and forth between hands.

"We will take our leave and never return to this horrible place. I can assure you of that." The lieutenant made his way out and picked up the head of his ex-commander with the intent to bury it properly.

"Lieutenant, please leave the head and banner." He gave him an angry look and dropped the head on the floor, and it rolled to Aycelin's feet. Aycelin looked down and the head was staring at him through dead eyes. The Lieutenant finally left the room, limping from the battle.

"I was always fascinated with the mastery of warfare since my youth. Do you like my trophies?"

"I really don't care for desecration of the dead. The dead should always be treated with respect." Cardinal Aycelin continued pointing at the arm over the mantle. "That arm over there must have once belong to someone's son." He walked toward it and tried to mimic his own arm the same way as the war trophy was displayed on the mantle. Further, analyzing the specimen he noticed the darkened peat colored skin; surely evidence of a taxidermy process that he was not familiar with. He spoke in a preaching tone, "This arm must have belonged to a child once. Must have held his mother tight… even maybe his father. Eventually, he must have grown and held a sword, lance…maybe a lover, a wife or even a mistress or maybe…not even that."

"Cardinal, we are all children of God. But that particular arm over there was from my biggest enemy if I didn't kill him first, he would for certainly would have my cock over his mantle at his keep. Cardinal these are here to remind me of my victories and, sometimes," he glanced at the head that was last brought into the room, "my failures, as well."

"You are not concerned with all the blood on your hands?"

"How long have you been a Cardinal?"

"I would say not very long."

"Well, all cardinals have blood on their hands."

"How dare you?"

"Now, now, what is the purpose of your visit? Remember, I have my own problems and war cost lots of gold; but how can I help the Holy Church?"

"I'm here to inform you that there is an English Great Company that is in the vicinity that can help you." Cardinal Aycelin sidestepped the decapitated head.

"What English Great Company? Are they the ones that took Pont-Saint-Esprit?"

"Yes, my Lord. The White Company are on the move now and they have completed a great victory against the Green Count."

"What they defeated Amadeus the Green Count of Savoy?"

"Yes, my Lord. They have over five thousand men consisting of two-thousands of longbowmen."

"According to my information, Sir Konrad von Landau has about fifteen thousand men strong. They would be fighting three to one." The Marquis was back, swinging his mace back and forth but, this time, giving it a little spin between tosses. "The last company I hired was also English and was defeated. That is their captain's head on the floor that just winked at you. What makes you think these will fair any different?"

"My Lord, these are English longbowmen all the major battles have been won by them with those type of odds. Great victories such as Sluys, Crécy, and Poitiers. I already spoken with them they said they would be amenable to the prospect of working for you."

"Invite them to my wife's birthday celebration. I will make a proposal for them that they will just have to accept. My Lady Isabella does enjoy such gatherings. After all our marriage is the reason for all these Visconti territories disputes. My marriage to Lady Isabella of Majorca came with land patrimony and the Visconti family must respect the land I inherited. I will make them respect the new boundaries no matter the cost."

"Thank you. I will let them know." The Cardinal turned around to leave the room.

"Cardinal, please place the head back on the table before you leave." Cardinal Aycelin didn't like the task, but he did it anyway. Cardinal Aycelin politely bowed and walked away. He made it to the doorway when the Marquis asked, "Cardinal Aycelin de Montagu, please look at your hands." Aycelin looked at his hands, they had blood on them. The Marquis started to laugh out loud coldheartedly; then, he motioned to his attendant. "Send a word to Sir Konrad von Landau not to leave just yet."

At the contract gathering, all the major cavaliers were there. With the exception of Cavalier Riis, who somehow excused himself from such an important gathering. Sir Godwine was well pleased to act as his proxy on such an auspicious occasion. This will be the White Company's first mercenary contract. The Marquis used Italian scribes to execute the document. The scribes kept insisting on changing English names into Italian. After reviewing it, Sir Godwine couldn't recognize his first name but at least his surname was correct. In discussions with other fellow companions, he found out that they rather appreciated that their names were changed due to some of them being wanted for crimes in other kingdoms. When the ink was drying on the contract bearing the date, *twenty-second of November in the year of our Lord Jesus Christ 1361*, the Marquis was very happy; he just hired the White Company to battle the Great Company. Finally, he would get his revenge over the Visconti family of Milan. The White Company had agreed to battle the Great Company at Canturino.

After the execution of the contract, Sir Godwine separated from the group mostly unnoticed; except by one guard, who asked him where he was going. He excused himself for having the need to relieve himself. The guard pointed in the direction of the garderobes. Walking through the empty hallway he came up to an ornate door; the feeling of curiosity was over baring for Sir Godwine, so he began pushing on the door to see if it was unlocked. That's when a servant girl walked by on her way to the kitchen. She had a large tray from the contract gathering. The tray consisted of empty glasses, half eaten bread, and other scraps of food that was not eaten from the gathering. She said laughing, "that is not the door to the garderobe, my Lord." He saw that she was very beautiful, and asked, "where are the garderobes?" She responded, "keep straight in the direction of the curtain wall and there you will find a narrow passageway this will lead you to the garderobes, my Lord."

"Thank you for your courtesy; I am a guest here at the Marquis request. I was wondering to what chamber this door leads?"

"That chamber belongs to the mother of Lady Isabella. I believe no one uses it in her absence. I most go now; they will get angry at me if I don't return soon."

"Don't worry about that my beautiful Rivarolo goddess. I am a guest here at the Marquis request himself. I'm the Lord and commander of the White Company."

Hearing this, she politely bows and said, "My apologies my Lord. I'm here to serve at my capacities."

"Aye. I'm sure he would want you to provide all the services that I require." Sir Godwine pushed on the door, and it was unlocked with the inserted key on the inside. "Come with me show the chambers to me."

"I don't think I'm allowed."

"Leave that to me, to think what is allowed or not." She reluctantly agreed and followed him inside. It was a beautiful chamber lit by a picturesque stained-glass window and with an equally exquisite bed and side table. He walked over to the bed and put his hand on it. It was so soft to him. Come over here and put that tray down on the table and come feel the bed."

"We shouldn't be here."

"I told you, I'm an honored guest here so do what I say." Then he said out loud but mostly to himself, "I don't even remember the last time I laid on a decent bed." Sir Godwine ordered, "Come help me with taking off my armor." The girl obeyed. When he was without armor he lay on the bed. It felt like heaven after such a long campaign. He said, "lay down next to me." She obliged.

"How does it feel?"

She said, "Wonderful." He closed his eyes and before he knew it, she was kissing him. "Something tells me this is not your first time. Is it?"

After all was over, he woke up and remembered the night's celebration for Lady Isabella was about to occur. He put on his armor by himself, something which he had done before;

nonetheless, it's not an easy task. He puts on his sword, surcoat and conceals his long bow underneath his surcoat. The girl was left there unmoving laying there charmingly on a royal borrowed bed; he said, "don't worry my dear no one will be angry with you tonight." He took the key and locked the door. He went to the curtain walls and reached the narrow passageway to the garderobes. The garderobe was lit by a small arrow loop. The seat, as customary, was a simple slab of stone with a round hole cut in it. He relieved himself and then dropped the key down the hole. He made his way to the great hall by following his ears and nose.

In the great hall, the command staff were all invited including Sir Ruffin, Dame Janet, Squire Richard, and Sir Lajos to celebrate the Marquis wife's birthday. In the great hall, the walls were specially hung with colorful banners, and a fresh covering of reeds and sweet-smelling herbs was spread over the floor. The Marquis and his ministers sat with Lord Albert Sterz, Sir John Hawkwood, Sir Nigel Loringe and Lady Isabella of Majorca behind a long table on a raised platform at one end of the hall. Everyone else sat at tables set up on the floor close to the walls. Food and drink flowed continuously from the kitchen and entertainment was provided by a variety of acrobats, jugglers, and musicians. "This is a new age we live in. Our armor is plated, swords are better, longer, and more available to the common soldier."

"Not really, Lord Sterz. It only appears like yours!" Someone in the crowd shouted and laughter ensued. Lord Sterz grunted, turned to the spectators, and laughed. Then, he drank some ale and continued his speech. "Where no more nobles have to go fight in open combat and risk their life or the life their sons.

Professional men-at-arms will settle disputes in a civilized fashion. This is also an age where a squire can become a knight if he or she has a strong enough arm. The great White Company is here to serve and to battle," Lord Sterz exclaimed.

One of the jugglers was juggling a set of oddly shaped leather balls into the air. One of the balls in his routine went high into the air to impress the celebration party. At this moment, Sir Godwine took out his longbow from his surcoat; no one seem to notice except Sir Riis who was startled and thought, *"Does Sir Godwine has a personal vendetta against the Marquis that I didn't know about?"* Nonetheless, Sir Godwine shot the leather ball when it was at its highest zenith. The arrow hit the ball and pierced it into the great hall's wall. Everyone was surprised then cheered and laughed at the same time. They also turned to see where the arrow came from. Soon it became apparent that it came from Sir Godwine's handy work. The Marquis stood up and said, "Thank you, Sir Godwine, for showing us your mastery of the longbow. But, to tell you the truth, I'm not quite sure what I'm more impressed with your archery skills or…" the Marquis' face hardened, and his tone of voice became somber, "or how you got a longbow into the great hall… past my guards."

The guards moved forward around Sir Godwine with their armor making lots of noise of metal hitting against metal. The Marquis motioned to his guards, "Confiscate his longbow – until…" the tone of his voice turned again but this time back to a joyous one, "… until our celebration is over!"

The Marquis laughed, sat down, and grabbed his wine goblet. "Sir, I think I will leave your arrow there as one of my trophies. It will be a testament of your archery skills and of your boldness tonight. For I say, there is nothing better than to show your martial skills around your fellow knights. I myself – when I was younger – competed in many tournaments and jousting events. Winning a few and even once winning best at sword." He pointed to a large wooden sword gilded with gold hanging on the wall. "I will always cherish that moment as the best time I ever had. I still remember the following day; everything looked and felt different – the sun, my tent, the landscape, even the air smelled different." The Marquis got up and started to walk around to the others sitting at the tables. He walked with an apparent old injury that left him with a limp. "To be the best of the best; at a grand tournament! There is nothing like it! Even better than having your cock suck by a serving wench!" He slapped a serving girl's ass as she went past him, and laughter ensued again in the great hall.

Sir Godwine, relinquishing his bow, said, "I understand completely my Lord how you feel. Hopefully, we all can have a tournament soon to test our mettle." He reached to his side. "Might as well take my long sword because I forgot to relinquish it when I came into the hall." More laughter ensued because the Marquis' only order was no bows or long swords into the great hall, and it was apparent that Sir Godwine was guilty of both. Most lords will require no blades, but he believes in a warrior should always carry their side blade. The daggers which some knights wore were almost short swords were even allowed.

Sir Riis lean over to Sir Godwine ear and asked, "How did you get past the guards, and, most importantly, why?"

"Hum, to tell you the truth I just walked in. I didn't see any guards." Great laughter arose and mixed with other laughter in the great hall.

"Very impressive, I thought you were only a master swordsman, but you are a master archer, as well."

"Oh, no, I just got lucky. And besides, there are a lot better archers here in this company than I. I guess that's why I don't pursue it as I used to." Sir Godwine said, sitting down, "Archery was my first love. Then came the mastery of swordsmanship." Sir Godwine reached for something to drink.

"Yes, Sir Godwine, please tell me about your mastery of weapons. Did you learn in a knighthood order?" Sir Riis reached for some more ale.

"I discovered myself that the mastery of arms is all intertwined. How do I explain it; it's like spokes on a wheel; all types of weapons: spear, bow, sword, mace, all the weapons you can think of, are like spokes on the wheel but link by the axis of the wheel. Some weapons are closer to the axis. Swords, maces, daggers are weapons that are closer to the center. These are weapons that bring out the warrior spirit clearly more personal. While weapons of missiles like bows and slings are weapons that take us away from the savagery of the ancient fight – the personality of the kill. But regardless of which weapon you use; you must experience the dragon to experience mastery of the weapon. For instance, once I had seen the juggler in his act, I knew; I could achieve the act of shooting the ball at the highest point in the air. It told me it was possible, and I saw myself doing the act before I did it. When I drew the bow, I didn't let go of the arrow, but the dragon did that for me."

"Ah yes, in the center is 'the dragon' – some sword-masters or archery-masters may call it by other names like 'the spirit', 'spirit of the warrior', 'the dragon', 'Saint George's Breath', 'the eye' or some may just call it simply 'it'. One thing is for sure – once you have 'it', no one can take 'it' away from you."

"Yes, that's it, you know of it. Then you had training from an ancient order, didn't you?"

"Ah, let's just enjoy the night." Sir Riis turned to his plate in front of him. "What is this creature from the sea that they want me to consume, anyway?"

"I believe it's called a lobster."

"How do you eat it?"

"You start from its tail and work yourself up."

Sir Godwine thought to himself, *Strange, he is familiar with the ancient order that only my crusader great grandfather taught me with a strict vow of secrecy. Ah, his ale is at the edge of the table. Now no temple master will let his drinking ale fall to the ground. I will slightly bump into it with my scabbard of my long dagger as I get up from the table.*

"Well, I will take my leave. Goodnight, Sir Riis," Sir Godwine said turning around quickly so there would be no chance of the cup survival, but his scabbard struck only empty air. He quickly noticed Sir Riis with a big bright smile and his ale in his hand bidding him good night. Sir Godwine thought he might be the one that could best him in a duel. He took a few steps forward. Then, he turned back again and looked at him struggling with the main course of the meal – the lobster. Sir Godwine quickly shook his head as to wipe away any thought of Sir Riis beating him in any contest of lances, swords, axes or daggers, or for that matter archery.

All eyes were also on Dame Janet that night, who wore a new shiny breast plate armor that Lord Sterz had commissioned for her. It was designed to show cleavage with correct female breast plates designed with anatomy correct auroras and nipples. She also wore makeup on her face and fashioned her hair. Essentials that never would have been done before if not for her reveal at the trial by combat. Janet toasted, "To the White Company, which to me is a lot more than just a company of mercenaries; it's more like a free society with gave me the opportunity to become what God intended for me to become."

"Excommunicated and condemned by Almighty God!" shouted Sir Konrad von Landau walking in making lots of metal noise with his armor.

"I decided to invite Sir Konrad to this gathering. I thought it would be interesting. Seen that the next time you professional soldiers see each other will be on the battlefield at Canturino."

"Interesting indeed. I'm sure I will have to instruct the White Company like I did the other mercenary company you hired."

"Now, now Sir Konrad. This Company made short work of the famous Green Count Amadeus."

"The Green Count had a reputation of being chivalry and honorable but lack men and tactical knowledge or some would say common sense. Of which I have both. I have tactical knowledge from experience, and I don't care to tell you that I have twenty thousand men at my disposal. I'm sure I will make mincemeat out of your Company, as well."

"Well, we will see about that… you chicken bird!" Janet shouted.

"What have we here… a women warrior? What a strange age indeed?"

"That's Dame Festu! My title is Dame Janet Festu! Can't wait till I see you in the battlefield."

"Now, Dame Festu, be nice to this exotic bird," said Sir Riis walking over, "yes, a bird of your caliber reminds me of a bird I once experience when I was traveling down south a long time ago. What did they call it? A royal peacock. Yes, that was it. You remind me of that bird called a royal peacock. No, with that golden face shield on your helm a Golden Peacock." Laughter ensued in the great hall.

Sir Konrad got really close to Sir Riis and asked, "Who are you, sir? I'm I acquainted with you?"

Sir Riis came even closer but said in a low voice, "I am Lord Riis von Ruffin coming back from the shadows of death. I will be the knight that will cross swords with you in the battlefield and defeat you." Then he said in a loud voice so everyone in the great hall could hear, "I'm going to have me some chicken bird! That is you! I'm going to kill you and eat you up!" Sir Riis acted like a chicken and made chicken noises. Sir Konrad was taken aback, and his skin color turned pale. He grunted loudly, "Well, sir, let's leave it for the gods of war to determine the outcome."

"Where is Canturino?" asked Dame Janet.

"It's over the Alps; on the Italian peninsula," responded Lord Sterz.

"We will be taking Hannibal's trail?"

"Where did you ever hear that? There is no such thing my lovely, but we are going to take the Maritime Alps pass. If you must know."

Some of the handy work that Sir Hugh Heton left behind could be seen over Janet's shoulder. The Marquis wife noticed, and Janet seemed to turn away as if ashamed. "Don't be ashamed wear those marks with pride. Wear them as a badge of honor of what you have accomplished so far. I envy you."

"Thanks. I'm not ashamed. I'm just not accustomed to people looking at me with, with–"

"...Desire? Well, get accustomed to it. You are beautiful and very special. You are a female mercenary... a lady knight. I don't know any other person like you. The stories... I heard of you already. Your reputation you carry. And at such a young age!" The Marquis' wife moved closer and whispered, "I want you to be my favorite at our castle in Montferrat." Lady Isabella of Majorca was a lot younger than the Marquis and very beautiful.

"Isn't this your castle where you live?"

"Oh, heaven's no child. This old family cottage," she said while looking around her surroundings. "This is just our ancestral hunting cottage... a chateau if you must, at the very edge of our northern territories. Our real castle lies at Montferrat. Montferrat the most beautiful province of the Italian peninsula. You must come and witnesses it for yourself; instead of this dreadful place." After a pause of looking around, she turned her gaze back at Janet and continued, "The Marquis likes it though; he likes to keep all his war trophies here. Besides, I'm scared for your life. You may share the same fate of the last company my husband hired. Be my favorite please. All my children are over at Montferrat. I would love to introduce them to you."

"My Lady, I don't know what that really entails. Besides, I'm not leaving the White Company."

"Well, can you spend time with me? Together?"

"I still don't know what you really mean. But I don't think you can have me. My heart belongs to another. I shall have no other. Besides, I'm a lady and you're a lady?"

"Oh, there are lots of things we ladies can do together that require no men's permission. And besides I only want you as a friend... for now. But I'm curious who is this man of yours?

Janet motioned that she was not going to answer.

"Is he in this celebration gathering?"

Janet nodded her head, indicating yes. "Is he Squire Richard?"

"No. He is too young and immature. But he wants to have me for his wife and run away with me." Janet laughed in a playful kind of way.

"Wow. You have been a busy young lady. Is it Sir Godwine Quatreton? He is very handsome, and I heard very courageous in the battlefield, a master swordsman and tonight he has shown an exceptional archer?"

Janet shook her head in disagreement.

"I know your head knight the men in charge."

Janet was getting flushed and thinking what she was going to do next.

"Lord Sterz? He is absolutely beautiful and those eyes one blue and one green. I can be with him all night long."

Janet let out a breath and said, "No. Not him. I believe he likes to query for his game in other fields." She giggled when she said these words.

"Heavens why would you ever say such a thing?"

"When I observed him in the taverns; ladies and prostitutes would gravitate toward him, and he would always send them on their ways. Sad really… seating there all alone with his ever side sentinel… old Sir Thomas."

"Be careful how you speak girl, for that's an abomination in the sight of God; punishable by death in our domain."

"Oh, maybe I miss spoken my Lady. Please… please pardon my lady and forget what I said, I don't want any trouble for him.

Lady Isabella responded waiving the thought, "Most likely he is of a noble morality and, therefore, he doesn't want to get tainted with the filth of this sinful world. His love of only chivalric knighthood… faithfulness and pureness are all that he endures for."

"I only want good fortune for him. He got me this beautiful breastplate."

"It is stunning." Lady Isabella came close to touching her plate armor. "And from what I heard it is all anatomy correct. You should wear it with pride just like you wear your scars. Well, I couldn't guess who is the one you love. I don't know your company well enough. Do you want to tell me?"

Janet looked over where Sir Riis was seating and struggling to eat a lobster.

"Oh my, you have your work cut out for you. How does he

feel about you?" Janet shrugged her shoulder. "He is not really old he just so… so… so un-kept. He needs to cut his hair, shave his beard, clean his nails, etc. But I'm concerned if he doesn't feel the same way about you. I'm motioning for him to come over. I want to see how he will interact with you."

"Oh, please don't do that." She tried to hold her hand down but it was too late.

"Cavalier Riis Ruffin."

"My Lady. And how are you enjoying yourself, Lambert?"

"You can call me Janet now, remember."

"Sorry, old habits." Then, Sir Ruffin stared at Janet's face really close and started to chuckle. "What is that stuff on your eyes, hair and… your lashes?" Janet's eyes started watering and she left very quickly.

"Sir Ruffin, it appears to me you don't know nothing on how to treat a lady, and especially about what you have with Janet." Lady Isabella of Majorca was raising her hand and pointing at Sir Riis.

"And you know her better than I do. You just met her."

"Well, that lady is in love with you."

"I can't be in love. My real love died a long time ago."

"You must bury the dead and go on with the living."

"I don't feel love any more. I'm a tormented soul." At this moment, Lady Isabella slapped Sir Riis on his face. He pretended that it hurt a lot more than it did. He turned his body all the way around and, then, dropped flat on the ground. "Oh, my lady has got me." Laughter ensued in the great hall.

"Well, did you feel that?"

"Actually, I did, and I understand your point. Should I go after her?"

"Yes, if you don't you are a very stupid knight."

When Sir Riis finally caught up with Janet, she was with Squire Richard at the great hall side balcony. They were embracing in a kiss. Sir Riis thought, *It would be better if I left and let them be. They are both the same age. They will be better together and will be happy together one day.* Sir Riis left the celebration without making an announcement.

"Janet why did you kiss me? Don't get me wrong; I liked it, but it was kind of sudden, without notice?" asked Squire Richard.

"You don't know anything about women's desires. I just wanted to know how a real kiss felt like. Now I'm tired and I want to leave. Will you escort me back to our camp?"

"Certainly, my lady."

"Walk me to our tent but don't get no funny ideas."

"I wouldn't dream of it. In our tent that would be too weird."

Leaving the gathering, Sir Konrad turned to his lieutenant. "Did you get the information on how they defeated the Green Count?"

"It wasn't easy, but it seems everyone has a price. I can go over into the finer details later, but it seems that the good Count was expecting a traditional mounted cavalry charge; they surprised him by attacking him dismounted, "Konrad's lieutenant said as they walked down a long set of stairs.

"Thank you. We must prepare for this battle; we don't want the same thing that happened to the Green Count happen to us."

"If you don't mind me asking, what was the exchange with that White Company cavalier at the great hall?"

"Oh, that. A ghost from the past. Nothing you need to concern yourself with."

Chapter XVII

"Routiers! Routiers! Routiers, Tard-Venus are at Avignon's Gates!" cried the pontiff heralds and palace guards.

"Impossible! Routiers never have attacked a wall city." Cardinal Aycelin de Montagu strained to look over the parapets.

"This is not any wall city. This is Avignon... a holy palace with walls, turrets, and gold," said a Priest, spectating the view of thousands of routiers pouring over the ridge and plains before the walls. The soldiers were approaching in bands of various kinds of men-at-arms. Some of them wore plate armor and sometimes they had on just mail or leather for protective coverings. Few had no protective clothing at all; but they still carried crossbows or pikes. Very few were mounted showing little sign of cavalry ability or competence. As a result, no cavalry formations were evident.

"Routiers were never thought that they would be organized enough to come this far."

"Are they really capable on overrunning Avignon?" the Priest asked as he leaned on the parapet wall. He made his way through the maze of parapets, hallways, and chambers until reaching his destination, the pontiff's great hall.

"No matter, Priest... we must attend to the Holy Father at once." Cardinal Aycelin turned around to face the task of mediating between Tart-Venus and the Vicar of Christ.

"Holy Father, there are thousands of routiers outside the gates. We theorize about three thousand men. They demand hundreds of thousand florins, or they will storm the palace. I have tried to reason with them, Holy Father. But the problem is they don't really have a leader or one captain that we can appeal to. I have spoken with different leaders like Seguin Badefol, Naudon de Bageran, Espiote, Camus Bour, Creswey and Robert Briquet. And they all claim to be in charge, and I get different demands from each. Each demand is usually over a hundred thousand florins." The Pope was seated on his chair in one of the grand rooms of the palace. This was the room that he would greet princes, princess, dukes, earls, kings, queens, and emperors. Now he was getting ready to greet thugs, brutes, ruffians, and criminals. He was never without a word to say but today. He looked defeated. The pontiff treasurer spoke up. "We don't have that kind of amount in the pontiff coffers, my Holy Father."

Cardinal Aycelin continued his report. "Moreover, I fear we have reports that they already have laid waste to cities such as: Lyon and Forez and Macon."

"Is this the apocalypse then, Cardinal Aycelin?" The Holy Father finally said something. The Pope thought that maybe the solution was in the history of the Catholic Church. "In the year of our Lord 452, Attila the Hun threatened to destroy Rome, but Pope Leo went outside and confronted him. It was said… that Attila before reaching him stop and saw two Angels of the Lord with swords ready to strike him down. Attila the Hun stopped short the invasion of Rome. He didn't even set a foot south of the Po River. I must be brave like Pope Leo. Prepare my staff, so I can meet these ruffians at the gate." The Pope struggled in his chair trying to stand up, but his attendants quickly begged for him to remain seated.

"Holy Father your condition! There must be another way?"

"My condition? What does it matter? If we are all dead. I

must meet them and save the Pontiff Seat that is Avignon!" His attendants rushed to make provisions and his travel chair ready to bring it to the main gate. The progression walked through the winding streets, pathways and steps until the Pope was atop a rampart where he could view the horde of the, left over, the Tard-Venus, that King Edward left him. And he hated the King of England even more than ever now. He had seen them all adjacent to the main roadway in front of the gate. The mighty Rhone River still is a level of protection since it lies in front of them. The horde of Tard-Venus will have to storm the gate first to access the main bridge. Still there is a form of buffer and time left. The horde amassed with no organization. Their lust for gold and ransom was too great. They didn't seem to be thinking logically any longer. They seem more like animals, something primitive.

At this hour sending Cardinal Aycelin to parley would be plain suicide. Then he saw at a distance, coming over the ridge and highland before the roadway and gate, stars in the midday sun. Then these stars turned into shiny metal lances pointing toward heaven. The Pope thought, *Is this some kind of vision that I'm having? Instead of the enemy getting the vision I got the vision instead?* He quickly ruled that out when he saw the reaction of the people around him. The knights then started to encircle the entire Tard-Venus horde in a gigantic half circle. The Tard-Venus had no place to escape with the mighty Rhone River at their backs.

"What is happening? Who are these brave knights?" asked the Pope. But no one knew.

Cardinal Gil de Albornoz finally responded, "My Holy Father, those are Castilians knights! What you would call Castilians cock suckers. I wrote to his Royal Prince Henry of Trastamara to aid us."

"Why didn't you say anything?" The Pope finally sat straight on his chair throne.

"I didn't want to give any false hopes, my Holy Father. I did not expect the letter to reach the prince in time; what is more, for him to be able to send us aid." They all viewed the spectacle from the ramparts far away from the battle. But they could see that the horde was no match for heavy cavalry troop lances followed by a light cavalry troop swinging their axes, maces and swords. It was all over for the horde they were cut to pieces all within an hour or so.

The commander of the Castilians knights made it to the pontiff who was back at his great hall. The Castilian Commander had a thin mustache and beard, and his armor was covered in blood. He knelt in front of the Pope and said, "We are here under the authority of Henry of Trastamara to humbly lend aid to the Vicar of Christ. He sends his apologies that he could only lend four hundred Castilians knights at this time."

"No apologies at all, my son. This is a most auspicious occasion indeed. Scribes mark this day; as the third of June, in the year of our Lord Jesus Christ 1362, as the day when four hundred Castilians knights saved Avignon the seat of the Roman Catholic Church from destruction. Generations from now, hundreds of years from now, pilgrims and devoted followers will look back at this date and rejoice whenever they come together and venerate the Pope at Avignon, France."

Cardinal Aycelin asked, "Commander, since the fighting is over, I would like to tend to the men before the shadows of death comes upon them?" The Castilian commander acknowledged and motion to his men to escort the cardinal and a small group of monks and priest that left with him.

"Cardinal Aycelin! Isn't your place here at the Pope's side!"

Cardinal Albornoz yelled, which echoed in the great hall.

The Pope answered, "Let him go. He is pulled to do his Holy calling. He is not made from the same mold as you are Cardinal Albornoz. You may have advised him to me because of your political motives but I persuaded him to stay because the dark figure behind the curtains left when he arrived."

Several months passed, and Avignon was back to its normalcy. The Pope is requesting an audience with Cardinal Gilles Aycelin de Montagu. He was led to the Pope's bed chamber but before he entered, he was notified by the attendant priest. "Your Eminence should know that the Pope's condition has taken a turn for the worst. His last rites have already been executed. He wants to see you very badly." Aycelin enters the papal bed chamber and stood next to the Pope. He looked around the room and on top of the Pope's personal desk, he saw the decrees that he helped draft of the Pope's last counsel to the new Pope. He kissed his ring like he had done so often before. The Pope slowly opened his eyes. "Oh, Gilles Aycelin de Montagu. Thank you, God, for giving me a chance to see you before I die."

"It's an honor to have a chance to spend these last moments with you."

"Tell me how it went?"

"Holy Father, how did what went?"

"How did it go with the Marquis of Montferrat? I didn't have time to ask you with all the commotion we had around here."

"The Marquis hired the White Company just like you predicted. It is all set. The White Company will fight the Great Company at Canturino."

"Oh, if God could only give me the health and time to see those cock suckers kill each other on the open battlefield," he said, chuckling.

"Holy Father, I met Sir Konrad von Landau there and he

implied that the Church was behind the Visconti Family attacking the Marquis. Is this true?"

"Cardinal Aycelin, we need to get rid of this plague of mercenaries from France. Who cares if they all kill each other or go over to Iberia or Italy as long they are out of France."

"Are you going to rescind the excommunication for the White Company? They did all what you asked them to do, and they are going to battle soon. A lot of them may die. We should be concerned for the salvation of their souls. I still have time to travel there and give them the news of our blessed Church accepting them once more. I can have mass with them like I once did, have communion, and help them with giving last rites if need be.

"Cardinal Aycelin," he started to laugh, "you're the dumbest Cardinal I ever ordained. Soon my life will be snuffed out like one of these candles. I had an experience once where I felt my heart stop and my memories leave my mind. One set of memories after another. Then, I lost the use of my entire left side for a while. A brilliant physician nursed me back to health; you met him before. He is the old physician who still takes care of me now. He nursed me back with his secret tonic or I like to call it the elixir. I always have him teach my confidant cardinals on just how to mix it. Didn't he instruct you on how to prepare it?"

"No Holy Father. You had Cardinal Albornoz teach me instead; don't you remember?"

"Oh, no matter. It's in the past. Let's concentrate on the future, my Cardinal. I want us to have a legacy that we will be proud of. What we put to ink and parchment will outlast us. Trust me, I can feel it in my bones. The recommendations we leave behind for the new Pope is our masterpiece."

"I didn't do much, Holy Father. I just inscribed your ideas onto parchment."

"You did more than that. The arguments, the persuasions, all was impeccable. And the concepts and opinions really came from our conversations. We must guide the new Pope to influence the French King to have a national standing army and to outlaw all free companies of mercenaries. The age of relying on the noble household knights is over. A unit of trained men with pikes can dismount the most chivalrous of knights. Kingdoms and countries will have to realize this, or they will perish." He started to cough and grab his heart in pain. "Aycelin please give me some water." Cardinal Aycelin grabs a cup from the bedside table and offers it to him. The Pope drinks and Aycelin assists him by raising his head until he was done. The Pope grabs his blanket tight as he glanced at the huge chamber's windows. He is startled and starts to tremble. "The man is back behind the curtains again. Do you see him, Aycelin?"

"Oh yes, I see him."

"Make him go away! Cardinal Aycelin, make him go away!"

"I can't – not this time. He says it's time."

"WHAT! You can converse with that thing?"

"Not in an audible voice, Holy Father; but he is signaling that it's time."

The Pope continued to cough and, grabbing his heart, said, "Get my physician… get my priests…" The Pope kept repeating these words, but his voice was trailing off. Aycelin thought, *What an evil man. So much death was caused by him persuading monarchs and armies as if they were mere chess pieces.* But more importantly Cardinal Aycelin has seen this before. He was well familiar with the face of death. Unlike other priests, he earned his place in the Church. He didn't use his brother or nephew influence to get him promoted. He had done his time administering final rites and consulting with people before their final time on earth. He has seen plenty of death when the plague ramped more than anybody cared for. And on the bloody battlefield he had done his task. He learned to feel and to even see the shadow of death. One thing was certain; the Pope would die within moments. He was sure of it. Even now, he saw the shadow of death hovering over him as they were speaking.

"What did you just say? That you forgive the White Company?" Cardinal Aycelin got closer to the Pope. So close that he could smell his bad breath. The Pope couldn't speak any longer, but you could see in his eyes that the terror of the end was near. Then, the Pope's eyes were wide open, and he was still holding his chest. "Rescind the excommunication for the White Company? I will get on with it right away, Holy Father. I will get my traveling clothes on, get the fastest steed available, and travel there as soon as possible!"

"Huh…ugh…ahhh." The Pope finally let out his last disgusting breath. No more hovering dark shadow. The shadow of death was gone. Aycelin finally closed the Pope's eyes. He thought of destroying the Pope's last decrees to the new elected Pope, but he noticed the Pontiff Bull Seal on the document. This meant that a copy of the document was already distributed and archived. Getting rid of that document would do no good. Then he thought, *I need to get started on what I can still do. "I have to get ready right away; I still have time to make it to Canturino."* Aycelin called out to the sleeping priest attendants on the other side of the door. "Get the physician! Right away! The Pope doesn't look well!"

Later at the papal scribe halls. The scribe halls were a vast multi chamber building with large stacks of parchments and books for archives and pontiff documentations. The secretary scribe was seating behind a small wooden desk reading the parchment letter that Cardinal Aycelin handed to him. "Yes, your Eminence. It's an edict from the Holy Father to abolish the White Company's excommunication. Who is the witness to this degree so I can write in his name?"

"I was the witness."

"Yes, but I will need another." The scribe informed with his blue colored lips and tongue.

"Another! How dare you question a Cardinal?"

"But you need at least two witnesses; it doesn't really matter if it's a cardinal or a priest."

"I can't believe this… I–"

"…I will sign as the second witness," a familiar voice said.

"Cardinal Gil de Albornoz."

"Yes. Cardinal Gil de Albornoz is the second witness." Cardinal Albornoz signed the document and walked away. "Please place the papal seals. Hurry, man. I have no time to waste," Cardinal Aycelin demanded with haste. He turned around and moved quickly to his room but first he wanted to thank Cardinal Albornoz.

"Thank you for this. I will be leaving to Canturino to deliver the good news to the White Company myself."

"My dear Cardinal, no one is leaving anywhere anytime soon. The Pope appears to have passed to be with Saint Peter. Of course, there will be an inquiry and then… well then… It is the time of the conclave. Cardinals like yourself will be the only be arriving not leaving until a new Pope is elected."

"I forgot about that. Is there a way I can send a message to them?"

"The only messages going out is that the Pope is dead, and we need all the Cardinals at Avignon. This affects millions of devout followers on earth. What are a few mercenary companions in comparison? Sorry, we are not going to waste any valuable resources on them." A large sound echoed throughout the hallways as the chain lock of Avignon doors closed for the official Catholic conclave.

Chapter XVIII

The White Company mobilized again and was on the march, but this time toward Canturino to meet in open combat with the Great Company. Canturino was located near Romagnano, on the Italian peninsula just north of Milan. As a result, the White Company proceeded south to head toward the Mediterranean pass of the Alps. This pass to some extent hugged the coastline. The White Company needed continual supplies and provision for this long journey. First, the company reached settlements near Marseilles. Marseilles is a considerable fortified wall city, not like Pont-Saint-Esprit. The White Company lack siege engines to take on wall cities like Marseilles. Their ladders night attacks tactics would not be enough. Therefore, the White Company would not be able to take Marseilles or for that matter Nice. The smaller villages and towns were the White Company only preys now. The villages had provisions and loot that the company needed for the journey. They travel with each contingent traveling on their own discretion. Cavalier Ruffin's Contingent traveled in the middle of Cavaliers Nigel Loringe's contingent on the east side and Cavalier Andrew de Belmonte's contingent on their west side.

Two riders were making their way through the thick forest until they came across a small village. It was Dame Janet and Squire Richard turn to do a far reach patrol. These far patrols were coined as the "hawk patrols." If they encountered a village or settlement their role was to get back to Cavalier Ruffin and report. They traveled lightly dressed just with a cuirass and side arms.

"This one is bound to have loot and plenty of rich nobles that we can ransom. I bet we ran into their summer homes!"

"Let's hope so. So far it looks like Cavalier Nigel is the only one finding loot. The last two settlements were just too small and Cavalier Ruffin directed to barter with them and paid off for their small provisions we got."

"Yeah, you know Cavalier Nigel's men don't do that."

"How do you know?"

"Rumors are that they just rape, pillage and burn without any mercy. And you do see and smell the smoke on occasions; Don't you? Did you hear me, Janet?"

"Don't mind me. I have an earache because of the fever sickness I had recently."

"When we get back to our tent, I will treat you with an old knight's treatment."

"What? You are not a healer! What are you planning to do with me?"

"Don't you trust me? All it is: you take the metal residue from sharpening your sword and mix it with oil. Next, take the oil mixture and drop it into the ear. It always works, Janet, believe me."

"We will see when we get back. Now, mount back up you will need ride like the wind and get the news to Cavalier Ruffin on what we found."

"No, Richard, you have the fastest horse, and you are a better rider. You go. I will stay here. I will be all right."

"Aye, stay hidden. And if any other scouts come you let them know we were here first." Squire Richard got on his horse and rode as fast as he could to the rest of his contingent.

Janet watched the daily life of the village, which was somewhat like her own that was destroyed. She reflected on the events in her life that brought her from her complete innocence to a place where she would be willing to destroy the life of the inhabitants of a peaceful village. They had a father like she had, once a mother, a brother, a priest. Every aspect that would make a community in a village. At least she thought that Sir Ruffin seemed different from all other Cavaliers or other commanders. He seemed to be a fair man and he had shown it on several occasions. She was watching a young man who was cutting wood and she thought of her brother when he had to go and cut wood himself, then, suddenly, an arrow pierced his neck. She recognized the arrow by its length and feathers that it came from an English longbow.

Next, she saw precise arrow hits on male targets, all at the same time. Next came in the knights in full battle harness. Hundreds of them covering the entire village. The villagers didn't put up any resistance. She could see the heraldry on the lead horse; it was Cavalier Nigel Loringe. It seems Janet and Richard were too late for this prey. The hunter has captured it already. Janet thought, *"We lost the prey. I should just leave, there is no point in me staying. But I'm curious about the rumors about this contingent. I want to know the truth. I will get nearer so I can get a closer look. No one will see me if I stay hidden in the wood line."* Janet left her horse behind and moved ever closer to get a better vantage point. She crept closer and laid down in patch of overgrowth forest. While she was watching, she knew stealth was of the utmost. Suddenly, she noticed a bee land on her arm. She remembered from her childhood to leave the bee alone and the bee would just fly away. She looked at the bee crawling to her unprotected hand and the bee stinging her unprovoked. She thought, *What! I didn't do anything to you Sir Bee! This isn't fair.*

She quickly swiped the bee and she saw it move on the

ground as it gave up its life. She thought, *"that's what you get for messing with the She Devil of the White Company."* Janet rubbed the stung area. *Ouch, that sting hurts.* She continued watching as an inner group of men dismounted of which one was Cavalier Loringe. He took off his war helm and yelled so loud that she could make out words clearly, "I love the sound of victory! Now, men what are we going to do now?" One could hear one of his lieutenants sounding off, that they were going to rape, rob, pillage, and burn! "Yeah! We are going to rape, rob, pillage, and burn!" He and the rest of the knights singing this chant was something primeval. He also had his drummers hit a beat to this chant. Janet covered her ears and then she watched as ladies were dragged from their homes and their clothes were ripped off their bodies.

Janet got up from her hiding spot. "I can't take this anymore." Once she turned to get on her steed, she ran into one of Cavalier Nigel's man.

"Where are you going, little one?" He grabbed her with a hold of an arm behind her back which inflicted great pain and with his other hand her hair. He drags her to the center of the spectacle of the raping and pillaging.

"Cavalier Loringe, look what I caught – a little French spy. It appears the rumors are correct; you are a French spy after all. Spying on us like that."

"I am not a spy. I'm part of Cavalier Ruffin's hawk patrol. We spotted this village, and we were in the process of getting word back to Cavalier Ruffin. I was left behind to make sure no one else made a claim on it."

Cavalier Nigel acted very bored as she explained her situation, and said, "All I know is that' the time of raping, violating and fornication is at hand. Is it not, men? And right now, you are my captive. So, men…" He made a motion toward his men for the chanting to begin again. Cavalier Nigel came close to Lady Janet and said, "Lady, to tell you the truth, I was there when you killed Sir Hugh that day, that made me very hot in my groin area for you. I'm going to very much enjoy raping you in front of all these men." Janet was terrified to think of being rape once more. She started shaking, struggling and her thought processes were lacking its normal course. "Settle down and listen to me very… carefully. I got hundreds of my men surrounding this place and no one comes in or out without my permission. Listen here, I will make a deal with you. If you don't fight me too much. I won't let another one touch you. I will return you back to your contingent myself safe and sound. What do you think? Pretty generous?" He laughed and started to release the portion of his armor that was needed to commit the crime.

Janet heard the lamentations of the poor women being raped in the village and looked around and saw the madness and horror of what was going on. "You won't hurt me, will you?"

"No, my Lady, I won't hurt you. In fact, you can hurt me instead; I don't mind at all."

"I will agree if we do it in private. I need it to be private… in a room. And then you can have me."

"Like that house over there – you want me to take you there?" Cavalier Nigel pointed to a nearby pillaged house structure.

"Oui, Oui, I beg thee." Janet said in a quivering voice. "Not here with everybody else? Like my guards? Sir Nigel raised his arms walking and looking around his fellow knights with a questioning gesture. Then, he stops on his track and look straight into her eyes. No, it must be here. You will be all right; my men are obedient to me. I will tell them to turn around. They will form a barrier so no one could see…You heard the young lady, turn around!"

One could hear the metallic sound of armor against armor but not only from the guards turning around but also from the street leading to their location. Three lone riders approached, and Nigel's men made way for them to pass. The three riders all had just cuirass for protection and a side weapon. Except one of the riders had the White Company command banner which only Lord Sterz or Lord Hawkwood would bear. The White Company command banners were rectangular in shape instead of typical contingent's extended triangular banners. At this time of day, the sun was very high. Nigel looked up to see who was interfering in his "by-the-dagger" seduction. After his eyes adjusted it was Lord Sterz, Cavalier Ruffin and Squire Richard. "Alt! Alt! You filthy English scum."

Lord Sterz screamed, jumping from Titan, and separating the two. He then comforted Janet in his arms. Then he said, "Please explain your actions Cavalier?"

"What do I need to explain? A knight carrying out your orders… Sir."

"My orders did not include raping another member of the White Company, did it?"

"It isn't rape if we had an agreement between us. Is it?"

"Well… what are you talking about?" He looked at Janet's face. Her face said that there was a shred of truth to it.

"Ask the wench? I made a bargain with her. Ask her to swear it by Holy God."

"Sir, this must have been done under a dagger! Cavalier Nigel, you have here a contingent of men against one Dame even though she is a fine fighter I think the odds would have been against her!"

"I was under pressure… I had no choice." Janet trembled,

trying to regain her composure.

"Sir, take your men and your loot and leave. Do not burn anything in your way out."

"It's not fair! It's not fair!" Janet said, franticly seeking last-minute justice. She sprang toward Sir Nigel and spit at his face. Her arms swung about, and Lord Sterz held her back. "Stand down, my Lady. There be another day another time to exact your vengeance." He whispered in her ear. "I know. Lots of things in this world aren't fair." Lord Sterz reassured her before handling to Sir Ruffin, "Go with Cavalier Ruffin, he will take care of you."

"Come, I will take you to our tent. Tomorrow is another day," Cavalier Ruffin said as he lifted her on his warhorse. When they got to a safe distance, they saw the rest of Lord Sterz contingent coming into the village.

"Was you scared, Squire Richard?"

"Petrified, Sir Riis. I almost pissed in my harness."

"Well, you didn't look like it. You look like you were ready to jump off your steed and cut someone with your sword. You did well, really well. It's a scary situation going alone like that. Things could have gone really wrong for us tonight. We must celebrate tonight. Sir Nigel could have ordered his men to kill and bury us and that would have been the end of us."

"Don't remind me. Why do you think he held back?"

"I don't know. God's providence perhaps. All I know is that when you are under authority you can sometimes get away with something like that. In other words, we were fortunate. Time was of the essence, so we had to move fast and just do it. Now we have Dame Janet back. It would have been a great lost if we would have lost you."

"How are you, Dame Janet?"

"My ear still hurts and now my hand where a bee stung me."

The White Company pushed forward and continued to the outskirts of the wall cities. Later the company passed by the Riviera toward Nice, then across to the Maritime Alps. These villages and settlements were rich and bountiful compared to the countryside where the company just came from. The White Company would offer payment for the provisions. If the locals refused, the White Company would take it. The company men took from the nobles what was needed which proved to be very lucrative. There were hundreds of nobles that the company took into custody and demanded ransom. News came to Lord Albert Sterz at his tent by Lord John Hawkwood. "It appears that Sir Nigel Loringe took his five contingents of men to fight for the Kingdom of Castile."

"What! Under whose orders?" Lord Sterz said, getting up from his chair.

"No one. He said he has the Pope authority to do so."

"I guess he finally got what he wanted. He has been a thorn at my side every step in this venture so I can't say I will miss him."

"But this will hurt us in the battle with the Great Company. We are already outnumbered." Lord Hawkwood sat down and got comfortable.

"We can't do anything about it now."

"Very true; we will have to believe that this is God's providence. And hope there is no more desertion from any more cavaliers." Lord Hawkwood took off his gold signet ring and started cleaning it. He did this so the impression of the hawk seal would come clear when sealing his letters and documents.

"I don't think we are going to have any more desertions. Sir Nigel always wanted to leave for a crusade to kill infidels. Each cavalier is sworn to this cause so we should not worry."

"How can you be so sure?"

"All those nights and days at the Green Bore, Blue Mug, the drinking tents, etcetera my Lord."

"What? Now all this time together Sir Albert and I don't understand you at all."

"Sir John, all those nights and days at the drinking establishments, the inns, taverns, drinking halls were not for nothing. I was gathering information when I'm there. And I tell you, most of his men, didn't even wanted to go, on his crusade. They wanted to stay with us. There were rumors awhile back of him leaving and his men will go to the drinking places to argue this. They are fond of what the White Company is accomplishing. Heck they had never seen so much gold in their lives. To leave all this and fight a religious war and make little gold. I actually believe it will be the other way around – Sir Nigel Loringe will get some deserters of his own soon."

"Lord Sterz, I almost feel that I must apologize. I thought you were just drinking and having a good time and sleeping in those places."

"Oh, I was but you still pick up everything else that is going on around you. Plus, I always had Sir Thomas Marshal looking out and keeping an eye and ear on such things."

"Well, no matter how you do it, very well done my friend. What's next?"

"Order the men to mobilize and keep them moving. Keep each contingent space apart; it will be less trouble that way. And look out for deserters from Sir Nigel's contingents."

"Aye, sir."

"Sir you joust well! May I offer another lance?" a muffled voice came from an oversize war helm.

"Ah, I'm just beginning to get my spurs on!" When Sir Ruffin passed his opponent knight's view of sight, he opened his visor and showed his extreme pain written on his face. The rest of his lance group was waiting for him with another practice lance. Janet quickly grabbed the reigns of his horse while Squire Richard carried off the broken practice lance. "Sir Riis you have him now!"

"Richard the only reason I wasn't dismounted was because you tied my harness to this prow horse you call a charger."

"This prow horse has a lot of spirit if you ask me. And don't talk about him like that he might hear you and be offended." At this moment, the horse let out a loud snorting sound with a spray of saliva spreading all over them.

"Nevertheless, this competition is over. It's easy to see who's best. Who am I against again anyway? I must have forgotten from that last hit."

"Cavalier Andrew de Belmonte."

"Cavalier Belmonte, I know him," Janet said, giving Sir Riis some water. "He winked at me once at the swordsmith shop at Pont-Saint-Esprit. Remember, Richard?"

"He did what?" He gave her an inquisitive look at her when he was trying to control his horse and then brought down his visor.

"Maybe what you need is some lady luck!" She lifts back up his visor and kisses him on the mouth and slams it back down shut. He gripped his lance tightly and took in a breath. He felt something was wrong even before spurring his steed. If he was younger, he would have heeded his old lance master and just not take his opponent offer of another lance; 'if the spirit is not right, do not lance!' rung in his mind, old voice, and all. Something was off but he could not explain it. He had been doing this for a long time, ever since his childhood. Yes, maybe a younger squire would yield but a veteran knight as himself. No more thinking. It's time to do what he taught his muscles to do as naturally as taking a piss. Bring the lance to the correct horizon. His horse jumped up to a great gallop charge.

When Cavalier Ruffin woke up, he was sitting on a small field chair. Then, he noticed he was completely wet. Then he heard, "Cavalier Ruffin? Sir Riis Ruffin?" Lord Hawkwood said this, trying to open his eyelids.

"Did I win?"

"No. You were unconscious when you were brought in."

"I was at a royal jousting tournament and won the hand of a princes. She opened my visor and kissed me on my lips," said Sir Riis, touching his lips, and then he closed his eyes. Lord Hawkwood said, shaking his head, "Another bucket of water, he is still hallucinating." A young page did as he was commanded. "Cavalier Ruffin you are in the White Company's command tent with Lord Sterz. And you were just practicing jousting with Cavalier Andrew de Belmonte in your spare time. You have to be careful. Hits like that can cause brain damage. I read it once. I believed the knight's name was Sir Robert FitzNeal. He was struck in the head while jousting and it caused him permanent brain damage. He speech was that of a child and he reverted to sucking his thumb."

"Oh, I must be a little out of practice that is all." Sir Riis grabbed his head to ease his pain.

"Well, what matters is how good you do at an actual tournament not at practice anyway. I brought you here because I wanted to bring to your attention that several of your men wanted to leave your contingent."

"I was not aware of this. Who is requesting this reassignment? And why?"

"Oh, it doesn't matter, they are all low ranking. I will deal with them. The main grief, it seems, is that you don't let them maximize extractions from the local nobles."

"I wonder what type of extractions they are talking about. Because I make sure we all get a fair share of ransom. Now that I think about it, I know what type of extractions they are referring. They want to rape, rob, pillage, and burn. If that's what they want, they are welcome to join Cavalier Nigel Loringe and his other cavaliers. They seem to love unnecessary pillaging, robbing and destruction. You know those type of tactics are no good for anyone."

"I know. I will handle the reassignment, don't worry about that. And I will get you some good replacements. And you will need not worry about Sir Nigel Loringe any longer, he and his men has left us."

"Where did they go?"

"They have left us for a crusade to drive the infidels out of lands of the Kingdom of Castile. The replacements I have for you are some of his deserters that wanted to stay with us."

"If they are deserters, then I don't want them either. Give them to another White Company cavalier."

"Take them you will need them. They are all good knights. I interview them myself," came a voice from a corner of the tent it was Lord Sterz.

"Sir Ruffin you are given the task of Sir Nigel's men. It is a big task. You and your men will be doing the job of five contingents of well-trained knights. So, you are going to need every knight I offer to you."

"Those jesters and acrobats! We are true knights. We are milites nobiles."

"Well, those jesters and acrobats were going to be the spearhead of our frontline against the Great Company. Now that weight will fall on your shoulders. Can I count on you and your men?" Lord Sterz commanded, handing him a towel to dry himself.

A dispatcher from the Catholic Cardinal reached the company near Nice. Sir Riis was in the command tent when it arrived. Lord Sterz took the message and read it out loud, "*Reap where thou hast not sowed; spread thy claws; Italy I give thee*. Signed Cardinal Gil de Albornoz."

"He didn't mention anything about the Pope rescinding the excommunication on the White Company?"

"Nope, that was it. How strange."

"Well, it was nice of the Catholic Cardinal to bless our journey and wish us farewell." Responded Lord Hawkwood.

"Oh, is that what it says? I thought it was more like, he is taking credit on our victories and a threat not to come back." Said Lord Sterz.

"Should we respond?" Lord Hawkwood asked.

"No. We should heed not. We are not under his authority."

Dame Janet and Squire Richard were tasked in escorting the captured nobles to a coral. They were using the war machine wagon to escort the captured nobles. The captured nobles were led tied by ropes and tied to the wagon. Lady Janet had the gigantic crossbow aimed at the captured nobles. She sees a familiar face on the side of the road. She signals Richard to stop. She jumps off the war machine wagon. "I can't believe that you are here!" She rushes over with a warm embrace and a kiss. "What are you doing here big brother Sir Lorens Festu?"

"An errand for the Cardinal or maybe the Pope? Not sure. I just delivered it. My God you look so beautiful and different. I would swear that you have grown taller and more refined. This new look suits you. And what are you doing with this fine group of poor souls?"

"Big brother, this how I earn a living. These are all rich nobles who have been captured for ransom. We will receive rich rewards when their families remember them."

"They are tattered and barely dressed… are you sure that they are real nobles?"

"Most of them, I have captured myself. Trust me we will get fat rewards out of these."

One of them spitting at her said, "Yeah, you will eventually get your reward!" Janet hit him with a lash. The man instantly lowered himself to the ground, hanging on to the rope and crying with pain. "You see – that was just one lash and he scurried like a dog. If he ever got twenty lashes he would die. What do you think about that, big brother?"

"Yes, these people are really rich nobles."

"Oh yes, big brother. Let me show you something." She guided him to the back of the wagon and showed him a chest full of gold florins. "This is just a portion of what we collected so far. If I was close to my tent, I will show you my share of the loot."

"I never seen so much gold in my life!" Sir Lorens put his hands in the gold.

"We are almost done here. Let's meet later at the drinking tent."

"How will I find it?"

"Just follow the smell and the shouts. Here is a clue it's next to the whore wagons."

"Oh, you should have said that in the first place!" He laughed and walked away. Sir Lorens walked through the maze of tents until he found the drinking tent. Janet was right, it was next to the whore wagons. At front of the tent entrance was Sir Godwine. He seems to be entertaining a small crowd. The crowd was marveling at his display of swordsmanship. One of the men would throw him a melon into the air. Sir Godwine would cut it three times before it fell on the ground. He would cut them three times from a low guard position and loop back to a low guard position again. The feat would be easier when it is done in a natural downward and then back to a high position. But what he was doing was taken notice because he would go back to the starting low guard position to swing three times before the pieces would ever reach the ground. Spectators would reward Sir Godwine every time he did this with ale. They would also beg for him to do it again. He would go late into the night never missing. Sometimes there would be friendly challenges. Today, it was Squire Richard that would try. "Let me try!" he shouted. Richard only got two cuts. "If I still had my scimitar, I could do it!" He said defiantly and taking a large gulp of ale. Finally, Sir Lorens walked into the drinking tent. Lady Janet was already sitting down waiting at a small table. "So, what was the important message you delivered?" she asked, taking a huge gulp of ale.

"I'm not sure, because it was sealed. But I think Cardinal Aycelin had an important message for the White Company but when we were leaving Cardinal Albornoz exchanged it with his very own message instead at the very last moment. Church politics I gather. It's really a despicable thing. I had time to talk to Cardinal Aycelin about things mainly what you told me when we reunited. And for the most part you were correct in every aspect," said Sir Lorens, seating down and adjusting himself on his seat.

At this time, Lord Sterz comes over. "So, is this the famous brother that you suffered so much for?"

"That is right, Lord Sterz; let me introduce my brother Sir Lorens Festu from the Dauphin army but reassigned to escort the Cardinal's biddings."

"I knew your face looked familiar. I heard good things from Sir Remon about you." He said this glancing over where Sir Remon was seating. "So, are you happy doing the Church's bidding? We are always looking for a young recruit. We can arrange for you to stay. Just say the word." Lord Sterz walked away to his reserved seat with Sir Thomas Marshal.

"You heard that? To join us just talk with Lord Sterz."

"I'm not saying that I'm joining but if I did, who around here has captured your heart? I don't want to start any trouble with the wrong person. I don't want to step on the wrong spurs."

"Capture my heart, yes. But I'm not sure he feels the same way about me."

"Is it Squire Richard? He always seems to be around you like a puppy dog?" He made a motion to the tent keeper to bring two drinks over.

"No way. He says he's in love with me but we can never have anything together."

"Why? I'm curious."

"If you really want to know, it is because of him our mother is dead."

"What!" he shouted, standing from his chair.

"Sit back down. The English were in the process of rescuing me. Maman just got in the way. So, I really don't know if he really loves me, or he is just saying that to appease me somehow."

At this time, a young lady sat at their table. "Good evening. I thought I would introduce myself since there are not many ladies in the mist of five thousand men. I'm Nicole from Pont-Saint-Esprit."

"I know who you are. You are Sir Thornton's woman. Aren't you?"

"Yes. I came with him…. Like I was saying, us ladies should be together. The rest of the ladies here are either, whores–" she said in a low voice, "or kitchen maids and, oh, yes, and an enchantress."

"What – we have a witch? Where is she?"

"Her wagon is next to the whore wagons. Her wagon is painted with many colorful flowers and many different symbols. That's how you will know it's her wagon. They say she comes from Egypt."

"Egyptian! I didn't know that. Maybe we should check our fortune before you make any decision – Lorens."

"Stop fraternizing with the enemy and retire for the night, Sir Lorens. That's an order! Tomorrow, we leave at first light," Sir Remon demanded.

"Maybe it's the ale talking? But you know what? I think; I'm going to accept the offer. After all we are the only family left and if you travel to Italy with this group, I may never see you again," he said, looking at Janet.

"Sir Remon, please make preparations to go without me."

Sir Remon grabbed him from the chair and asked, "Where is your loyalty to the king?"

"You mean the king that is held for ransom by the English King?"

"I should kill you right here and now." He held him by the throat. "You know treason is a capital offense."

"We are not having any trouble with my newfound friend… are we? Sir Lajos placed his oversize hand over on Remon's shoulder.

"I don't know who you are! But you are impeding on the king's justice!"

"King? I see no king and no king's men; look around." Sir Remon looked around the room. He could see none of his men. But a lot of men on the side of Sir Lajos.

"I think it's time for you and your men to leave."

Sir Remon let go of Lorens and said, "You haven't seen the last of me. I pledge to hunt you down like the traitor you are." Looking at Sir Lajos, he said, "I said we are leaving in the morning."

"You and your men will be leaving now or never." Sir Lajos said this while holding the handle of his sword.

"How dare you! We have Lord Sterz protection," argued Sir Remon.

"Oh, Lord Sterz; what do you want me to do with this filth?" Lord Sterz was seating on the other side of the tavern on his usual spot with Sir Thomas Marshal.

"I think you have outdone our hospitality. Do your knightly duty! And throw him out of my camp!" commanded Lord Sterz. Sir Remon was escorted out of the tent and out of the camp.

Janet and Lorens walked over to thank Lord Sterz. "Lord, I'm ready to join the White Company," said Lorens.

"Ah. Yes. I think Dame Janet needs a squire." A depressive look fell on Lorens. "I'm an accomplished man-at-arms and I know my craft."

"I know. I'm only jesting. You can join us as a man-at-arms. Do you have any preference on which contingent?"

"It will be with Sir Riis Ruffin," Janet answered.

"I see. Janet, show him around."

Janet grabbed Lorens' hand and they both walked away. Lorens whispered to Janet, "Who is Sir Ruffin?"

"He is our lance leader. He taught me swordsmanship and he is the one that captured my heart. Let's go to the witch so she can tell us our future." She and Lorens felt like school kids again. Together again, running and laughing along the way. Finally, they made their way to the witch wagon. The wagon was easy to pick out because of the description. The most notable graphic symbol other than the colorful flowers was the spread wings coming from an oval shape. This image was right over the doorway. Oddly, they had to wait for her to finish with a customer. All you could here was a man crying lamentingly. They looked at each other and laughed. "One of our big strong knights crying like a baby; how pitiful," said Janet, laughing discreetly with her brother. When the young man stepped out, it was Squire Richard. Janet quickly stopped smiling and said, "So, you came to see the witch too?" Saying this he ran off.

"Janet, I don't know if we should do this." Lorens half pulled her away.

"No, we are here now. Let's just go in."

"Come on in. I hear you out there," said a voice from inside the colorful wagon. When they walked in, they were greeted by an elderly woman with a huge birthmark on the middle of her forehead. She was sitting down in the middle of her wagon that was full of occultist materials of her trade such as crystals, snake skins, roots, herbs, etcetera. The interior was cramped but there was just enough space for two more people to sit with her inside. "This will cost you a gold coin for each."

"Here you go; but please read my brother's fortune first. He's got important decisions to reflect on." Janet paid the old lady.

"Here spit in this cup." Lorens did what she asked. She took the cup and smelled it. "Ah, you will travel far. I see you as a cavalier on your horizon. You will be admired by your men." She took another sniff. "They will go to the ends of hell for you."

"That's it? Will he be married and have children? Is there love in his horizon?" Janet snickered. The old lady took a taste of his saliva. "Oh yes. A wife and children…" She tasted the saliva again, "and a broken heart because of a forbidden love."

"That's enough; now read mine." Janet spit in a cup and handed it to the witch. When she sniffed it, she was automatically repulsed by it.

"This is not good. Not a good fortune. You don't want to hear it. Now, please leave," said the witch.

"I paid for my fortune, and I want to hear it, old hag. Will I be married and have children too?"

"No."

"No, to what? I won't have a husband or, no, you are refusing to tell me?"

"No husband, no children. Now get the hell out!"

"Go deeper you old hag; tell me the rest of it!" Janet grabbed her by her head and opened her mouth and empty the cup's saliva into her mouth. The witch jerked back on her seat and cried, "Get out, you ANIMAL!" At this, Lorens pulled her out of the wagon.

"Let's go. This is all a sham. She probably is a witch just because of the hideous birthmark on her forehead. This is how she makes a living. Please calm down and show me where I'm going to sleep tonight."

"You are probably correct. Let's go. Tomorrow the company will be on the move again so we must make proper preparations. Come and I'll introduce you to Sir Ruffin and Lucifer. You will love Lucifer."

"Lucifer?" Sir Lorens was very confused as to why she wanted him to meet the Devil.

Janet could not sleep in the night, thinking about what had transpired. "Why would the witch say such things about myself?" she said out loud. "She doesn't fucken know me. She doesn't know how much I suffered." Early the next morning she excused herself from Sir Ruffin's tent and ran to where the whore wagons were located looking for the witch. "If I find her, I will beat a confession out of her," she said to herself. When she did reach her destination, already most of the whore wagons had left including the witch's wagon.

When Sir Lorens was helping with the horses, he had a chance to talk to Squire Richard. "If you don't mind me asking, what happened with the witch? You seem very upset when you left her wagon."

"I was upset on what she told me."

"What did she tell you?"

"Well, my fortune. I asked, her if I was going to get married to the one, I truly love." Richard became silent and kept brushing Titan.

"What did she say?"

"That I would not."

"Sorry to hear that." Sir Lorens thought, *God, it's probably my sister after I have seen how he looks at her.* "Maybe soon you will meet someone else?"

"There will be no other! My heart only belongs to her."

"Does she know how you feel?"

"I told her this, but she does not believe me."

"Did the witch said something else?"

"She said something about I was going to be a great Condottiere. I didn't even know what that meant, anyway. Then, she said, it was a high military rank. And I told her she is a fake because the first time I have enough wealth; I am out."

"Then, what did she said?" trying to control Titan.

"Well, she said, she was only reading what is revealed to her. And not to get so upset with her. You can't escape it. That's when I left. Now, come let me show you how to handle Lucifer." Walking through the stables, "Who's beautiful horse is this one?"

"Oh, that's Sir Riis. He doesn't have a name for him, but he keeps referring to him as a prow horse. I really don't know why."

"What? He's a very well-defined courser; a credit to his breed. He is not a great horse; but I would rather have him as a charger instead of a destrier. Coursers are very fast, swift, and strong. I wished I have this one for this upcoming battle with the Great Company."

"What do you ride now?"

"Oh, I have the horse I had as an escort… courtesy of the Dauphin. But it's not a very good charger. I'm having trouble thinking of the battle ahead. What am I to do? I'm really scared. I'm an infantry soldier armed with a crossbow not a cavalryman."

"What? If you're not a cavalryman, I would highly suggest getting out of their way and behind them when they call for a cavalry charge. Do you know where your place in the battle will be?"

"I don't know. I think that is why I'm so troubled because I'm not sure what my role will be. Maybe I will probably be with Janet."

"I don't think so. You are a knight and will be expected to be up front while I will be with Janet on the war machine. And I don't think Sir Riis would be able to take care of you. He will be too busy. Most likely, Sir Riis will put you with Sir Goodwine with his troops or maybe Sir Lajos. But don't worry so much about it. It's still in the future so there is no need to worry now."

The campaign continued till the White Company reached Romagnano, Italy. At Romagnano the company set up an encampment. A hawk patrol was sent to see the layout of Canturino. Canturino is located adjacent to a river and bridge. There is an open field that is adjacent to the river. The Great Company was already encamped there and waiting for the White Company. In the command tent tactic conversation later ensued. "How many knights does the Great Company has?" asked Lord Sterz staring at a map that was on top of a table.

"Our patrols counted less than fifteen thousand men total. Mostly cavalry and crossbowmen," reported Cavalier Riis Ruffin as he leaned over a map of the subject area.

"Sir Konrad said he had over twenty thousand. I guess wanted to keep us in the dark. He's an old fox. Well, that five thousand less that we don't have to worry about. What else have you found out?"

"They also have what appears to be a contingent of Magyars. They are light cavalry, and they love to shoot bows from horseback. I think he was planning to use them as the counterattack of our dismounted knights and how we use our English longbowmen."

"Interesting how so?"

"Well, their ability to be mobile and fast. They can shoot and cause havoc in our unmounted formations and the longbowmen."

"This is very problematic then; we will need to break them. Maybe with a preemptive skirmish attack?" Lord Hawkwood said as he leaned on the table.

"The odds do not look so good. But English trained and disciplined longbowmen have proven better, time after time. We can still win the day. Look what happened in Crecy and Poitiers. Both times we were outnumbered. The key is knowing where Sir Konrad will be within the battlefield. I will need an advance force to capture the bastard. Then the lieutenants of the Great Company will sue for truce. I guarantee it. I also need the longbowmen to be in a good flanking position to take advantage of the situation. Maybe a diversion, that way it will be easier to flank them and get the upper hand on them. Where are the Magyars located?"

"On the east side my Lord." Sir Ruffin answered as he pointed to the map.

"Cavalier Lajos, can you do a skirmish attack on the east side? And take care of these Magyars pests? Present company excluded – Cavalier Lajos."

"Don't worry; and you leave the pest problem to me," Cavalier Lajos volunteered.

"And don't worry about the Golden Peacock. I will personally take care of him. He is mine I will have me some chicken bird tonight!" Cavalier Ruffin said sharply. All in the tent laughed.

Lord Sterz said, "Cavaliers Andrew de Belmonte, William Boson, Adam Scoto and Rubino de Pingo do flank attack from the west side when I give the order. You will know the order is given when you hear the second trumpet charge. Cavalier Ruffin when you hear the second trumpet get your men behind the battle line with the Golden Peacock or not. Cavalier Andrew and the other cavaliers will be coming down on you with four contingents of knights. But that will be the last of the chess pieces to play in this game. If we don't get Sir Konrad and get them to sue for peace, I fear all will be lost."

"Let's hope God is in our side," Lord Hawkwood said as he did the Christian cross on his chest.

"Amen," said Cavalier Andrew as he also did the sign of the cross. Then they all said, "Amen," as they all walked out of the command tent.

That very evening in the drinking tent, Janet caught up with her brother. "I don't like these odds, Janet," says Sir Lorens, drinking a down a huge gulp of ale.

"So, what if we die tomorrow? Do you want to go back and escort the rest of your life? Very little pay to show for it. Trust me we made the right decision. Don't dwell on the number so much we will win I feel it in my bones." Janet drank her ale trying to keep pace with her brother.

"Are you relying on the fame of the English archers?"

"Yes. And why not they have been beating the French on the last few battles?"

"Janet – we are not engaging the French this time but this experience mercenary company. They are called the Great Company because they have been doing this for a long time and have not lost a single conflict. There was supposed to be no other company like them. They have a great reputation. That's why they are called the Great Company."

"We will win fear not. You weren't there when we defeated the Green Count at Savoy. We have great mercenary tactics."

"I heard the Green Count forces was about even with the White Company."

"You weren't there, big brother. He could have had three times as many men, and we still would have won with our tactics."

"Yes, Janet but this Great Company has three times as many with the same mercenary tactics."

"Well, they don't have the War Machine," She got up to where he was sitting. "They don't have Lord Sterz with his warhorse Titan, or the meanest warhorse of all time Lucifer, or Dame Janet, the "She Devil" herself and her big brother Sir Lorens Festu." Patrons at the drinking tent were overhearing and were urging her on and applauding.

"All right, all right, settle down, people are looking and laughing at you. You can't just give yourself a warrior moniker. You must earn it."

"That's where you are wrong!" Then she got up on top of the table to address the crowd. "Mercenary men lend me your ears who is the "She Devil" of the White Company?"

Everyone in the tent responded, "You are *the She Devil*!"

She got off the table and sat with her brother, "So, you see big brother. You are wrong about me and about tomorrow and remember what the witch said that you will have a long life."

"She didn't really say that I was going to have a long life."

"No but she said all those other things about you that haven't come to pass. I will most likely be with Squire Richard with the war machine wagon. Do you know where you will be by now?"

"Oh yes. In the mist of the fight with Sir Lajos."

"Do me a favor… keep an eye on Sir Ruffin?"

"Shouldn't he keep an eye on me?" he said, laughing.

"Seriously, keep an eye on each other. I feel something might happen to him if you are not there." She embraced her brother. Then, Sir Lorens spotted Squire Richard walking into the tent when his head was over Janet's shoulder.

"Guess who walked in. It's your little puppy dog."

"Oh, Richard!"

"You know, he really is in love with you."

"Well, I'm not really in love with him."

"So, what are we talking about gentle people?" asked Richard, bringing fresh libations to the table.

"Oh, about tomorrow and facing the battle, death and all that comes with it."

Sir Riis was also in the tent and drinking maybe more than he should have. Janet invited him to sit at their table. Sir Riis stumbled to the seat and seated himself which brought laughter to them all. They immediately offered him another drink. He chose wine. Squire Richard thought maybe this would be a good time to ask him a question that he had on his mind for a long time. "Tell me, sir; why you call your war horse a prow horse. He is nothing of the kind."

"So, what do you know? You think you're an expert because you're a noble squire! You're not even a knight. You're not even a man-at-arms." He violently pushed and slammed the table which caused the drink to fly and spill; this causes the others to stand up. People stopped enjoying themselves and stared at his spectacle. Then he realized he was out of order, especially for his rank as a cavalier. "Sir, I must apologize. I got a little out of line with you. Tomorrow we all may die, or worse be capture, torture, assassinated, etcetera. Sit back down and I will tell you my humble tell." They seemed a little apprehensive in sitting back down. "Sit, sit, bring more drinks and a fresh bottle of wine no make that two bottle of wines – Sir Lorens, and that's an order." A long time ago, I awoke from my madness on a prowled field completely naked covered with blood. I could not remember… how I got there or where I was, or who I was… that sounds funny: who I was… or anything else… really. There was a horse in this field. This horse was there on this field with me. I know he is not a prow horse. He is a charger, a warhorse, a courser. What I hate the most is that I do remember little bubbles of memories. For instance, I remember that I had a bigger horse once. A destrier that I loved very much. He was completely black in color a beautiful a credit for his species. We jousted like no other in my kingdom. Well, at least, I believe that we did. Like I said bubbles. I know I had a lovely wife, a baby all taken away in a span of a day… foams of memories; but now my new life gave me this. So, this horse signifies my new life a low-class beast, a low-level life, a mercenary, a man-at-arms." Sir Riis took from his wine cup. "True noble knights are being hunted. They are disappearing."

"You don't remember the kingdom you come from?" asked Richard.

Sir Riis shook his head as no. "I remember a few things here and there. A few important things. Like I know it's destroyed. The things that I've loved once and who I must kill. I know I must kill this chicken bird. Will you help me to this kill peacock bird?"

"I will. We all will." Sir Godwine move toward the table, "The men are ready. I encouraged them about what we must do tomorrow on being the spearhead of the White Company. They are so motivated that they changed our white banner so it will represent our contingent. They added a blue chevron to represent a spearhead but if you ask me it looks like a blue triangle on a white field."

"Did you ask for permission from Lord Sterz or Lord Hawkwood?"

"No. We thought you would."

"Great. Tomorrow, tell the men we will gather around the Spearhead Banner to lead the White Company into victory!"

"Aye, sir, aye." Sir Godwine left to make preparations. "I think; I will retire for the night." He grabbed a bottle of wine and started to walk away. "I will try to capture some of those good bubbles of memories that I lost once, for tomorrow there is a chance for death and vengeance. You two should try to make some good memories of your own… for tomorrow we are under God's providence."

Squire Richard said, "Good night, sir." He then looked into Janet's eyes and clasp his cup a little tighter and then he moved his other hand closer to her hand. Janet looked at Richard like a scary cat does when one comes too close. Janet said pulling away from him, "We need to get some rest if we are going to help Sir Riis with killing the Golden Peacock tomorrow. Oh, he is such a troubled soul. He needs a real woman to wake him up from his bad dream."

Sir Riis stumbled into his tent and fell flat into his sleeping cot. Janet was right behind him. She quickly took off her chess cuirass and aketon and sat next to him. She slowly began to caress and embrace his arms, shoulders, and neck. Then, she noticed his bared back. It was full of brands. They were all shapes of crosses. Templar crosses of different sizes all over his back. She strokes his bare back with her fingers. Riis turned and passionately kissed her. Squire Richard had a suspicion when he left the drinking tent that Janet gave him the slip and followed Sir Ruffin to their tent. He thought, *maybe she wanted to make sure that he reached our tent all right since he seemed to be drunk.* When he was close to their tent, he paused instead of just bursting in, like was his accustomed. He slowly came to the entrance of the tent and noticed Janet in the same sleeping cot as Sir Ruffin. He stopped and thought, *Maybe, it was always meant to be between those two. They deserve each other's love.* He turned around and headed toward the war machine in which he has a comfortable spot where he usually got cat naps during slow days. When he made himself comfortable and was almost dozing off to sleep broken hearted, he heard a familiar voice from the entrance of the war machine.

"Hey, it's me. Let me in."

"Why should I? Don't you have Sir Riis to keep you warm tonight?"

"Don't be stupid. I'm coming in. He was with his ghost again that is all."

"I know you, Janet. Don't lie to me!"

"Lower your voice. I'm not lying. I did try to have something with him tonight. I admitted it; but his mind is in another place, another time. He kissed me and then started…well never mind. He grad me, held me tight and kissed me like I always wanted him to; but then he called me by another lady's name. That's when I realized what I was doing was wrong. Which it didn't matter anyway, because that's when he realized I wasn't her and he violently pushed me away."

"So, that's when you came here. I'm supposed to be the one to care for you now?"

"No. You are such a stupid noble squire. I could go to my sleeping cot. I could go to the drinking tent and pick up any mercenary there. But I'm here with you now." Janet started to come closer, letting her aketon to slowly fly open revealing that she was wearing nothing underneath.

"I see."

"I'm here to properly thank you for the sword that you gave me. I want to give you a gift as well." She went to kiss him as she had done before but this time feeling his manhood at the same time. Richard replicated with sensually touching her as well.

Ultimately, this engaging erupted in mutual love making. This was what he had been longing for ever since the time he first met her.

Very early in the morning, Janet woke up by the sound of a passing horsemen. She peeked through the canvas of the war machine to see Lord Sterz riding Titan. She thought, *He must be surveying and inspecting the encampment.* Squire Richard woke up as well and began to comfort her from the morning chill. "Richard, I was a virgin till tonight."

"A virgin, Janet?"

"Yes, the day the men had their way with me, I didn't enjoy it because it was an act of violence, pain and humiliation, but tonight I felt joy and delight."

"I'm glad. Now maybe we can leave together. Let's leave today before the battle. We can be married and start a new life together."

Janet was quiet for a moment and then she said, "That will never ever happen. I would rather die in the battlefield. This is my chosen profession; I will not change it. Moreover, I don't want you to tell anyone about the gift I gave you tonight. You hear me! No one must know! This day we start like nothing ever happened between us. *Saisir*?"

Chapter XIX

Nicola di Rienzo ascended the dreadful stone staircase escorted by a young catholic page. The same dungeon staircase that he descended many years ago. The experience took him from the edge of death to the limit of madness. He relied on the strength of the young page since it was impossible for him to climb the staircase by himself. Rienzo squinted his eyes when he was reaching the top of the staircase; his eyes had to adjust since he spent so much time in subterranean darkness in that cell. It was a bright sunny day at Avignon, so the colors of the stained-glass really shown magnificent throughout the great hall. When he reached the top, he marveled at the architectural space and the beautiful stained-glass windows. The great hall stone windows frames were carefully cut and fitted with pieces of colorful stained glass. Rienzo was greeted by a couple of young nuns with garments ready for him to wear since he was still wearing his only possession – his loincloth. Rienzo thought that he had died, gone to heaven and these were angels escorting him to almighty God.

"Cardinal Gil de Albornoz will see you later, Senator Rienzo. We will escort you to his Eminence. But first there is a room set aside for you. We will wash you and mend your wounds. Do you require anything else of us, Senator?"

"I hope the water is warm and can one of you lovely angels cut my hair?"

As soon as Rienzo came into the cardinal chambers he knelt

in front of Albornoz and kissed his hand. "Forgive me for I doubted you; but I doubt you no more. I have sinned against you." He was sobbing and shaking, kissing his hand. The Cardinal thought that Rienzo looked a lot better with his body clean, clean shaven, and his hair cut really short to get the bugs out. But he had to ask to measure his mental strength and his alliance. "Rienzo that's enough I need you strong. How are you?"

"My Lord, my body is weak from my time in purgatory for such a long time, but my mind is clear, and more resolute and stronger than ever. I know what we must do now!"

"Good. I will nurse your body back to health." Cardinal Albornoz cut a slice of an apple and fed it to Rienzo's mouth as if it were communion bread. "Soon it will be the both of us again raising havoc at the Italian city states. We will do what we do best conquer and tip the balance back in our favor. What says you?" He patted Rienzo's head like a well-trained hunting dog. Rienzo looked around the Cardinals chambers. It was a grand room with a great fireplace. There was a balcony that overlooked the chapel and the pontiff great hall. "I'm so happy that you could join me at my moment of triumph." Cardinal Albornoz helped Rienzo off the floor and walked him over to the balcony. "And you may also be wondering how I'm not locked up in that conclave. I have a secret passageway from there," he pointed at the great hall, "back to my chambers. Besides, it doesn't matter anymore. The die has been cast your Holiness – the Visconti family has a Great Company on move to battle against Marquis of Montferrat." All the votes have been accounted for. The college even offered me the mitre hat. But I don't need it. Once you become the vicar then you are a target. That is not for me. We just haven't announced it yet. All in due time. In God's perfect time." Rienzo held on to the stone railing and said, "We will unite the entire roman peninsula under one pontiff banner."

"Yes, that's right my son. I have a company of mercenaries obedient to the pontiff that we will join us along our way to Rome."

"My Eminence, why did you do it?"

"Did what?"

"Kill Pope Innocent? Wasn't he who pardon my death sentence? Doesn't he want the pontiff states united in Italia?"

"Rienzo, his vision was not our vision. His vision was too small. He wanted the Vicar of Christ to stay in France. The pontiff seat should be back in Rome like God intended; you know this. The old power of Rome needs to be restored to its former great self. How can the Pope rule from France? It's like Israel being taken away into captivity by the Babylonians. Besides, don't concern yourself with these matters. The new Pope I selected see things our way. Oh, before I forget, I have something for you." Cardinal Albornoz walked over to the other side of his room where there were two armors prop up on stands ready for their owners to wear them. He led Rienzo to a bright shiny one. "Rienzo, I had this one commissioned just for you. It was done by an Italian master craftsman." The armor had a medusa emblem engraved on the chest piece just below the neckline. Cardinal Albornoz, pointing at the medusa head, said, "This was something that was very common for the ancient Romans and Greeks. Do you like the motif?"

"Yes, the ancient soldiers were trying to invoke the power of the medusa head. To be able to turn men into stone by her gaze. The belief was for the enemy would freeze just for a moment from glancing at her engraved image. This would give the holder just enough edge to get the upper hand on a fight."

"It's said that even Alexander the Great wore one on his

armor," Cardinal Albornoz interjected. Rienzo said this while getting very close to the medusa face and touching the relief on the fine sculptured face. You usually see Medusa represented as a hideous face; this one far from it. Do you know who the craftsman used as a model?

"Actually, I do. She is a sister at one of our nunneries… Sister Sofia. She is of uncanny beauty is she not?"

"Oh, yes, she is. I must have her." Rienzo said this while he pressed his face on top of the sculpture face.

"Now Sofia is not like the other nuns I sent you. She is pure…married only to Christ. On our way to Rome, we might stop by and pay her visit so you can meet her."

"I see you made a new armor for yourself as well." Rienzo said looking at the armor on the other side of the room.

"Oh yes, do you like it?" The armor consisted of plated armor in a crimson color, a metal wide rim hat that of a Cardinal would wear with an armor face visor. "I was going for a grotesque closed face visor reminiscent of the ancient Romans."

Rienzo looked back and forth at the grotesque face visor and Cardinal Albornoz's face. "Aye, I see the resemblance."

Cardinal Albornoz said, "I have one more item for you." He went to an oversized wooden chest that was seating between the two armors and pulled open a drawer. He reached in and pulled out an object that was wrapped in cloth. He pulled out a long shiny metal object and handed it to Rienzo. "Is this not your sword, Senator Rienzo?

"Hum, I believe it is." Rienzo took the sword, and it was like he was getting energy from the object itself. He took it off its scabbard. He held it pointing upward as he inspected one side and then the other like getting reacquainted with an old friend. "Oh, you took good care of it. Others would have just neglected it." Then he read the inscription on the fuller on the blade out loud. "Nomini domini… In the name of the Lord." Holding his sword, he closed his eyes like someone would remember an old song and said, "We will gather the lost sheep back to the fold. Vengeance is mine, says the Lord."

"Yes! Yes," exclaimed Cardinal Albornoz. As Rienzo swung his sword and made a noise as it cut through the air. He said, "The city states will fold and pay for what they have done. They will pay for their betrayal."

"Ah, that's right my old friend! In the name of the Lord, we shall unite the entire roman peninsula under one holy pontiff banner!" At this moment, the white smoke came out of a small chimney signaling to the world that a new pontiff had been elected.

Chapter XX

It was the twenty-second day of April in the year of our Lord 1363, and everyone was getting into their position and making last minute preparations before the battle. Everybody prepared differently for a coming battle. Lord Sterz didn't sleep during the night. He rode Titan to inspect the fighting positions, the battle line and, more important, the field of battle. He didn't want any unexpected surprises from the Great Company. He was envisioning the future battle that was to come in his head. He didn't feel the urge to drink that night. He felt fully satisfied and fulfilled in this type of situation. He moved himself to the predetermined battle position for him to give orders. He was so excited about the coming day's events that he forgot his newly forged sword that he had commissioned in his tent.

Lord Hawkwood was praying at his Catholic alter. He was kneeling and made the sign of the cross on his newly plate armor that he had commissioned. The armor had engraved a large portrait of the Virgin and Child right on the breast plate. In his tent Sir Lajos was completely naked warming himself up practicing with his weapons. He put on his aketon, armor and weapons and ran out of his tent jumping and screaming in his native tongue. Now Sir Ruffin cut his hair, shaved his face, and used fragrant ointment that he got back at Pont-Saint-Esprit. He also put on new engraved plate armour that he had commissioned from the Pont-Saint-Esprit blacksmith. It had a roaring lion motif right on the chest plate. Decorative engraved plate armor is very expensive. Typically, it was only reserved for nobles due to its high cost, but it seemed more and more mercenaries had them acquired these days. What else will they spend their gold florin coins? The reflection of Cavalier Ruffin looking back on the polished metal mirror is not of an old man, even though he feels like one. Then, he noticed a mark on his neck from when he was tortured. The unkept beard did a good job covering it up. He also thought to himself that if he ever gets through this battle maybe he needs to rethink his relationship with Janet.

Through the tent door flaps, he saw Dame Janet all dressed for battle with Squire Richard. Squire Richard was within the war machine getting it ready. Sir Riis walked over toward Dame Janet. Dame Janet came closer as well, looking surprised. "I like your new look Cavalier Ruffin. But it looks like you cut yourself shaving." She came very close to him and touched the flesh cut on his face and then licked it off her finger. "You should be more careful young man."

"Thanks. I'll be more careful next time." Looking at Squire Richard, Sir Riis said, "Both of you are my family now. I would hate to lose any of you. So be careful out there and don't take any unnecessary risks."

"We won't other than getting, what you called him? Oh yeah… the Golden Peacock," Janet said.

"I know you will. Now move this machine into position and don't accidentally cut off your hands!"

"Cavalier Lajos are you ready for your skirmish attack?"

"I'm ready for the grand diversion. I have my men on the eastern side ready for battle." Sir Lorens walked over. "Keep this man-at-arms close to you," Cavalier Riis said, pointing at Sir Lorens. "And thank you, Cavalier Lajos for being a noble chivalric knight."

"I'm not milites nobiles. That is why I'm in this knight's errand. To amend for my pass sins."

"Sir Lorens if you are not a noble knight then who is? Take care of yourself and this one for me?"

"Aye, I will."

Everyone else was still getting into their battle position including the command staff. Lord Albert Sterz was moving into his own battle position. "Cavalier Ruffin please bring me my new sword that I commissioned. It's in my tent; you will find it in a wooden box." Not everyone was at the frontlines yet. Cavalier Riis thought, *This might be my chance to get satisfaction on Sir William Thornton. I might die in this battle, and I don't want that evil filth left on Earth.* Sir Riis walked to Sir Thornton's tent and asked permission to enter it. A familiar white cat ran out between Sir Riis legs, and he heard an acquainted voice.

"How can I help you – Lord Ruffin?"

"Lady Nicole?" She was dressed in a fine long garment and even made a proper curtsy. "Lord Thornton is getting into his armor–"

"…Come inside, Cavalier Ruffin. I have an idea why you are here. So, let's converse together like brothers," Sir Thornton answered.

"I think we are past that, don't you?"

"Is this about the death of Jean-Luc or his widow?" asked Lady Nicole.

"Something similar, my Lady. But, if you must know it's about chivalry, honor and satisfaction; so, get your sword and I will meet you outside."

"Lady Nicole, he's upset because I killed Jean-Luc."

"You said, Sir Ruffin had to kill him in the Pont-Saint-Esprit attack?" Nicole acted very surprised and upset at the same time.

"He was a sodomite! He enjoyed having sex with other men or worst with boys. And he was going to run away with Olark; his lover and leave his wife and child behind." Sir Thornton standing up in his defense.

"Sir Thornton, you didn't know him like I knew him," Nicole said arrogantly. "Everything he would say was a lie that was the type of person he was. Maybe, it was out of protection, or he was just plain strange. And he did not like to have sex with men or boys. Trust me on that. He and Olark grew up together, so yes, he was going to take him and his wife and daughter who he loved very much. Surely, you must have met someone like that before. Think back I bet he said that his wife was ugly? Cavalier Ruffin you said you met his wife? How did she really look?"

"Beautiful, and an attractive daughter at that," Sir Riis said.

"Now that I remember that whorehouse didn't cater to that type of clientele." Saying this, Thornton sat down acting like he was going to vomit.

"He feared the French crown. He thought Pont-Saint-Esprit defenses were lacking. He thought all you needed was a handful of men to open the gate and then an army of mercenaries can take it over before anybody would even notice."

"How do you know all this?"

"I was the whore that night when you were in the other room. He took an interest in me because he thought I was too young to be there. So, he purchased me out of the whorehouse. He knew you were next door. Later, Jean-Luc and Sir Thornton secretly met and hatched out a plan. Or I should say, Jean-Luc convinced his plan on Sir Thornton. Sir Thornton merely agreed with it. He was hoping and waiting that you would come, and he would execute his part. And he was right. Now what really happened to

Jean-Luc?"

"We made a deal to let him go. Then, Sir Thornton killed him," said Sir Ruffin.

"Ah, you just gave me the last stitch that I needed to sew this whole garment together."

"How so?"

"I wasn't brave enough until now; but this whole plan was conceived by Jean-Luc himself and it was him who gave instructions to Sir Thornton. This was not Sir Thornton's plan like he led the White Company to believe."

"Shut up! Shut up! Bitch! I should have left you behind!"

Cavalier Riis Ruffin said with authority, "No. Sir Thornton. You shut up and let the lady finish."

"It was Jean-Luc's plan all alone. The French court papers were given to Thornton by Jean-Luc. And once Olark notified that he had encounter Thornton with the court papers, Jean-Luc could set into motion his part of the plan in Pont-Saint-Esprit. I was part of it. I spiced the soup with herbs that would cause relaxation and sleepiness, that was why Pont-Saint-Esprit personnel were so calm that night. Later I was supposed to bring a bowl to Jean-Luc himself that was going to be the signal that everything was going according to plan. But instead, I walk into you two and death. But I learned to survive and kept quiet. I guess that came from being in a whorehouse from a very young age."

Sir Ruffin thought, *I should have guess Sir Lajos jests are not that bad to put people to sleep.* Then he asked in an audible voice, "How come our vanguard party in the great hall weren't affected? They were hungry from the ride. I know they don't refuse a good meal."

"Olark had one of his trusted men to look after your men. And he and I made sure that the soup that they received was untainted. I believe you met him blade first, Lord Ruffin."

"My apologies, but that's what happens because of lack of knowledge. Please continue, my lady."

Lady Nicole's eyes started watering as she continued saying, "If everything had worked out as planned, I would have left with them. I was supposed to act as Olark's wife, at least that was the story we were going to tell his wife and child. Cavalier Ruffin what you need to be asking yourself, whatever happened to the widow and her daughter Marie because I tried to check up on them and no one has seen them since the White Company took over Pont-Saint-Esprit?"

"But I… took care of her?"

"Did you really?" Thoughts came to Sir Riis about what happened that night and other instances. As a result, a fire was lit in Sir Riis heart that would only be extinguish through blood. "Sorry for the inconvenience. I will take my leave."

"I will also take care of it!" Lady Nicole had a dagger that must have come from Thornton's belt, and she was about to plunge it behind the neck of its owner. Cavalier Riis pulled out his sword and decisively cut her nearly in half. When Thornton noticed what had happened, he recoiled back and landed on the ground covered in her blood.

"Sir Thornton, today, you are one lucky dog. I was going to dispatch you to the underworld, but I ended up saving your pitiful life. Get on your knees and give thanks to almighty God, and repent…Thornton or next time I will not change my mind." Sir Riis wipes his sword on Nicole's dress before putting it away in its scabbard. Leaving Sir Thornton on his knees crying on the floor of his tent. Sir Riis walks over to Sir Godwine's tent. He was hoping that Sir Godwine had not left to his appointed fighting position, yet. "Sir Godwine, are you still here?"

"Aye Cavalier Riis." Sir Godwine lifts his tent's flaps and walks out ready in full armor.

"Come with me. I have a task from Lord Sterz." They walked into Lord Sterz's tent and no one else was in there.

"What are we doing here?" asked Sir Godwine.

"We are here to pick up Lord Sterz new sword that he had commissioned. Ah, here it is still in the swordsmith wooden box." Cavalier Riis took it out of the box and drew it from its scabbard. It was longer than most swords that were being used at the time. "This is a new design, a little longer and stronger to pierce armor."

"Very nice. I think we should be going," said Sir Godwine, sounding eager to get out.

"Oh, yes. Wait, we have a little time left. Please tell me Sir Godwine, where is your squire?"

"I don't know. Doing his business, I suppose. I said he was a common thief!"

"Yes, I heard that story already, but no one has seen him since he was assigned to you. Where is he?"

"All right, I caught the little thief stealing from me, so I killed him and got rid of his body. Later, I regretted killing my young squire; I found the bag of florins that I thought he stole from me. It turns out, I just misplaced it. It is a knight's duty to kill all thieves like the Spiripontain swordsmith."

"What you killed him too?"

"Oh yes. He was a thief who made good swords. That sword you have he forged it himself, but he passed it off as an Italian blade. He offered me a bag of florins to keep my mouth shut."

"Speaking about a bag of gold florins, did you give the florins that I gave you to give to Jean-Luc's widow, as I instructed?"

"Oh, yes of course I did."

"How come no one seen her or her daughter ever since that night?"

"Oh, that's because I killed her."

"You did what!"

"Well, after I got my way with her, she went for a dagger, so I killed her."

"What did you do with her daughter Marie; did you killed her too?"

"Oh heavens no. I took her to the next village over and sold her to the local whorehouse. Virgins command a premium price. You know."

Cavalier Riis was glad that he had the advantage of having Lord Sterz's sword drawn and pointing right at him. But Sir Godwine was a master swordsman. "By the order of St. Mary and all that is Holy, I sentence you to DEATH!" Sir Riis went straight for a thrust for his bare neck. Sir Godwine drew his sword with incredible speed, had it over his head with a two-handed high guard and was in the air going for a straight downward lethal cut. Sir Riis' sword initially missed the neck, hitting and bouncing off the breast plate, causing a metal spark but then going through some of the chain mail, into Godwine's neck and then deep into his skull. Sir Godwine was impaled with his warm blood covering the front of Cavalier Riis face, tabard and breastplate.

Cavalier Riis removed the sword from Sir Godwine's head by pulling on the sword back using his arms and hips muscles. It was a hard pull since the sword was impaled deep into his skull. After the struggle of getting sword out of the skull, he checked to see if it was bent. It was straight as an arrow; he thought any other sword would have bend. But this one flexed and went back to its original shape. He wipes the sword on Sir Godwine's body and inserts it back into its scabbard.

Cavalier Riis made his way back; everyone was in position by now and all the men in rows dressed in steel looked like rows of steel walls moving up and down the open field like chess pieces. This was especially visual since one company was dressed in white, and the other side dressed in almost all black armor. Walking to Lord Sterz and Lord Hawkwood position, Sir Riis noticed some of the men staring at him. It seems Sir Riis was some sight since blood was covering his entire front and no battle has yet started.

"What happened to you cavalier?" inquired Lord Sterz.

"I cut myself shaving," Sir Riis said laughing, "A duel of honor to serve chivalry and justice; I'll give you all the details if we get out of this alive."

At this, Sir Hawkwood said, "It must have been some duel. Looks like your back and bottom half of your surcoat was also cut." Cavalier Riis didn't notice this before, but Sir Godwine must have cut the back of his surcoat in the struggle.

"Thank you. Good Cavalier Riis Ruffin for doing what is expected on chivalry duties. You are *milites nobiles*."

"I'm not a true knight. I have a lot of faults. And I'm beginning to think none of us are, especially, in this profession of mercenaries...all we care about is fortune. We are all just fighting for gold and wealth. I would venture to say true chivalry is even dead these days."

At this moment, Cavalier Lajos and his page broke rank. Running toward the enemy with a banner staff and his page close behind him.

"What is he doing running toward the enemy by himself like that?" Sir Thomas said.

"Come back! You're going to get yourself killed!" yelled

Lord Sterz.

One can see a few arrows that were shot but he was just out of range. Just then, he ran up a slight hill and plants the staff on top of it. Cavalier Lajos and the page start unwrapping it. It was a massive banner. No one has seen it before. It was very colorful and glimmering in the sun but still the colors had a relic look to them but quite impressive. It looked wonderful on the wind and Cavalier Lajos stood there with his arms cross, straight like an arrow looking chivalrous. His page by his side. And then absolute stillness, no arrows, no noise, complete quietness. Then suddenly there was unrest in the enemy side. There was a great commotion and then a portion of soldiers were breaking ranks. At first, Cavalier Riis thought maybe they were doing some type of maneuvering or battle tactic; and you can hear them saying something that he couldn't understand because it was in Magyar. A voice that could be heard and understood was Sir Konrad who was yelling, "Alt! Alt!" at Magyars cavalry but to no avail. Cavalier Riis turned to Lord Sterz.

"You speak their language can you hear what their saying?"

"I believe, *we haven't forgotten what your family did for our country or heritage* or something like that." They were leaving the battlefield. These were his own countrymen. Out of some sort of loyalty or respect to a forgotten kingdom or, in this case, not so forgotten. Cavalier Riis thought, *I've never seen or most likely will never ever see anything like this again. Or for that matter, I never heard of anything like this ever happening before.* With this incredible act, Cavalier Riis came to an awareness that chivalry, honor, and respect still lives… even among mercenary knights.

Cavalier Lajos and his page ran back. "I told you; I was going to take care of it. This should help our day some." He came back just like that, like it was just another day for him.

"More than you think by the count of them that left. I estimate at least three to four contingents have broken rank! Ha, this gets even better they want to retreat via the bridge. To do this, they are causing havoc because they are going through the rest of the formation of the Great Company!" Lord Sterz said, pointing and with great laughter.

This gave time for Lord Hawkwood to move half of his longbowmen into position. The other half is going to form a V-shape in front of the men-at-arms. This was the traditional formation for an English army that the Golden Peacock would expect. But with a flank as well as a frontal attack of arrows it would be devastating to the Great Company.

"Cavalier Lajos, I need to ask another favor. I need you to help me get to the Golden Peacock. I need you and your men… your loyal countrymen to form a V-shape formation, just like we do with our lance group. Then, my contingent will be in the center. And when the fighting starts, my contingent and I will spearhead directly to that Peacock."

Cavalier Lajos turned around and started to bark out orders in his native language. Cavalier Riis grabbed his lance tightly, checked his axe, sword, and helm. He looked at Janet and said, "Dame Janet as soon as you can get close enough, I want you to shoot one of your beautiful rocks right at the Golden Peacock."

"I'll shoot his head clean off for you."

"Good. Squire Richard, stay with her. If we get the Golden Peacock, we can win this just like a game of chess."

"Got it. I don't know how to play chess."

"I'll teach you if we get out of this alive."

"I would like to volunteer to drive the war machine wagon for you, my Lady." Lajos' page giving a small bow at Lady Janet.

"It will be my honor." Janet said as she helped the young

page up onto the siege wagon.

Cavalier Riis finally made it to his contingent. His contingent was in the place just where he had ordered Sir Godwine to position them the day before. A familiar man-at-arms asked, "Cavalier Ruffin, where is Sir Godwine?"

"Sir Godwine will not be joining us in battle today or ever again – Sir Gold. You will be my second in command of our contingent from now on."

"Sir, I?" Sir Gold stature started to drop by bending his knee. Cavalier Riis held him before he lowered himself any lower, "No need to thank me now, my good knight. I need you to continue to lead our men after you don't see me any longer."

"After I don't see you any longer?" questioned the newly appointed lieutenant.

"Aye, I will explain: You push the men through the defenses and follow me as I make my way to their commander. The aim is to capture the Golden Peacock and sue for peace. It's the only way to win against such a large force. Do you understand – Sir Gold?" Sir Gold rubbed his chin, looking a little confused. Cavalier Riis took out his dagger from his belt and drew on the ground, "'Cavalier Lajos is leading his men like a spearhead. Our men will be the shaft. Once the spearhead breaks through the initial line of defenses.' He continued drawing on the ground pointing at the enemy positions, the direction of attack and objective. "Our men will rush in and do what they do best with axe, mace, and pike. Then you get them to form a defensive perimeter back to our rear battle line. Hopefully I will try to reach the commander and I need a way back."

Sir Gold asked, "Initially where will you be?"

"I will be at the center of the spearhead where the action is."

He pointed on the ground. "And one last thing, I need you to help me with a boost up; lances are heavy, as you know. Now raise the Spearhead Banner high so the whole White Company to see that we are ready!"

Cavalier Riis had thoughts of his late sword master and his explanation of the hour of the dragon. *The hour of the dragon is the time of battle where it was only do or die, no thoughts of techniques, or even breathing only of battle and the melee at hand. At this time, one thing was certain the hour of the dragon was nigh:* Sir Riis haven't prayed since his wife and child death but somehow felt compel to do so. He looked up and said, "God grant us this day a victory, if it is in your will, and not because we deserve it more than the bastards on the other side. But because we are small in numbers, and we were told, that our souls would be destined for damnation, but I don't believe that a man on earth can dictate what you almighty God's providence. So, give us today victory, oh God to prove all of them wrong! Amen!" Then he heard from behind him the rest of his contingent saying together, "Amen!" They must have overheard his prayer.

Cavalier Riis thought, *It's the hour of the dragon.* The departure of the Magyars cavalry from the Great Company really affected the Great Company. Lord Sterz gave the order to begin the battle. He signaled Lord Hawkwood to begin his terror of the English longbows. He relays to his lieutenants to begin the alternating hails of arrows. The first arrows strike came from the visible front chevron formation. The Great Company reacted to the strike as they were accustomed to with their counterattack. The crossbows had a shorter range compared to the mighty English longbows. Soon they would have to move within range of the English longbow surprise, courtesy of the Magyars' diversion. As predicted, the Great Company moved up their crossbowmen to return, fire with fire, but it was too late when they settle in position they were met with a rain of deadly English arrows. Then another rain of arrows from the first V-shape line of longbowmen. The enemy was caught in a deadly crossfire. The longbowmen did their job well. The Great Company had a sea of death in front of them. Sir Konrad gave the order to move forward unmounted in formation.

Lord Sterz seen the movement from Titan, "I guess Sir Konrad set the stage. This battle will be knights versus knights." He cried in a loud voice, "White Company dismount! Into your pike phalanx formations lads and get ready to move forward! Let's show them our mettle!" A great shout came from the men of the White Company. He slid off Titan got out his new commissioned sword that was already baptized by blood, a few hours ago this morning. Lord Hawkwood ordered his lieutenants to stand down. When the last few hails of arrows were over, the order was given for everyone to advance at a slow even pace. One didn't want to start running too early or you would be exhausted before the fighting started. And have no energy to win. The running charge command really must be close to the enemy in order to be effective. This was the mastery of war. Lord Sterz had all of this in his mind when the White Company were advancing closer and them in turn, likewise. Until Lord Sterz gave the order of the trumpet charge and he cried with a mighty voice, "WHITE COMPANY CHARGE!"

Cavalier Ruffin's contingent ran ahead into the enemy rank with Cavalier Lajos' men forming its spearhead and came into the resistance of the enemy rank and then they all came to a complete stop with an explosion of men and metal. Cavalier Riis was in the center, so he used the momentum to jump over Lajos' rank and the enemy rank with the help of Sir Gold. Cavalier Riis flew and landed on the ground and did a rolling stop with his long lance imbedded in the closest enemy in front of him. It went so deep that it went through his body. The lance was useless for him now. He grabbed his axe. Cavalier Riis cut off a sword arm on his way and kept running toward the Golden Peacock. He is getting closer. The Peacock got his personal guards around him, just then Cavalier Riis thought maybe he went too far into enemy territory by himself; how would he take care of all these men-at-arms and Konrad's personal guards at the same time? Then, he thought overthinking like this may get himself killed. The first guard came up, Cavalier Riis parry his sword and gave him a taste of his axe. The next one, he hit his sword, and it took a severe L-bend.

The guard looked at Cavalier Riis with a surprise look. Riis looked at him like, *Yeah, sword verses axe, what do you expect?* But he couldn't think; Sir Riis next axe swing cut his head clean off. At this time at the corner of his eye he could see Cavalier Lajos and his men advancing getting ever so closer. He could also see Janet and Richard going at it with the war wagon and the rock-crossbow. Also, he noticed their driver getting shot by an arrow. Not good!

Squire Richard said, "Our driver is hit, Janet!"

Richard leaned over to the driver and asked, "Are you all right?" Cavalier Lajos' page was badly hurt but still breathing.

"Shit! Let's throw him to the side. We'll pick him up later."

"No, Janet. That's cruel – this boy always loves you. He will stay with us, or we will all die together."

"All right. You still must drive and get me a little closer to the damned Peacock."

"I will try but this is not easy. Looks like his almost there. Look!"

"Shit! I'm taking my shot now! Load me now!"

Squire Richard took one of the rocks and kissed it and placed it on the shaft. Janet stuck her tongue out as she bit into it to aim and shoot. The rock hit one of the enemies that was closer in the same line of sight.

"Shit! Richard, you need to drive to get me closer!" Squire Richard went to the driver's side next to Sir Lajos' page.

Cavalier Riis counter with his axe then took out his dagger and buried it deep into the enemy's chest. This gave him a moment to catch his breath. He thought, *This axe is getting heavier as the day is moving on. I must be getting old.* Cavalier Riis put his dagger away. He looked around to see most of the Peacock's personal guards were dead. He was down to six – make that five – guards. Good old Cavalier Lajos. Cavalier Riis mustered all he had left for another charge. He calculated that with Lajos there he would make short work of three guards and that was just when he got there to kill one more, which would leave one unknown. No time to think. He ran toward the nearest guard and drove his axe so deep he was unable to take it out. By instinct, he grabbed his sword and then saw a projectile going over his right shoulder. It landed on the Peacock's helmet. You could hear the snapping noise of metal breaking. And the Golden Peacock was down. Sir Riis thrusted his sword at one guard, pulled it out and reached for the Golden Peacock. It was one of Janet's rocks; she did it.

His face was bloody; the helmet flew off with the broken golden nose piece still imbedded deep into his face. Cavalier Riis looked around. Behind him was one more guard with an overhead sword, ready to strike him down. And then his head fell off his body and the appearance of Sir Lorens with his own bloody sword was left standing. Cavalier Riis didn't take into consideration that young Sir Lorens would be there to take care of the last unknown. Now, Cavalier Riis could Cavalier Lajos and the rest of his men coming around.

Cavalier Riis grabbed Sir Konrad tightly and said, "I told you I was going to get you, didn't I? Do you remember me? I am the ghost from the past!" Lord Konrad was even more shaken by these words than by the wounds he had just inflicted. But he couldn't temporarily speak due to the impact on his face. "Well, speak! Man! Speak! Soon your men will see that you're captured, and they will throw your banner."

Cavalier Lajos came over and said, "Cavalier Ruffin, we must be going if Lord Sterz sounds the second trumpet charge, we don't want to be here." Sir Riis barked out the orders quickly. "Sir Lorens start moving the men back to the main battle line slowly. Cavalier Lajos, see if you can get the attention of a Great Company Lieutenant without first cutting off his head. Quick, get me a lieutenant before Lord Sterz gives the order!" Then he looked at Lord Konrad. "I want you to see that, but I want to kill you for what you did." Then, you could hear the blood gulping voice of Lord Konrad. "You can't remember, can you? Maybe that's a blessing from God not being able to remember." He spit a large amount of blood-infused saliva. Cavalier Riis slipped open Lord Konrad's breastplate, and let it fall to the ground. "There, now you can breathe better; so, we can talk."

Cavalier Riis took out his long narrow dagger. "I remember that there were two more of you… knights of the order… No, they were not called that…" Riis hit his opponent's head with his head to help jog his memory. "… They were Teutonic. Teutonic Knights, were they not? Of the Teutonic Order? Where are they now?"

Lord Konrad shook his head indicating no, and said, "The Order does more than just kill; they rip your life out of you. That's what we did to you: your memories, your home, family, children, wife. Do you remember her? I tasted your wife just before she begged to die!"

"I will kill you!" He thrust the dagger right between his ribcage to puncture the heart. Sir Riis kept that dagger there because as soon as he pulled it out, he would die. Sir Riis did not let him speak any more. All you could hear was the painful sound of a man's last breaths. The sun was setting and the whole sky was filled with shades of crimson which blended with the blood red stained battlefield. Cavalier Lajos finally brought a Magyar lieutenant. This lieutenant remained faithful through the Magyar desertion and was currently bearing the Great Company banner. "I am Sir Nicholas Thod, Lieutenant in the Great Company." After he quickly ascertained the grave situation that Lord Konrad was in, he ordered his page to sound a retreat call on his trumpet, and when he got the Great Company knights' attention, he lowered the banner to the ground. The rest of the Great Company, when they noticed that their Condottieri, Lord Konrad von Landau, was a captive, gave up and rapidly sued for surrender. A great cheer arose from the mass of the White Company and Lord Sterz stood down the rest of his knights. Sir Thod said, "Sirs the White Company has won the day. Please extend to us the courtesy of collecting our dead." Cavalier Ruffin acknowledged, "Take him to Lord Hawkwood. Cavalier Lajos will show you the way. Lord Konrad hearing these words moved and struggled a little that's when he remembers that he had cold steel in his chest and that his time on earth was short.

Then, Cavalier Ruffin asked Lord Konrad, "Surely you must

know by now that you are going to the other side. Consider yourself privileged enough to know when you're going to die. Why don't you come clean and tell me where the rest of your brothers are?"

"One is a Condottieri, like myself, and once he hears what you've done... he will be coming for you... so there is no need to seek him out!" Sir Konrad speech was wavering even more now since he was having difficulty in breathing again. "The other I don't know where he is. And that's the truth my SWORDBROTHER!" Cavalier Ruffin pulled the dagger out from his heart very slowly and said, "Teutonic filth, I'm tired of smelling and listening to you. To the shadows of death and the underworld where you belong." Lord Konrad quickly collapsed onto the ground and said,

"I'll wait for you there my brother." Then Lord Konrad let out his last breath. Cavalier Riis von Ruffin was sickened and disgusted in remembering his suppressed memories of his Teutonic heritage. Then he thought, that's where you are wrong Teutonic filth. I'm not going where you are going, for I am a true knight – I am miles Chrisi.

In Trial by Combat, it is believed that whoever is innocent in the eyes of God wins. We were greatly outnumbered, did not have the experience, and were condemned by the Holy Catholic Church. That day we won and proved vindicated by God. We also proved to the world that the White Company bow down to no men, lords, kings, or God.

Given at Pisan, on vii day of February in the year of our Lord Jesus Christ 1364
Anonymous, Chevalier

CODA

On April twenty-second, 1363, the inexperienced and greatly outnumbered White Company met against the Great Company. Inexplicably, the Hungarians in the Great Company refused to fight and left the battlefield. The Battle of Canturino terminated on a truce, the death of Konrad von Landau and the total demise of The Great Company. Concluding in a great victory for the fledging White Company.